French film director and filmmaker...
...for films...

...graduated from... University, he pursued
a career in advertising management, after managing... ...
...later he switched to... for... with... ...his
for... ...India's largest... ...his... films are...
...directed... ...films include Uncle, American King
of comedy, and... ...

He lives in his beloved Mumbai, where he can often be
seen... ...that... ...

D0994862

MUMBAISTAN
A TRILOGY OF CRIME THRILLERS

Piyush Jha is an acclaimed film director, ad filmmaker and a first-time novelist.

A student political leader at university, he pursued a career in advertising management after acquiring an MBA degree. Later, he switched tracks, first to make commercials for some of the country's largest brands, and then write and direct feature films. His films include Chalo America, King of Bollywood and Sikandar.

He lives in his beloved Mumbai, where he can often be found walking the streets that inspire his stories.

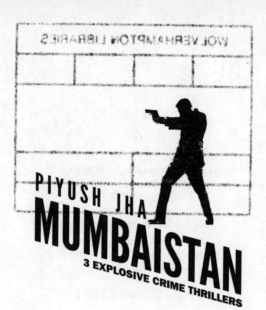

PIYUSH JHA
MUMBAISTAN

3 EXPLOSIVE CRIME THRILLERS

RUPA

First published in 2012 by
Rupa Publications India Pvt. Ltd.
7/16, Ansari Road, Daryaganj
New Delhi 110002

Sales centres:

Allahabad Bengaluru Chennai
Hyderabad Jaipur Kathmandu
Kolkata Mumbai

Copyright © Piyush Jha 2012

ISBN: 978-81-291-2017-5

10 9 8 7 6 5 4 3

Piyush Jha asserts the moral right to be identified
as the author of this work.

Printed in India by
Replika Press Pvt. Ltd.
310-311 EPIP Kundli
Haryana 131028

To my wife Priyanka, whose unwavering belief
in me is the force that fuels my imagination

Bomb Day

Bomb Day

'If I don't marry Tanvir today, I'll die!' Rabia's words tumbled into the phone that fateful morning. Standing at the STD booth on the corner of Khetwadi Lane No. 10, she spoke with just the right amount of determination to put an end to any further discussion. This manner of speaking, with threatening undertones, was uncharacteristic of the otherwise demure beauty. Most of the time, her soft voice was in concert with her even softer mannerisms. The placidness with which she copulated with her few customers made them use a not-so-flattering adjective for her: homely.

Perhaps that was why there was silence on the phone line. The person on the other side seemed to have been taken aback by Rabia's resolute pronouncement. Waiting for a response, Rabia now began to display her true self. She fidgeted, letting her mind wander down to the street corner where Tanvir had walked up to her one evening and looked at her with those earnest eyes of his. 'Will you go with me?' was the question he had posed. Without answering, she had gestured towards the seedy entrance of Friendship Lodge.

'*Allah Hafiz*,' the two words, spoken with calm finality on the other end, jolted her back to the present.

Now, as she stood with the phone receiver lying limp in her hand, she shivered, wondering if those words were meant to be good wishes for a long life ahead, or an ominous farewell.

◉

Aalamzeb put down the phone after his conversation with Rabia. The rat-faced teenager sitting next to him, reading an Urdu newspaper, glanced at him and sneered, 'I told you so!'

Aalamzeb didn't reply. The expression on his lean and craggy young face was incomprehensible He sat silent, staring out of the window of his sparse tenement in Mumbra, a far-flung suburb of Mumbai. His eyes were focused on the Mumbra harbour that lay in the distance; on four Koli fishermen, who were passing through in a thin tapered wooden fishing boat. It was a sight not normally seen in the small harbour, usually home to rusty sand barges and tired tugboats.

Silence had always been Aalamzeb's friend. People would wonder what wheels were turning inside that broad forehead whenever Aalamzeb lapsed into those long silences. While some said it was just his way of unnerving people, others felt he always thought four steps ahead.

After a few minutes of being ignored, the rat-faced teen couldn't take it anymore. He folded the newspaper, threw it down and said, 'We should have killed this Tanvir long back.'

At the harbour, the man sitting at the fishing boat's prow broke into a song. The lilting Koli melody energized the others in the boat, and harmonized the dip and pull of their arms to its rhythm. The boat now rose smooth and proud against the tide, and slipped merrily out to sea, past the silent line of sand barges.

'Everything happens in its own time,' was all Aalamzeb replied .

He began to type a message on his mobile phone.

◉

As she trudged back up the stairs of the Friendship Lodge, Rabia remembered how she had led Tanvir up the same dark staircase the first time, past the corners infused with a stench of urine and lacerated with paan stains, to her handkerchief-sized room on the third floor. Locking the door behind her, she had let her clothes drop to the floor. The blue light of the bedside lamp had given her bare body a strange glow. As his hungry eyes had roamed over every nook and corner of her incandescent skin, she had felt a warm feeling growing behind her ears. She had wondered why. Perhaps it was his lean rugged face, or his rock-hard muscular body. It was his eyes, she had concluded. His eyes had an honest expression she had never seen in any other man's.

He had undressed himself and taken her into his arms. Then he had lifted her up, laying her with utmost care on the bed. Every pore in her body had opened up for him.

He had left the next morning, after handing her a small wad of money, and promised that he would be back soon. Somehow, Rabia was drawn to believing that he would be back.

Her roommate, Zohra, had raised an appreciative eyebrow as Tanvir had passed her by in the corridor on his way out. Rabia had blushed. Zohra would laugh if she told her what she felt. Here, in the busy red-light district, no prostitute could have the luxury of believing her customers' promises of returning. In fact, there was a mantra chanted by every prostitute on Mumbai's streets: *'Khao, khujao, batti bujhao'*. Enjoy them till they last, turn off the lights when they leave. And yet there was an ache, a yearning somewhere deep inside her.

But true to his word, Tanvir had returned two days later and spent another sweat-soaked night with her. He had visited her again and again over the past three months, till Rabia could almost feel that his desire for her was more than just physical.

Tanvir's expression was always sincere, almost childlike. He seemed to be a gentle man with a certain earnestness, something that made him immensely attractive to her. He had a promising job as a gym instructor in Juhu, and was constantly in demand for private training by the loaded Gujarati businessmen who frequented his gym.

Soon, Rabia began to sense signs of her own eagerness at Tanvir's impending arrival. For every little tryst with him, she chose her clothes with care, making sure that she wore only the fresh-smelling ones. Using only imported lipsticks and kohl to highlight her features, she always added a tiny drop of attar on her pulse points as a finishing touch. She needn't have bothered, for each time he stepped up the stairs for their hurried moments of togetherness, he brought with him a breath of fresh air. Blotting away the fact that Friendship Lodge stood in the narrowest of the narrow stinking lanes of Kamathipura.

The night before her phone call, he had told her that he had been offered a lucrative opportunity by one of his wealthy clients, to become a managing partner in a small gym in Dubai. He wanted to take up the offer, but only if he could share his good fortune with her.

An involuntary 'yes' had escaped her lips when Tanvir had proposed a nikah, to be solemnized the very next day.

◉

As he strode through the already teeming narrow streets of Pydhonie, one of the oldest parts of 'inner' South Mumbai,

Tanvir Khanzada was in a pensive mood. Dodging between the early morning bargain-hunters, the handcarts delivering bartans and dry fruits and the already bumper-to-bumper traffic, all he could think of was getting the task at hand over and done with, in the shortest possible time.

Tanvir had just left Rabia with the promise of meeting her at noon at Sultan-e-Hind Restaurant in nearby Dongri. He had promised to be there with a pliant qazi, who would seal their marriage vows, sitting across the sunmica tables at the restaurant. After the nikah, they would have the choicest falooda at Sultan-e-Hind as a treat, and though their relationship had been consummated three months ago, he had planned a motorbike trip to a hotel in Khandala for a symbolic 'suhaag raat'.

As Tanvir walked past small shops crammed with jewellery, zari-embroidered saris, fabrics and assorted knick-knacks, and turned a corner onto Kolsa Street, he saw a sight that stopped him in his tracks.

A police constable, standing right in the middle of the street, was beating a mangy beggar with a stick of sugarcane.

A crowd had gathered around, but was standing silently. A man in the crowd whispered that the beggar, a Muslim, had made the mistake of trying to steal prasad from the puja thalis at the Pydhonie temple. Pydhonie separates the middle-class Muslim inhabitants of the eastern part of the inner city from the Hindu-dominated areas to the west. Although there is harmony between them for most part, situations, such as the one at hand, tend to spark off communal flare-ups. The crowd watched, seething inside. Tanvir hesitated, wondering if he should do something. He was about to step forward and attempt to stop the atrocity, but someone else got there before him. It was a clean-cut young man, who looked like a computer salesman. The young man casually picked up a stone lying on the street and hurled it with force at the police constable. Before anyone else could notice his act, he turned and slipped away into the crowd. The stone hit the constable on his head, and he doubled over in pain. Blood gushed from a wound above his eyebrow. 'Run!' came a loud cry. True to form, the crowd dispersed without anyone thinking twice, running helter-skelter, leaving only a few broken slippers and an angry bleeding constable alone on the street.

◉

Back at Friendship Lodge, Rabia's mood turned upbeat as she packed her best clothes into a cheap plastic suitcase. She was trying hard to maintain a calm demeanour, but the quiet smiles to herself didn't go unnoticed. Zohra, in her trademark blunt manner, confronted her. 'Are you up to something which I should know about?' she asked.

After a moment's hesitation, Rabia let slip, 'Tanvir is going to marry me today.'

Zohra didn't break into an ear-to-ear smile, as Rabia had anticipated. Instead, a worried crease appeared on her forehead.

'Will he be able to take care of you…financially?' was her first reaction.

Rabia walked away from her, irritated and pouting. She busied herself with packing her few belongings. 'In our business, when love knocks on your door, you don't start fixing a price with it,' said Rabia.

But, Zohra didn't back down. 'But what about Aalamzeb?'

Rabia, who was busy folding a shimmery maroon duppatta,

didn't turn towards her. 'He said he loved me. But where was he all these months?'

Zohra didn't back down. 'There will be consequences! You know Aalamzeb's temper. And what about...'

Rabia cut in, speaking as one would to an uncomprehending child, 'Aalamzeb doesn't own me. He cannot keep using me whenever he feels like it. Don't worry about anything. It's all been taken care of. We have a *plan*, Zohra. Long before anyone realizes what's going on, we will be gone'. Rabia smiled and waved her slim hands in the air as she added, 'Poof! Like dhuan!'

Zohra didn't quite understand Rabia's attitude sometimes. The orthodox Kashmiri household that Zohra had been raised in did not condone flights of fancy. She had grown up under the dark cloud of militancy, fearful of every little shadow. But as soon as she had attained a semblance of puberty, she had run away from her cloistered existence. Away from home in Kupwara, all the way to Mumbai, into the arms of the only trade that would embrace runaway girls like her. She didn't mind her chosen profession; it had provided her with a safe haven. Apart from the occasional 'rough up' by a drunk client and some close scrapes with sexually transmitted diseases, she had lived a carefree life.

Rabia's voice cut through Zohra's thoughts, 'You know what the best part of a nikah is?'

As Zohra took in Rabia's flushed face, she couldn't help flashing back an indulgent smile at the best friend she had ever had. 'Shopping!' she replied, as if reading Rabia's thoughts.

◉

From a terrace two buildings away, a tall dark man, dressed in a municipal corporation worker's dirt-stained khaki bush-shirt-and-pant uniform, watched Rabia and Zohra's exchange through a powerful pair of binoculars. He was smiling, as if in sync with Rabia's enthusiasm. He put down his binoculars and packed it away into a moth-eaten jute sack. He slung the bag over his shoulder. Then he picked up a worn-out broomstick propped against a water tank and walked off the terrace, down the stairs and into the teeming Kamathipura streets.

The uniform, the sack and the broomstick might have conveyed a 'municipal jamadar' to the casual observer, but a closer examination of the man's face would have revealed intelligence and education far beyond that of someone belonging to that particular profession.

◉

For the past fifteen minutes, Tanvir had been zigzagging as fast as possible through the streets, hoping that no one had identified him as a member of the crowd that had assaulted the policeman. His breath was ragged, and there was a patina of sweat on his forehead. Tanvir's eyes were darting over the passers-by, trying to spot anyone with an interest in him.

After a while, he entered a hole-in-the-wall teashop and found himself a broken bench in the innermost corner, next to the stinking kitchen area. The bench was at a strategic position, close to a possible escape route through the back door, which opened out into a kachra-riddled back lane with an even more overpowering stink.

He sat with his back to the wall, facing the street. Without taking his eyes off the street, he ordered a special chai. Almost instantly a cutting chai, with a small wisp of vapour seeping over the rim, was slammed in front of him. Tanvir was about to take a sip of the oversweet brown fluid when he froze.

The young man who had thrown the stone at the constable entered the shop and sat down opposite him. Tanvir's body tensed but he sat still. The stone thrower, too, ordered a special chai, which was once again slammed onto the table within seconds. He took a sip and shook his head, shuddering, as if the tea had rejuvenated his being. Tanvir, all this while, had been silent, watching him. A fly had fallen into Tanvir's tea glass. The stone thrower dipped two fingers into Tanvir's glass and scooped up the fly. He flicked the fly onto the dirty sidewall of the restaurant in an exaggerated action. He then flashed Tanvir a wide hyena-like smile. 'That's the way to deal with the irritating elements in our lives.'

The stone thrower's smile cut the edge off the tension. Tanvir relaxed and smiled back, 'I was about to stop him…'

The stone thrower cut him short, 'But you were going to confront him, and thereby, expose yourself. Do that only when you are ready to lose everything.'

Tanvir nodded in understanding. His eyes took in the black taviz that peeped through the buttons of the stone thrower's thin polyester shirt.

'There is so much atrocity happening against our people. Sometimes, I want to do something. But I don't know what…' Tanvir trailed off.

The stone thrower's eyes shone. 'Are you sure you want to do something?'

Tanvir's face was hard. He nodded a firm 'yes'. The other man's eyes bore a hole into Tanvir's, but Tanvir managed to keep steady eye contact. After what seemed a lifetime, the stone thrower took out a pen and scribbled a mobile number on Tanvir's palm.

'Fearless men like you are needed all the time in the struggle against injustice.' The stone thrower winked as he got up. 'That is the direct number of our leader. Call him when you are ready', He got up and, with a few quick steps, was lost in the crowd outside the teashop.

◉

As Rabia and Zohra, clad in black silk burqas, made their way to the main road en route to the nikah shopping spree, Zohra couldn't help but think about the fateful night, five years ago, when she had first met Rabia.

After a week of incessant downpour, the rain had finally settled into a drizzle. As was always the case during such times, Zohra had been low on customers. Things would have been okay, were it not that she had been down with the flu the previous week. Her pimp was tightening the screws on her for the weekly protection money. Though she wouldn't have done so otherwise, this time Zohra had thrown caution to the winds and decided to go out looking for clients on the same main road to earn a quick buck. On drizzly nights like this, the road had big cars with fat customers and fancy tips. But on the flip side, there were also 'beaters', who liked to rough up prostitutes after sex.

Her worst fears had come true. Despite being choosy, Zohra had been trapped inside the plush leather interiors of a fancy car with one such 'beater' that night. She had been taken in by his stylish clothes, his perfume, the soft toys in the backseat that seemed to suggest a child and a wife waiting for him at home, and had decided that he must be a gentle soul. But, in the safety of the small lane behind Maratha Mandir Cinema, he had turned around and slapped Zohra as soon as she had unzipped him and found that his manhood, instead of responding to her ministrations, was in desperate need of medical intervention. The goddesses' photos on his dashboard had made Zohra laugh at the irony of it all. This had made him hit her harder.

After the first two blows, Zohra had been mentally resigning herself to a bruised face, when, out of the blue, a petite woman had smashed a rock on the windscreen of the car. The man had heaved with all the might left in him and pushed Zohra out. Backing out of the lane, he had zipped away to the safety of Malabar Hill or whatever posh neighbourhood he reeked of.

Zohra had picked herself up from the ground and turned to look at her saviour—the shivering, emaciated young woman with the rock in her hand. Zohra, at once, had known that she had found a kindred spirit in this innocent-looking girl-woman, She had taken Rabia's hand and led her out of the lane. Neither had thanked the other for the mutual help, for both realized that some things are best left unsaid.

Later, Zohra had come to know that Rabia had not eaten for four days. She had run away from her home in Haryana after being raped by the village sarpanch's son, a slick-haired youth who was being groomed to take over his father's position. 'Well-meaning' villagers had egged her on to complain against the rapist. But before she knew what was happening, it had blown up to become a communal issue. She would have been strung up on the same tree that provided shade to the village panchayat. But some humanity was still alive within the elders. They had passed an externment order instead, and pushed her out onto the highway.

One never-ending rape-cum-lorry ride later, she had found herself deposited on Mumbai's mean streets. Not wanting to be raped anymore, she had curled herself up under a cardboard carton in the nearest lane, prepared to die of hunger.

Rabia had shivered uncontrollably as she recounted her story to Zohra.

◉

Tanvir still sat quietly in the teashop. The thoughtful expression had returned on his face. He took small sips from the now tepid tea, as if trying to prolong the experience. His reverie was interrupted as a man in a khaki bush-shirt and pants emerged from the stinking back lane. This was the same man, the municipal jamadar who had been keenly observing Rabia through the binoculars across the building. He passed through the kitchen and entered the small sitting area of the teashop.

He sat down next to Tanvir, eyeing the road in a similar fashion. He didn't say a word, but a glass of chai was put in front of him. Ignoring it, he kept his eyes on the street.

After a while, Tanvir opened his palm and levelled it to the jamadar's line of sight. The jamadar let his eyes move across the number a few times, as if memorizing it. Satisfied, he smiled to himself. He now whispered without glancing at Tanvir, 'Call the number. Do as he says.'

He then looked away into the distance, and was about to get up and leave when Tanvir spoke, 'What about Rabia?'

The jamadar sat down again and, without a change in expression, said, 'Forget Rabia. It's Aalamzeb we are after. You have drawn him out, *ab apun uska game baja dalenge.*'

Tanvir looked amused. 'Speaking like a tapori doesn't suit you, ACP Hani.'

The jamadaar/ACP Hani replied, 'Okay, so if you'd like me to speak plainly, it's time we finished Aalamzeb.'

Tanvir's eyes flared. 'ACP Hani, I have done as I had promised; now *you* finish whoever you want, by yourself. I don't want to be involved in this any further'.

The ACP looked towards Tanvir for the first time. His eyes were cold, his face stony. 'The three attempt-to-murder charges against you will ensure your involvement, won't they? Or should I order an encounter to seek your further cooperation?'

Tanvir didn't back down but he did modulate his tone, adding a pinch of respect in it, 'ACP saab, it's because you had promised to get the attempted murder charges dropped that I undertook this assignment. I had only promised to use Rabia to make the contact with Aalamzeb. I've done that, now please, don't go back on your zubaan. The problem is, if my people find out that I'm helping the police, they'll brand me a "khabri". My career will be over.'

The ACP also softened his tone. 'You are helping the anti-terrorist squad nab Pakistani terrorists. Don't worry. Your gangster friends will understand. And my word is set in stone. You will be a free man soon. Just do this last bit. Draw Aalamzeb out into the open. You have gotten his mistress, Rabia, to fall in love with you, so he's made a wrong move. He's contacted you. He doesn't want to kill you because he feels he'll lose her forever. Poor man, he really loves her. He now wants to show Rabia that you are not the honest, upright man she thinks you are, but a man as ruthless as him. Play along. We will be watching over you. Aalamzeb is sure to make another wrong move, and then we'll get him and the four other Pakistanis, who are hiding somewhere in this city.'

'And Rabia?' Tanvir asked.

The ACP emitted a dry laugh. 'Who cares about a two-bit whore anyway... Uh...don't tell me you've fallen for her?'

Tanvir's expression was hard to decipher.

'Love is a weapon. In the right hands, it can make a kheema of the hardest heart,' said the ACP, while his eyes searched Tanvir's face. Tanvir did not flinch under the scrutiny. This seemed to satisfy the ACP. 'Good. Now please go, you have a phone call to make.' He got up and flung a last steel-tipped glance at Tanvir. Tanvir smiled back, his manner reassuring. ACP Hani picked up his broom and entered the kitchen area, exiting on to the back street, unmindful of the stench.

As the ACP disappeared from sight, the smile disappeared from Tanvir's face. He spat into his chai glass. Then he cursed and cursed. He cursed the day he had befriended Firoze Fateh Ali, the hotheaded gangster from Byculla, and had been recruited into his extortion syndicate. He cursed the day he had listened to Firozebhai's missive, and had graduated from being a small-time 'vasooli' to a 'shooter', by firing a shot at their rival, Pratap Pote. He had missed. He cursed the day when Pratap Pote had sent two of his shooters to finish him. Although he had had the presence of mind to stab both of them in the stomach and escape, he hated the fact that at that crucial moment, he had lacked the guts to push his knife further upwards and slice their hearts.

All the three gangsters had survived. Fearing retribution, Ferozebhai had taken off for Malaysia and become incommunicado, and Tanvir had gone into hiding in Indore. He had been trying to go straight, and put the past behind him, when ACP Hani had caught up with him and offered him a deal. He had grabbed the deal, thinking it to be an easy way out. But now, he realized he was a puppet on a string that was firmly in the ACP's grasp.

◉

The nondescript Mumbai Central branch of the State Bank of Punjab, located at the northern end of Falkland Road, was the financial hub of the neighbouring red-light area. Rabia and Zohra weaved their way through the traffic snarls on the road and entered the bank. Inside, Rabia went up to the cashier and handed her the withdrawal slip for 'Rupees one lakh thirty-two thousand and eighty only'. The cashier, unaccustomed to such large withdrawals, excused herself and went into the branch manager's glass cabin. A few minutes later, a lazy-looking peon came up to Rabia and asked her to accompany him to the manager.

Looking a little worried, Rabia entered the cabin. The cashier looked at her as if she had tried to rob the bank, but the manager's genial smile put her at ease. 'Beti, do you want to withdraw all your money and close your account permanently?' he asked. Relieved, Rabia smiled and replied, 'I had saved all this money for my nikah. I'm getting married today. So I'm withdrawing it all.'

The manager nodded but enquired, 'Congratulations, but shouldn't your husband-to-be take care of the nikah expenses?'

Rabia puffed up her chest. 'A modern girl shares all expenses with her husband.'

The manager nodded. 'I wish my daughter were as modern as you.' He signed on the withdrawal slip and asked the reluctant cashier to encash the amount. Rabia, grateful and relieved, thanked the manager and left.

She counted the notes and then rolled them up, tucking the roll deep into her small Rexine handbag. Then Zohra and she went off for their shopping spree.

The manager, who had been watching them through his cabin's glass door, dialled a number on his phone as they exited.

'I have a tip for you,' he said.

◉

Tanvir stood at the far north corner of the footbridge across the train tracks, near Grant Road railway station. After the construction of the new underground subway that exited near the ticket counter, commuters wishing to economize on every second of their hurried journey had abandoned the footbridge. It was now used in the evenings by ragpickers, drug addicts and 'five-rupee whores' who spilled over from the nearby Kamathipura. Tanvir had chosen this place because at that time of the morning, it was almost deserted. A more important reason, though, was the height—he was at an elevated vantage point and could spot anyone coming towards him at a distance of 500 yards.

Tanvir dialled the mobile number scrawled on his hand. The 1990s Hindi film song *'Ek rasta aha aha...'* started playing. The song was cut short by a male voice. 'Yes?'

Tanvir began, 'I was given your number...'

'No need to explain, I know who you are. This number is not given to many people,' said the other person. Tanvir now fell silent, not knowing how to proceed. The man at the other end sensed his ambivalence.

'So, are you ready?'

'Ready for what'? Tanvir enquired, his manner cagey.

'Ready to take your destiny into your own hands and guide it to glory?'

'Yes,' Tanvir said, with just the right inflection of fanaticism in his voice.

The other man replied, 'Good, I will tell you what you have to do to join the jihad.'

But what he said next further parched Tanvir's already dry throat. His fingers went numb as he clutched the mobile. Somehow he managed to reply 'Yes' that came out as part croak, part cry for help. Thankfully for Tanvir, the man didn't catch on to his discomfort. '*Allah Hafiz*,' he said and cut the line, after giving detailed instructions.

The corners of Tanvir's mouth drooped. Using the overbridge railings for support, he closed his eyes to stabilize himself.

◉

Chhatrapati Shivaji Terminus Railway Station, still sometimes referred to as 'VT' (a nostalgic abbreviation for Victoria Terminus) by many a local Mumbaikar, is one of the world's most crowded places in the evenings. It has to bear the double brunt of the office-going crowds returning home and the out-of-town passengers leaving for various destinations across the country. Somehow, it survives this onslaught day after day. Such is its stony resilience that it has also survived a brutal terrorist attack with not a scar to show.

But in the middle of that morning, the terminus was quite empty. Tanvir stood on Platform No. 5 cursing the emptiness, while waiting for the Bhagalpur Lokmanya Tilak Express to pull in. He attempted to take cover, standing right in the middle of a knot of on-holiday taxi drivers who were heading home to their native Bihar. In order to avoid undue attention, he flashed an occasional smile and bobbed a cursory nod at the excited banter between the taxi drivers.

As the express train drew into the platform, he sidled towards the door of an approaching bogey. He extended his hand to grab the door handle, but was in turn grabbed from behind and pulled away from the train. Before he could protest, he was bundled across to the other side of the platform, into the bogey of an empty local train. Tanvir realized that his silent captors were two unsmiling well-built men, whose manner and clothing screamed 'plain clothes policemen'. He did not say anything but sat still, deciding to preserve his energy. He had a feeling he was going to need a lot of it that day.

The train lurched forward and rolled out of CST, heading to the repair yard. At the last minute, a man jumped on. Tanvir shook his head and sighed as the man, ACP Hani, walked towards him and sat down on the empty seat opposite his. The two plain clothes men let Tanvir go and receded in the distance. As soon as they were out of earshot, Tanvir blurted out the details of what the man on the mobile phone had asked him to do.

A crowded local train screamed past, on its way to CST. The ACP listened to Tanvir and kept nodding, poker-faced, while the rhythmic clank-clank of the passing local train filled their compartment. As soon as the train had passed them, the ACP looked straight into his eyes and said, 'Do it.'

Tanvir stared at him, aghast. ACP Hani didn't him give a chance to speak. 'This is war,' he said. 'Any measure for the greater common good is okay in a war.'

Tanvir set his jaw firmly. 'I won't. I will be labelled for life.'

'Aalamzeb will kill you, and a few thousand other people. How would you like to be labelled as the man who let that happen?' asked the ACP.

Tanvir's protests continued. But ACP Hani was past caring. He stood up and pulled the stop-chain. The train trundled to a stop near the Masjid Bunder station. The two plain clothes men grabbed Tanvir. Without warning, they pushed him out of the local train and jumped out behind him. To his luck, Tanvir landed on his feet. The men then dragged him through a break in the wall next to the train tracks. Before any passer by could react, he was bundled into a waiting police jeep and whisked away towards Chira Bazaar.

○

Chira Bazaar's narrow lanes comprise mainly old three-storey buildings with jewellery shops and wedding-invitation-card shops in front. However, over time, these buildings have begun to get 'modernized'. That is, to accommodate the ubiquitous new-fangled 'ready-made garment' shops at the street level, and the seedier 'massage parlours' on the darker floors above.

Tanvir was marched up the stairs of one of these old buildings. On the rooftop stood ACP Hani who, without a word of greeting, pointed at places along the rooftops of the surrounding buildings. Tanvir's eyes strained hard to notice that a man, with what seemed to him a powerful long-range rifle, was positioned at each of these points. These men had their eyes trained on the shifting sea of humanity on the streets below.

'These sharpshooters will protect you,' the ACP said, his manner terse but reassuring. Tanvir looked unconvinced. In a flash, the ACP's tone changed to his favourite cold one, 'And if you don't do Aalamzeb's bidding, they will shoot at you. They won't kill you, just maim you. But in such a way that, I promise, these wounds will stay with you for long.'

Tanvir snarled back this time, 'ACP saab, don't push me too far. Remember, I'm the one who's charged with three attempted murders.'

ACP Hani smiled, '*Arre, shabash*! That's the way! Channelize all your energy into hatred for my kind. You will not falter. Go now. Meet me at the saloon later.'

Tanvir turned away from the ACP. Seething with rage but managing to control himself, he walked down the dark wooden stairs into the street.

◉

At that very moment, inside a Chira Bazaar jewellery shop, Rabia's keen eyes were inspecting an exquisite green crystal floral motif crafted into the heart-shaped centrepiece of an exquisite kundan jhumar, one of the most coveted ornaments for a Muslim bride. Pinned on one side of the bride's hair, the flowing jhumar, with its special gem setting, lends her a dignified communal identity.

This particular jhumar was on display at Popular Jewels, one of the smallest but oldest jewellery shops in Chira Bazaar. Popular Jewels had earned a reputation for being one of the last few shops that provided superb traditional craftsmanship at affordable rates. The owners were known for their honesty, but on the flip side, the shop also had a reputation for a laid-back attitude towards security.

It was, therefore, not a shock when a gangly well-dressed young man walked into Popular Jewels without being stopped. He had been following Rabia ever since he had received the tip-off from the bank manager. He sauntered up to Rabia and without warning, snatched her Rexine handbag off the glass-topped counter where she'd placed it while trying on the jhumar. Rabia blinked, confused, not understanding what such a well-dressed young man would want with her bag. But when the man loped towards the exit, she displayed an alertness alien to her otherwise languid nature. She rose, screamed

'Chor! Chor!' and, with a speed seen only in professional sportspersons, sprang behind the thief, who had just about managed to reach the exit door.

The store's lax attitude was on full display—the security guard's chair by the door was empty. As a considerate afterthought, the guard had left behind his antique 12-bore rifle propped against the wall, perhaps hoping that its presence would deter a thieving mind.

In fact, this kindly act was what saved the day. Rabia, chasing after the thief, grabbed the rifle instinctively and emerged with it on to the crowded street. The sight of a burqa-clad woman brandishing a 12-bore rifle on the busy street, combined with Rabia roaring 'Chor!' had its effect. Most passers-by leapt out of the way. Fearing for their lives, they ducked down to avoid any errant bullets. This gave Rabia a clear view of the running thief. She raised the rifle, as if ready to fire.

'Stop!' she yelled, as the thief was clearly in her sight. But nearby was also a police constable, who had just turned the corner, curious about the source of the commotion. All of a sudden, Rabia seemed to come out of a trance. The realization of what she had been about to do hit her in the gut. In a flash, she lowered the gun. But not before the constable, too, had ducked to the side, fearing that he might encounter a bullet from her rifle. While doing so, he bumped into the thief, who was swerving past to avoid him. The thief was thrown off balance and landed on the dirty street with a loud thump. His head hit the ground and he was out cold. The constable, trying to regain his balance, saw that Rabia was still standing with the 12-bore in her hands, in a state of scared confusion. Equally confused, he grabbed the rifle from her and asked her to kneel on the ground. Between her gasps, Rabia tried to explain the sequence of events, but the constable would have none of it. A small crowd surged around, flinging questions at them and at each other.

To Rabia's luck, Zohra arrived on the scene right then. She lifted her veil and gave the constable a beaming smile. He blushed, self-conscious. She placed a soft hand on his wrist and took him aside, casually pressing her breast on to his arm as he stepped away with her. Having caught his absolute attention, Zohra started recounting the chain of events to him to prove that Rabia was actually the victim. Meanwhile, Rabia stood on one side, catching her breath and examining the contents of her handbag, which she had managed to extricate from the unconscious thief's grasp.

◉

Tanvir walked through the crowded streets, almost zombie-like. The weight of the world seemed to sit on his shoulders. The noonday sun beat down on his already hot head. Realizing that his energy was draining fast, he stopped at a roadside nimbu sharbat wallah. He picked up a chilled glass of nimbu sharbat on display. Downing the tangy-sweet syrup in one gulp, he experienced the surge of courage that he had been desperately looking within himself for. He asked for another glass.

Across the street, Tanvir saw a constable talking on his mobile phone, trying to explain something.

A woman in a burqa walked up to Tanvir and, without a word, handed him a small plastic carry bag that she withdrew from the folds of her burqa. She pointed towards the constable. Before Tanvir could react, she merged into the crowd.

Tanvir's body tensed. Drawing a quick breath, he looked heavenwards. Then, without another word, he strode towards the constable, the plastic carry bag in his hand. In the middle of the street, Tanvir put his hand inside the bag and took out a small revolver. He cocked the revolver without breaking his stride and stood in front of the constable, who was still engrossed in his conversation. At point-blank range he raised the revolver. The constable's jaw dropped. He froze with fright. Tanvir squeezed the trigger. But the hammer just clicked. He squeezed again. Nothing. Now Tanvir went crazy, squeezing the trigger in quick succession. But the gun just kept clicking. It was then that the psyched-out Tanvir realized that there were no bullets in the gun.

Tanvir and the constable both reeled in shock, staring at each other.

A woman somewhere let out a hysterical scream, breaking the spell. Tanvir turned and ran pell-mell. He kept running until he was far away from the scene of crime.

The constable, still stunned with fear, turned his attention towards the woman who had screamed. He realized that it was the same burqa-clad woman who had run after the young thief. The same woman who had been taken aside by her other burqa-clad friend, and had been sipping a cold drink while he called his senior to explain the incident.

The constable's blood pressure dropped and his eyes began to droop. Through the haze creeping over his mind, he wondered why she had been so hysterical. Just before he fainted, the constable also realized that the screaming woman's flirty companion had disappeared.

◉

Zohra stood shivering at an STD booth near the Jama Masjid. She had run all the way without once stopping to catch her breath. Running away was not new to her. In fact, she had been trained to run away at the smallest hint of trouble while growing up in her small village near Kupwara in Kashmir. The rule there was: 'If you see a gun, run. If you see a man near the gun, run harder. If you see a man holding a gun, there is no use running, a bullet can outrun you.' Today, she was thankful she had defied the rules.

But now, she was scared. The man holding the gun had been right in front of her. But she was not dead. She had had her veil down, so he had not recognized her. But she had. She knew that it would only be a short while before the police connected all the dots and came knocking at her door.

Zohra decided that it was time to break the rules again.

She picked up the phone and dialled 100.

◉

Tanvir was gasping for his life in a dark recess. He had run into an excrement-encrusted by-lane between two old buildings off Shuklaji Street. Every breath he took filled his lungs with revolting odours. But he had no choice. At this time of the day, this was the only place that would accord him a safe moment.

Tanvir was about to throw up when he noticed a burqa-clad woman entering the lane. He could only see her shape silhouetted against the sun-drenched outer street. But as she came closer, he realized that it was the same woman who had handed the revolver to him in Chira Bazaar. Her palm was extended towards Tanvir. As she reached him, she said, in a deep male voice, 'Give me the gun, quickly!' Tanvir noticed that her arm had dark hair curling above her wrist. Unsure, he slid further back into the dark recess. The burqa-clad 'woman' raised her veil to reveal the stone throwing 'computer salesman' who had given Aalamzeb's mobile number to him. The man flashed his hyena grin. 'Surprised? Don't be. We are only a few, but very effective. And now, you are one of us.'

Tanvir stood his ground by not placing the revolver into the man's hand. Instead, he spat out, 'Why were there no bullets in the revolver?'

The man stopped smiling. 'The whole exercise was only to make sure you are not a policeman. If you were, you would never have fired on another of your kind.'

Tanvir let the logic in the answer permeate into his mind. He had to admit it was an ingenious identity test.

'Our leader saw this trick in some old film. He uses it all the time. It never fails.'

But this time it had failed, laughed Tanvir to himself. Thanks to ACP Hani's killer instinct. Tanvir took out the revolver from his waistband and handed it over to the man. The revolver disappeared into the folds of the burqa. The man turned to leave. Just as he was about to disappear, he said, 'Keep your mobile on, you will be contacted soon.' He gave Tanvir a thumbs-up. Tanvir was sure that he was grinning away under the veil.

Tanvir had had enough of this hide-and-seek in dark alleys. He walked out into the bright sunlight.

◎

The A-1 Air-Cooled Hair-Cutting Centre, aka 'The Saloon', lay in the middle of 6th Cross Lane off Foras Road, in the heart of Mumbai's red-light district. In business for the past eighty years, it still operated in a manner that was quite anachronistic in this age of beauty parlours, hair stylists and spas. 'Air-cooled' by air-conditioners close to its own age, its rigid three-hairstyle menu appealed only to those unadventurous men that passed by it on the way to their daily sexual romps. In tandem with its age-old style of functioning, the staff took a three-hour siesta every afternoon. The third-generation owner, Mustafa Angiwala, had tried his best to make the staff give up this financially unviable habit, but to no avail. Fed up with their mutinous attitude, he had decided to let out the saloon premises to anyone who wanted a quick afternoon rendezvous, no questions asked.

It was here that ACP Hani sat wrapped in the white barber cloth, ensconced in one of the oldest 'barber chairs'. To all appearances, he was just another man waiting for his haircut, but in fact, he had been waiting for the past hour for Tanvir to show up. His patience was wearing thin.

Just when he was ready to tear off the barber cloth and leave, Tanvir entered the saloon. Without looking at him, the ACP proclaimed, 'They were too smart for us this time. But you didn't fail in your task. I'm proud of you, Tanvir, you would have made a good policeman.' As the acrid stench accompanying Tanvir burst across the closed air-conditioned room, the ACP scrunched up his nose in disgust. 'Have you been swimming in a gutter?'

Tanvir paid him no heed as he slumped down in an adjacent barber chair. 'I'm just being used as a pawn by Aalamzeb and you. It's time you let me out of this.'

ACP Hani shook his head, as if exasperated with a child's whim. 'Tanvir, you have to play out your role till the very end.'

Tanvir looked into his eyes and said, 'I'm a gangster. Not a policeman. I don't want to die in this crossfire between you and some terrorists.'

'The role you are playing, my friend is the most crucial. You are...'

'I'm just the bait. And the bait always gets eaten up.'

The ACP said, with a softness not displayed earlier, 'Why did I choose you, Tanvir? Precisely because you are a gangster and could never be seen as a policeman. Even if your cover of a gym instructor was blown, it would be seen as a gangster's attempt to go straight. These Pakistanis are ruthless. They know that you are not in the police force, and they also know that you are not the honest man you claim to be. Now, they appreciate the fact that you are a killer, too.'

Tanvir didn't say anything. The ACP shook his head and took off the barber cloth. Tanvir saw that he was shirtless. But what transfixed him was a black string with a silver cylindrical taveez around the ACP's neck. The ACP saw that Tanvir had noticed his taveez. He smiled. 'Yes, bhaijaan, I, too, am a Muslim like you. We are the chosen ones, you and I.'

Tanvir raised an eyebrow. 'We have to pay a high price for being a Muslim in this country.'

ACP Hani shook his head. 'No, my friend. You are paying the price for being a gangster who missed the nishana, and got caught by us. I'm paying the price for being in love with my job. And together, we are going to get these Pakistani terrorists who have invaded our country.'

Tanvir now looked at the ACP with beseeching eyes. 'ACP saab, I don't want to die.'

The ACP laughed. 'Are you afraid to die...the fearless Tanvir who attempted to kill three gangsters from rival gangs?'

Tanvir shook his head, mumbling to himself, 'You're crazy...we both will die.' The ACP got up and opened the saloon door. He gestured to Tanvir to step out.

◉

Tanvir stood lounging outside the Sultan-e-Hind Restaurant. Next to him stood a man who, by his attire, could be identified as an orthodox Muslim cleric. In fact, he was a retired clerk from the Public Works Department who had been summoned by the ATS to help out in the critical job at hand—performing a fake nikah between Tanvir and Rabia.

ACP Hani had ordered Tanvir to go to the Sultan-e-Hind and carry out his promise of marrying Rabia. This ploy would force Aalamzeb's hand and make him come out in the open. The ACP had assured Tanvir that the entire area had been sanitized since the morning, and no one had spotted any rooftop shooters taking position. This meant that Aalamzeb and his men would come by road. The road was crawling with ATS personnel, who would swing into action as soon as Aalamzeb or any of his men were spotted.

Tanvir had summoned up all his resolve and managed to muster a casual air, although inside, he felt ready to collapse with the tension. The fake qazi stood next to him, muttering something under his breath that seemed, to Tanvir, a spell to ward off evil spirits. 'Welcome to my world,' he thought, leaning against a street pole.

Across the street, Rabia stared at Tanvir. She was a little taken aback by his nonchalant attitude and questioned her own sanity. A part of her wanted to run away. But the part that wanted to run into the arms of the man she loved eventually won over. She began to cross the busy road at the traffic signal.

Across the road, Tanvir spotted her. His face broke into the open-faced smile that Rabia found so endearing. He raised his hand and signalled to her to come towards him. He pointed towards the qazi and smiled even more broadly. Rabia gave him a half-smile and stepped onto the zebra crossing as the signal turned red.

All of a sudden, two nondescript Ambassador cars pulled out from the traffic in unison on both sides of the road. One stopped in front of Rabia and the other one in front of Tanvir. Their doors were flung open; strong hands emerged and both Tanvir and Rabia were pulled into the respective cars. The signal turned green and before anyone could respond, the cars sped away in opposite directions.

On the rooftop across Sultan-e-Hind, ACP Hani screamed into his walkie-talkie, 'Hold your positions! Don't fire. They are policemen!'

◎

'I work for ACP Hani of the ATS!' screamed Tanvir. Before he could say anything further, a hard open-palm slap hit his bare body. He had been subjected to these slaps nonstop for the last fifteen minutes. They stung hard as they made contact, and yet, hardly left a mark. A few dozen of these at the right spots on the body caused immense pain to the recipient's internal organs, so much so that he would collapse in agony. Yet, to the casual observer, there would not even be a scratch on him. The police used these specially designed slaps on criminals so that they could not, in the future, have an opportunity to yell 'Police brutality!'

Tanvir was not alien to blows and knocks. Throughout his criminal career, he had received quite a few. But this was different. This was a virtual barrage. Just when he felt that he would pass out from the pain, a police officer, who appeared to be senior to the others, entered the small backroom of the Robert Circle lockup where this 'interrogation' was being conducted. He motioned to the other policemen to stop. Turning to the policeman standing next to him, he asked, 'How did we capture this gandu?'

'Parab Saheb, we received an anonymous tip-off by some woman who called the control room.'

Parab walked up to Tanvir, whose hands were tied to a rope that hung from the ceiling.

'Sir, please call ACP Hani and ask him about me!' pleaded Tanvir through his pain.

Without warning, Parab spat on Tanvir's face. 'You harami! I'm from the Crime Branch. If I have not heard of this ACP Hani, he doesn't exist.'

'He exists. Please believe me.' Tanvir swallowed as he launched into his story. 'From the way he operates, I think ACP Hani is from a top-secret section of the ATS. He contacted me six months back. He told me that after 26/11, a few more Pakistanis had entered Mumbai. A man called Aalamzeb was suspected to be their leader. The ATS had come to know that a big blast was being planned.'

The policemen in the room stood shocked. Tanvir continued, 'ACP Hani told me that these people were Pakistanis hiding amongst Muslims in Mumbai. Therefore, he needed an unknown Muslim, who would never be suspected and who could get to Aalamzeb's through a Kamathipura prostitute called Rabia, his mistress. I was instructed to visit Rabia as a client and then fake love for her. Since during earlier operations using regular policemen, their identity would get revealed and Aalamzeb would disappear, the need of the hour was to be discreet and operate using local people. That's why my help was important.'

Parab chided him now, '*Haan zarur*! A man with three

attempted murders on his name would be the perfect choice to save this crazy city'.

Tanvir controlled his anger at the police officer's pompous attitude. 'ACP Hani asked for my help in averting the carnage planned by these terrorists, and that was the reason I decided to be a part of his operation.'

Parab was still full of bluff and bluster. 'Achcha, so, how come we poor Crime Branch officers don't know anything about this so-called operation, whilst a third-rate chutiya like you does?'

Without hesitation, Tanvir spat out, 'I told you already, ACP Hani wanted to avoid details of the operation getting leaked out to stupid maadarchods like you, who don't know of anything beyond hafta vasooli.'

This time, the blow with a leather-booted foot was aimed straight at Tanvir's testicles. There was no attempt whatsoever to hide the marks. Tanvir doubled over in excruciating pain. Parab sneered, 'There will be no jail for you, lundfakir, just a straight "encounter" killing.'

Tanvir didn't hear the last part as he fainted due to the pain.

In an adjoining room, Rabia had been forced to stand and watch the proceeding through a one-way mirror panel.

She broke down in a flood of tears as she heard the story.

◉

It was not often that a senior officer like Parab visited the Robert Circle lockup in person, so the entire staff was in attendance. Parab sat like a feudal lord astride a desk in the office room. The mood in the room was upbeat, and the fawning inspectors and constables who had gathered were sharing a rare jocularity. Vada paos, along with chai, had been devoured, and the duty constable had just delivered his latest punchline in a string of bawdy jokes. But the laughter reverberating off the walls was cut short at the sight of the grim-faced ACP Hani striding into the main office area.

The ACP, still dressed in his municipal jamadar uniform, was accompanied by a group of plain clothes policemen, dressed in an assortment of street civvies. The laughing policemen of Robert Circle took one look at this motley group, and their mood switched from lax to alert. A policeman knows when he was in the company of the elite of his ilk. The ACP strode up to Parab and asked, 'So, are you the one who ordered the operation...sir?'

Parab was still recovering from the sudden shift in mood in the room. 'Who are you?' he asked in turn, confused.

Without replying, ACP Hani handed him two typed sheets of official papers, bearing the signature and seal of the Mumbai commissioner of police.

'I hope Tanvir Khanzada and Rabia Bano have not been harmed?' hissed the ACP through his teeth.

Parab, who was reading the official papers, now stood up, defiant. 'Just because you have letters from the CP, it doesn't make you something special. I will hand over the prisoners after their proper interrogation.'

The ACP stepped closer to him and whispered, 'I don't want to insult you in front of your juniors, so please, hand over both of them to me right now, and let me be on my way.'

Instead of complying, Parab chose to start grandstanding. 'You think you can march in here and order me around... Who the fuck do you think you are?'

The ACP said, 'My name is Hani. I am with the ATS. I am on a mission, and I have orders to do whatever it takes to achieve my mission. What my mission is, it's not important for you to know, but please understand that it is to ensure the safety of lakhs of people.'

'So you are the man who ordered that bhadva criminal to shoot at my constable?' said Parab, his face contorted with jealousy and hatred.

ACP Hani replied in a measured tone, 'I didn't order him. It was a necessity for a larger purpose.'

'So for a "larger purpose" you are ready to sacrifice a fellow policeman's life?' Parab was in no mood to let up.

The ACP sighed, 'The constable was never under threat. I figured that it was just an initiation strategy, similar to one used by the FLN revolutionaries in Algeria in the late 1950s. In those days, it was the ultimate act of courage, the act of shooting a policeman pointblank on the streets. The gun was not loaded, but the shooter believed it was. If the shooter refused to pull the trigger, it was believed that he was with the police, and he was executed. If he did pull the trigger, he was inducted. The men that we are dealing with are highly knowledgeable in various techniques and well trained.'

Parab was incredulous. 'How can you be so sure? It was just pure luck that the gun did not fire. What if my man was killed?' He spoke loudly, with the obvious intention of inciting his men.

The ACP shook his head, exasperated, then turned and nodded towards his men. Like a well-oiled machine, the ACP's men fanned out throughout the room in positions that blocked any movement in or out. From the folds of their clothes, they produced automatic machine guns. They kept their guns pointed to the ground, but the threat was clearly communicated to all. Parab and the other policemen in the room were stunned at the turn of events. Before they could recover, the ACP confronted the senior officer, 'Listen, you two-bit rat, my time is precious. I don't want to get into any politics with you...'

Parab was rabid now. 'I will show you politics... How dare you threaten me?' He punched a number on his mobile. 'I want to speak to Nandkar Bhau... Yes... Hello Bhau, there is an ACP here whom I don't know. But, he is threatening my men that if I don't release some prisoners...his name...I think it is Hani... What? Why? But...' he stopped speaking and extended the mobile phone towards ACP Hani. 'The home minister wants to talk to you.'

The ACP took the phone. 'Yes, sir...no problem, sir...okay, sir, thank you.' He handed the phone to Parab, who blustered, 'Sir, I want action against...' The corners of his mouth drooped as he listened to the minister. 'But...but...' he blubbered, then cleared his throat. It was obvious to everyone in the room that the line had been disconnected. He stood, looking at the ACP with a crushed expression, then put down the phone and cleared his throat again, but still didn't say anything.

ACP Hani spoke instead, 'Six months of planning have gone down the drain because you decided to play a political stunt to gain sympathy among your policemen. Today, you've only lost your posting... I hope that no lives are lost because of your stupid actions...otherwise...'

◎

Dr Chitrekar's Lie-in Clinic in Agripada was a semi-derelict two-storeyed structure. It stood at a slight distance from the chawls lining the thin gullies, opposite the YMCA. Its healthcare service had once been the pride of the people of the neighbourhood, who were very happy with the cleanliness and the sanitary environment at the clinic. So much so that it was rumoured that a famous local underworld don of yesteryears, who was afflicted with a potentially fatal disease, refused treatment at the swankier Jaslok Hospital, choosing Dr Chitrekar's instead.

Dr Chitrekar had died many years ago, and the clinic had passed into the hands of a trust under the administration of Dr Chitrekar's grandson, who was not a doctor, but a professional gambler desperate to sell the property to the highest bidder to feed his gambling habit. The other members of the trust had refused to indulge the grandson and he, in turn, had let the clinic languish. The few doctors who still visited the clinic only conducted a cursory examination there. If the patients were found to be lucrative catches, they would be called to meet the doctors at their own private clinics.

From time to time, however, some doctors used the clinic as a base for shady private treatments like inconvenient abortions for mistresses of valued clientele or hush-hush hymenoplasties for brides-to-be, who wanted to restore their virginity as a 'wedding gift' for their unsuspecting 'arranged' grooms. Sometimes, surgeries could also involve closing a gaping bullet or a stab wound. Needless to say, maintaining a high level of secrecy was crucial.

It was one such doctor who was treating the still-in-pain Tanvir in an inner private room of Dr Chitrekar's clinic. Rabia was seated in the adjoining room, under the watchful eye of a heavyset female police officer. The strained expression on Rabia's face was proof of her ordeal and that she was reconciled to face more.

As ACP Hani entered, the female officer took her cue and

left. The ACP sat down in front of Rabia, who looked prepared for the worst. 'Tanvir is a good man,' was the ACP's opening line. Rabia's expression did not change. The ACP changed tack and went flat out, 'Your…friend…Aalamzeb, is one of the gunmen who came into Mumbai along with the 26/11 terrorists.'

This piece of information did the trick, Rabia looked as if she was about to faint. But what the ACP didn't tell her was even more deadly. Six months earlier, the ATS had come to know that one more motorized dinghy had landed somewhere along the eastern coast of Mumbai, along with the 26/11 attackers. In that dinghy were five people, including Aalamzeb, with a cargo of enough RDX to blow up three or four high-rise buildings in Mumbai. These men formed a sleeper cell, who would blend in with the local populace and wait for the right time to strike. They would accumulate the RDX at an attack point in a slow trickle, so as not to arouse suspicion. When the time was right, they would carry out a spectacular bombing attack, akin to the one on the World Trade Center in New York. To stop this from happening, ACP Hani, previously a trainer at the Counter Terrorism and Jungle Warfare College in Kanker, Chhattisgarh, had been summoned by the Maharashtra home minister.

The scion of an aristocratic Konkani Muslim family, ACP Hani, despite protests from his genteel business family, had opted for the IPS after his graduation from Mumbai's St Xavier's College. During his probationary period itself, the dynamic young Hani had been spotted as 'a man who had a future' by his seniors in the Maharashtra cadre. He had been sent for specialized training to Israel with the Mossad specialists right after 26/11. Thereafter, he was deputed at the

CTJWC because he had stood first in his counter-terrorism course, performing better than many an Israeli commando. During the past year, he had been given charge of a special cell that reported only to the home minister. He had agreed to take on the mission only after the home minister had agreed to the ACP's intentions of 'taking on guerrillas like a guerrilla'.

ACP Hani had got a tip-off from an informer about Aalamzeb. But instead of nabbing him right away, his men had started tailing Aalamzeb to figure out who the other four Pakistani sleepers were and also to find out what had happened to the RDX. Three months earlier, an ATS officer had made a mistake while following Aalamzeb, and Aalamzeb had managed to give them the slip.

The ACP continued, 'We had been following Aalamzeb and discovered his regular visits to you.' He was now a little sheepish. 'So we recruited Tanvir to "befriend" you and find out whether you are clean or not.' He looked at the still-impassive Rabia. 'Tanvir told us about what happened to you, about the heinous crime committed against you, and that you were innocent. Aalamzeb, we realized, had fallen in love with you, so we had to use a ploy to force his hand, if possible. So Tanvir proposed to marry you, under my orders. I'm sorry for that.'

A single tear escaped Rabia's eye.

'Tanvir is a gangster, but he's a patriotic man who is helping the ATS. And now, I want help from another good person—you,' said ACP Hani, his voice as flat as possible.

Despite the tremendous pressure that Rabia felt in her chest, she maintained an even manner. 'You want my help?'

'Yes.' The ACP nodded. 'Call Aalamzeb and tell him that you have come to know about what he did to Tanvir. Beg for his mercy, plead with him to spare you and Tanvir. Ask to meet him one last time.'

For what seemed like an aeon, Rabia didn't say anything. She kept staring at the lazy billowing curtain at the dusty window of the room. The ACP sat patiently, waiting for her answer. Then, almost when it seemed that she would never speak again, she turned. 'All right, I'll do what you say. But first, I want you to set Tanvir free.'

⊙

Tanvir was being helped to his feet by a ward boy when Rabia was ushered into the room. Not wanting to reveal the extent of his discomfort, he pushed the surprised ward boy aside and stood on his own, albeit with some difficulty. Rabia walked up to him and placed a soft hand on his cheek.

'How are you feeling now?' she asked.

Tanvir reached out to hug her. But she stepped aside, taking care not to throw him off balance, to indicate to him that she was in command of this meeting. A hesitant voice rose from somewhere within him. 'Please forgive me, Rabia.'

Rabia allowed herself a tight smile. 'ACP Hani has asked me to perform a task for him. So I just came to say goodbye.'

Tanvir's voice instantly rose by a decibel, 'Rabia, listen to me. Please. I was caught in a trap. I had to do what they wanted me to. But you don't fall for their tricks. Don't do anything that the ACP asks you to do...otherwise...' he trailed off.

'Otherwise, what?' Rabia asked.

'Otherwise you'll become like me.'

She shook her head. 'I'm sorry. But I don't think I'll ever become like you.' The firmness in her voice surprised him. He stared at her, crestfallen.

Rabia looked him straight in the eye. 'Tell me this: do you love me?' she asked in a softened tone.

Tanvir shifted his stare to the ground. He still didn't speak. Rabia gave him one last look and walked out of the room.

◉

'Will you please forgive me?' asked Rabia, with a hint of a sob in her voice.

The voice on the other side of the telephone fell silent. 'When there is love, there is no question of forgiveness,' came a calm reply, after a long wait.

Rabia was speaking to Aalamzeb on a hotwired landline. Seated next to her, the ATS technology experts were trying to trace the location of the number that Aalamzeb was using. But they were failing miserably, as the connection was routed through four Indian states, as well as through Dubai and Tajikistan, back to Mumbai.

As promised, Rabia had placed this call at ACP Hani's behest. He had briefed her on what to say. 'First, greet him the way you normally would. Then ask him for forgiveness.' Rabia was following her script.

'Then you would know that one can't help falling in love,' she continued. A hollow laugh was all she got in return.

'I know that you got Tanvir involved in a criminal activity. Please don't. He is innocent and, sometimes, hotheaded. He gets easily swayed by people.' Another hollow laugh was offered in reply.

'Tanvir and I want to start a life together. Please spare us.' Aalamzeb fell silent now. Rabia seized the moment 'But before that, I want to meet you one last time, for the sake of all that you gave me. Will you meet me?'

The silence was prolonged this time. For a brief moment the ACP felt that Aalamzeb had left the line, but then his voice crackled through, 'Excel Godown. Next to the Sewree Christian Cemetery. In exactly two hours.'

The line was disconnected.

◉

Tanvir paced up and down the room that seemed to get smaller and smaller with every stride. He felt like shooting someone in the head, gouging someone's eyes out. The fury at his situation was burning an acid hole inside him. At the best of times, Tanvir was a man who hated being helpless and uncertain. The current scenario, where he was unable to 'fix' anything, was driving him up the wall.

His mind was screaming at him to walk away from the clinic and bid goodbye to Mumbai for life, but his heart was behaving like a super-charged magnet keeping him glued to his place.

He forced his mind to relax and focus on what was keeping him back. It wasn't the fact that he still had the three attempted-murder charges on him—ACP Hani had already told him that his services were not needed any more and he was a free man. It wasn't that he wanted to somehow avenge the pain and humiliation heaped upon him by the police officer at the Robert Circle lockup. All of a sudden, he stopped pacing the room and stood still. It dawned on him. Rabia.

As his thoughts became clearer, he realized that he didn't want to leave Rabia alone in this situation. He wanted to protect her.

An orphan who had made something of himself in the city, Tanvir did not get attached easily, but his connection with Rabia was something he was not willing to give up anytime soon.

He sat down on the bed as the full import of the feeling finally hit him like a punch in the solar plexus.

◎

Under the given circumstances, the appearance of a Turkish evil eye pendant, about the size of a child's playing marble, in the hands of ACP Hani, seemed nothing short of bizarre. Also known as the 'nazar bead' because of its appearance, the pendant is supposed to attract the evil eye and absorb its damaging power before it affects the wearer. Therefore, the bead is always on display, and not worn as a secret talisman. After a plain clothes policewoman, at the behest of the ACP, slung it around Rabia's neck, its bright blue hue seemed all the more striking against the jet-black of Rabia's burqa.

However, this particular pendant was not quite what it seemed. It contained a high-resolution chip-camera, no bigger than the head of a standard sized screw. Powered by a battery as big as a matchstick head, the camera could record high-quality video and sound for up to three hours.

Rabia had been briefed about the operation in detail. She was to enter Excel Godown, meet Aalamzeb and engage him in conversation. While doing so, she should ensure that she turned towards every other person in the room, so as to record their images on the camera. After concluding her conversation, she should leave the premises as soon as possible. Once she was back with them, the ATS would extract the camera. Then they would confront the terrorists immediately. Helped by the images retrieved from the camera, the ATS would know the lay of the land, and also be able to identify all the terrorists.

Even if one of them escaped, his image would be flashed in the media prominently enough for someone to identify him sooner or later.

Rabia was pacing up and down the ward, going through the instructions in her head. For a moment, her eyes rested upon a crack in the door across from her. To her surprise, she saw Tanvir in the adjoining room, getting strapped up in a bulletproof jacket. Agitated, Rabia called out to ACP Hani, 'ACP saab, I asked you to let Tanvir go.'

The ACP saw what she was looking at and then said, 'He has volunteered himself. He has seen the face of one of the others with Aalamzeb and can identify him instantly.'

'But I will get the images on this camera. I promise.'

The ACP shrugged. 'We need him as backup. You never know what might happen.'

Rabia lapsed into a frustrated silence.

◎

The Christian Cemetery is a silent oasis in the midst of the hurly burly of Mumbai's chemical manufacturing and port-warehousing area, Sewree. It was established by Arthur Crawford, the first municipal commissioner of Bombay, on a horticultural garden next to the saltpans and the ruined Sewree Fort. Consecrated in March 1867, it has served as the final resting place for many, Britishers of the Raj including F. W. Stevens, who designed the VT station and A. M. Jacob of Shimla, said to be the inspiration for Rudyard Kipling's jeweller-cum-magician-cum-spymaster, Lurgan Saheb.

As dusk fell, the shadowy figures of ATS men, now multiplied in numbers and adorned in 'attack gear', crawled on all fours through the cemetery. They were snaking towards the Excel Godown that bordered the eastern fencing of the cemetery. The godown had been chosen well. Its location gave a strategic advantage to the people inside. The daily business approach for it was from the open medium-width lane from the north that threaded through the maze of warehousing structures of all shapes and sizes. On the south and west of the godown were the Sewree Jetty and the saltpans, the famous refuge of flamingos during the winter months. Because of the acres of open expanse and marshy slush, the saltpans could not be used as an approach. The only approach that afforded any sort of cover was through the cemetery, that, too, only under cover of darkness.

Rabia arrived in a taxi driven by a policeman in disguise. The taxi parked outside the main gate and, as instructed, Rabia asked the taxi driver to wait for her. She walked up to the gate and was let inside by the lone sentry on duty. It was obvious that the sentry had been awaiting her arrival. He motioned her towards a small wooden side door that led into the godown. The wooden door opened by itself as soon as she neared. Rabia disappeared from the policemen's sight as the door closed behind her.

◉

In the adjoining cemetery, ACP Hani and the ATS men waited in the shadows. Tanvir, who was a couple of paces behind the ACP, crawled up to him in the dark. 'Now what?' he enquired.

The ACP raised his finger to his lips. 'Now, we wait,' he muttered, irritated. He got busy focusing his infrared binoculars on the upper glass windows of the godown, hoping to catch some movement inside.

The night was cool, yet small sweat droplets trickled their way down Tanvir's temples. He was not used to maintaining a prone position for a long time. He felt specially constrained because of the heavy bulletproof jacket and leather boots kitted out to him by the ATS team, and shifted in his position from time to time as the alien equipment chafed his skin.

They had been lying in wait for almost two hours now, yet there was not a single movement seen in the godown. Deep worry lines furrowed ACP Hani's forehead; he kept glancing at his waterproof wristwatch and then at the taxi still waiting at the gate. The taxi driver, in true waiting-for-passenger style, was lounging with his head thrown back. However, the ACP knew that he was just pretending to sleep. But what the ACP was not sure of was whether he could see any activity through the upper glass windows of the godown. Although the taxi driver was equipped with a walky-talky, the ACP dared not contact him for fear of the signal being picked up by someone inside.

ACP Hani now turned towards his deputies and made some hand signals. The deputies started crawling in the direction of the team clusters. The team members showed signs of pushing their alertness up a few notches. Tanvir, confused at this action all around, crawled towards the ACP and whispered in his ear, 'What is happening?'

The ACP ignored him but Tanvir persisted. 'What are you doing?'

The ACP turned towards Tanvir, irritated as before, but this time there was an edge to his voice that Tanvir found very dangerous. 'Your Rabia might have gone over to their side.'

Tanvir's face fell. 'But...but...she won't do that...please wait a little while more.'

The ACP seemed firm, 'I have to attack, or this chance, too, will be lost.'

He turned to check if all the clusters were ready and was about to give the signal to fire when, all of a sudden, he heard a voice coming through a loudspeaker. 'Shame on you police-wallahs, you hide and send a woman to face danger. Innocent people of our qaum have been ill-treated by you vardiwallas for too long.'

The ACP and his squad were ready for battle before the sentence was over. The taxi driver sprang out of his seat with a drawn gun and took cover behind the taxi. The sentry on duty shrank into a corner, confused and fearful. The ACP kept trying to identify the source of the voice, but he couldn't make anything out. The voice continued, 'If you have the courage, let us fight man to man.'

The wooden door in the godown building swung open, without warning. Rabia stood in the doorway. Her mouth was taped shut and even from the distance it was clear that her hands were tied behind her back. All the ATS guns were trained on her. The voice spoke again. 'First, we are letting this innocent woman out. We got all the information that we wanted from her. We don't want to hurt her.' Rabia started walking towards the ATS men in the cemetery. No one moved a muscle. As Rabia took her slow steps towards them, the ACP trained his infrared binoculars on her. Rabia was now near a broken gap in the wire fencing between the godown premises and the cemetery. Suddenly, the ACP sucked in his breath and raised his automatic pistol simultaneously. 'Bomb!' he shouted. Before anyone could react, he shot at Rabia. The bullet hit Rabia in the arm and she spun and fell backwards on to the cemented ground. Everybody dove for cover except the shocked Tanvir, who stood up and looked towards where Rabia had fallen. She lay prone on the ground in front of the wire fencing. Tanvir let out a cry of anguish and, without thinking, ran towards her. The ACP shouted a loud 'No!' from behind, but Tanvir paid him no heed. He bounded towards Rabia and reached her in no time.

Rabia's eyes were glazed. Tanvir fell on his knees next to her, took her in his arms and hugged her. Her wound was bleeding copious amounts of blood on to the ground. Tanvir cried out, 'Please don't die. I love you. Don't leave me, please!'

Rabia fainted. Tanvir hugged her tighter. Till he became aware that under her burqa she was strapped with bombs. The ACP shouted out to him, 'Tanvir, move away now. There must be a timer backup to blow her up.' Tanvir, instead, ripped apart Rabia's burqa and saw the mass of wires and bombs strapped on her. He looked for a way to remove the contraption. Luck was on his side, as he found that the bomb makers had found the easiest and fastest way to strap bombs without their telltale bumps showing outside the clothes—a corset. The whole contraption was sewn onto a wraparound corset, fastened only by a single Velcro strip on her right side. Tanvir tore at the Velcro strip and it started to peel off. As the last of the Velcro strip unfastened, the corset came loose. There was another attachment, a metal brace clipped onto her arm. Tanvir broke this brace with one hard twist. Without hesitation, Tanvir rose with the corset in his hands and flung it away towards the godown. He then grabbed Rabia and lifting her bodily, dragged her across the gap in the wire fencing into the cemetery grounds. He rolled along with Rabia, moving on the ground as fast as he could in the opposite direction. As he reached closer to the ATS men, a couple of them stepped forward to help him. The ACP, meanwhile, asked his sharpshooters to shoot at the upper windows. They let loose a volley of gunshots that shattered all the window glass and poured bullets into the godown. After a while, the ACP raised his hand as he realized there was no return fire. He shook his head in anger and slammed his fist into a tree. He then rose and spoke into his walky-talky, 'Bomb squad. Please come forward to incident point.'

◉

A state-of-the-art sound system and a small voice-recorder were lying on a wooden table inside the empty godown. Two old chairs lay by the side, atop which two powerful loudspeakers had been positioned. The ACP surmised that the recording must have been done as soon as Rabia had entered. Then the hapless woman must have been strapped with the bombs and told to walk out as soon as the door was opened. She had been through a lot. It was a surprise that she hadn't fainted due to fear of her imminent death. The infrared laser trigger beam that he had seen through his binoculars was supposed to trigger off the bomb as soon as she stepped across the wire fence. The backup timer that he had expected was not there, but a carefully –thought out trigger had been placed under Rabia's hand. Her hand had been encased in a metal brace attached to the corset. The metal hand brace was designed to lock down her hand on the trigger, should she fall to a bullet. But somehow, the trigger had not gone off. Perhaps his bullet that had hit a nerve in her arm that had immobilized her hand movement, perhaps it was the way she had fallen, or perhaps Tanvir had taken off the jacket before her hand could automatically lock down on the button. These thoughts bounced around the ACP's head as he watched the swarm of policemen and forensics department officials working on the godown.

Aalamzeb and the terrorists were long gone. In fact, they must have left a mere ten minutes after Rabia entered, after quickly carrying out the recording, strapping and positioning, thought the ACP, as he watched his men wade through the large indoor nullah that functioned as the escape route. Through what looked like an abandoned effluent pipe, the nullah wound out towards the south emptying into to a small rivulet that ran through the saltpans leading to the Sewree creek. A small fishing boat could take three, maybe four, crouched men through the rivulet without being detected by a casual observer. The rivulet led into the mangroves bordering the creek on the far eastern side of the saltpans. From there, anybody with the know-how could have trudged through the narrow walkway of the Sewree Mangrove Park, hopped into Sewree Fort and from there, melted into the night.

The ACP rubbed his chin as he was just coming to realize the degree of organization that the Pakistani terrorists had undertaken while visiting Mumbai. They were forming a bad habit of staying one step ahead of him, and he didn't like that at all.

◎

Usually, at nights, the silence in Dr Chitrekar's Lie-in Clinic assumed almost eerie proportions. Dim lights shone only in the few wards on the ground floor that were used by the ward boys and chowkidars as their quarters. The rest of the ramshackle building would be shrouded in an uncomfortable black veil.

But tonight, a bright light shone on the second floor. This housed the room that Rabia was being treated in. She had been wheeled into the room and put on a makeshift operating table in front of a reluctant surgeon, who had been pulled out of his mistress's cosy bed. Fearing the disclosure of his peccadillo to all and sundry, he had agreed to operate on Rabia's bullet wound. Rabia had lost a lot of blood, but luckily, her blood type was the universal recipient AB+, and sufficient bottles could be obtained from the government-run JJ Hospital through semi-official channels. The bullet had passed though the thick fabric of the corset and lodged in the fleshiest part of the right deltoid. The cheating surgeon was adept at his work, and dislodged the bullet with a few quick strokes of his scalpel. He removed the bullet with his forceps and shivered at the sight as he dropped it in the garbage. After that, he went through the standard procedures of swabbing, stitching and bandaging. His work done, he smiled in relief at the ward boy assisting him, and scampered out of the ward. On the way out he bumped into Tanvir and said, 'Your wife will be all right. In about an hour or so she'll be up. The wound will heal soon. Just make sure she gets proper rest and care.' Before a relieved Tanvir could thank him, he had exited the premises, fearing that his good work might be required for others too.

Tanvir tiptoed into the wardroom to spy on the sleeping Rabia. She had a hint of a smile on her peaceful face. She did not look at all like someone who had been through hell and back. Tanvir drew up a chair and sat next to her. All of a sudden, the day's proceedings hit his body with full force. A wave of fatigue gripped him. In a flash, Tanvir had fallen asleep, snoring softly next to the slowly recovering Rabia.

◉

Tanvir opened his eyes a crack. Rabia was staring at him with a blank look. He opened his eyes further. Rabia didn't shift her gaze. Tanvir sprang towards her. Her eyes flickered an acknowledgement as he went closer, but he stopped short as he saw a flash of anger in them. He didn't know whether to be happy at her having regained consciousness or to be sad at the hardness of her expression.

'My life is over.' She spat out the words. The anger in her voice was palpable.

Tanvir's voice was soft. 'Don't say that, Rabia. Allah granted you life. You are going to be fine.'

Rabia looked away at the dust-caked window, as if trying to spot any sign of normal life outside on the street. Tanvir continued, 'You tried your best, but Aalamzeb escaped. Now our work is over. We can go away. As far away as you want.'

Rabia screamed, 'You don't understand. Get away from me before you cause more harm. I don't want you in my life anymore.'

Tanvir reeled in shock. He tried to speak, but couldn't find any words.. He stood at the foot of Rabia's bed, shifting from one foot to another, unsure of what to do next.

ACP Hani's entry broke the pall of awkward silence that had fallen over the room. Unmindful of the swirling tension, the ACP ignored Tanvir's presence and strode towards Rabia's bed. 'I'm sorry that I shot you.' The accompanying nonchalant shrug indicated that he wasn't really sorry. 'It was something I had to do to save the others…and in the process, save you.'

Rabia didn't speak, but her eyes conveyed that she didn't really care for what the ACP was saying. The ACP, too, realized that he was not making much headway, so in his usual manner he abruptly changed tack. 'What happened to the camera?'

The memory of the chip-camera encased in the nazar bead came flooding back to Rabia's mind. But regarding its present location, her mind drew a blank.

Tanvir enquired, 'What camera?'

'The one we put around her neck to record the goings on in the godown. We have been looking for it all over, but it has disappeared.' said the ACP, his terse tone revealing that he was on edge.

Rabia replied, 'I don't remember. Aalamzeb must have found it when he was strapping the bombs on me. I was in a daze then.'

The ACP quizzed, 'How many men were there with Aalamzeb?'

Rabia gave a muddled answer, 'Two...or...three... Their faces were covered... It's hard to remember...'

Without hesitation, the ACP reached out and pressed hard on her bandaged wound. 'Try to remember clearly!' he said in a flat tone.

Rabia screamed. Tanvir sprang at the ACP, but Hani had anticipated his move. He pulled out his automatic pistol and asked Tanvir to stand back.

'I have failed!' ACP Hani shouted at Tanvir. 'Aalamzeb and his cronies are free to carry out their deadly mission.'

Rabia continued to cry in pain. Tanvir stood back with a murderous expression on his face. The ACP continued his tirade, 'Now Rabia is my only source to get any information on Aalamzeb. I will get it out of her, using force if I have to.'

Tanvir looked at the ACP with a disgusted expression. 'ACP saab, I had respect for you, but now you seem as crazy as the terrorists.'

The ACP didn't say anything because by now, Rabia had lapsed into unconsciousness.

Tanvir shook his head in disappointment. 'You and I have destroyed this woman's life.'

The ACP turned away from Tanvir as he holstered his gun. 'Don't stand around giving philosophical lectures, Mr Gangster. If you really want to save what is left of Rabia's life, you better help me find Aalamzeb and the other Pakistanis.'

Tanvir strode out of the room. From the corridor outside, his voice floated back towards the ACP, 'I'll be back soon.'

◉

Tanvir crept between a line of European gravestones in a remote corner of the Sewree Christian Cemetery, a torch in hand. He had been tramping about Excel Godown, where the search was on for the nazar bead camera, for the past hour. It was now just about midnight and the ATS men were losing their patience. They had shooed Tanvir away after initially allowing him to be a part of the search.

Like a drowning man clutching at straws, Tanvir was still searching the cemetery, in the faint hope that he might find the camera there. A slight movement behind a gravestone caught his eye. A thin figure detached itself from the shadows and ran in the opposite direction. Without thinking, Tanvir leapt after him. He ran behind the figure, cursing and swearing as his still-booted feet slipped on loose masonry. The figure seemed to know its way around and weaved its way expertly through the unkempt undergrowth between the graves.

The cemetery land opened up into a flat patch with a bald, grassless surface. The figure in front of Tanvir suddenly emitted a sharp cry and fell flat on the ground. Tanvir pounced headlong on to the writhing figure. He shone his torch into the face of his captive, only to realize that he was a young boy, no more than thirteen or fourteen years old.

'Ow!' cried the boy, clutching his ankle that seemed to have twisted.

'Who are you? Why are you here?' shouted Tanvir.

The boy now burst into tears. Tanvir thought that it was because of the pain, but then realized that he was trembling with fear. 'Please, bhai. Don't tell anyone about me. My father will lose his job. He'll be thrown in jail!' he pleaded.

Tanvir helped the boy up. 'Who is your father?' The boy was silent. Tanvir now repeated the question, this time with a threat attached, 'The police will beat it out of you in five minutes. Come on, tell me who your father is?'

The boy blubbered, 'My father is the sentry employed at the godown. Tonight, he came home shaken. The police let him go only after he promised not to tell anyone else what happened here, but he told my mother. I overheard him and I was very curious. I couldn't stop myself. I know this place well. Sometimes, my little brother and I come and play here when my father is on duty. I told them at home that I was going to study at my friend's house and I came here to see what was happening.'

Tanvir nodded in understanding. He then bent down and examined the boy's foot. It was swelling at the ankle. 'Come on, let me take you home'. The boy shivered, perhaps fearing the beating his father would give him. 'Look, you need to put some cold water on that. Don't worry, I'll tell him I saw you fall into a pothole on the road.' The boy smiled at him in gratitude.

'Where do you live?' asked Tanvir.

'We live in the Sewree Koliwada.' Tanvir gave the boy a supporting shoulder and helped him hobble through a gap in the fencing on to a small mud path that led away from the cemetery.

◉

Ganpat Suryavanshi was full of gratitude. Tanvir had wanted to leave right after depositing Ganpat's son home, but the sentry and his wife would have none of it. He had dragged the reluctant Tanvir inside and plied him with a hot glass of chai and some khari biscuits. Tanvir had initially relented because Ganpat had said that the gods would be angry if they let a good Samaritan go away without offering him anything, but now he was really thankful, as the first bite of sustenance was doing its bit in rejuvenating his fatigued faculties. He realized that he had not eaten anything since the morning. Without warning, the shock of the events of the day again reared its head inside him. But this time, Tanvir fought it. Ganpat Suryavanshi had been looking at him, curious, for the past few minutes and now, there was a flash of recognition in his eyes. 'You!' he said. 'You are the man who saved the woman in the burqa.'

Tanvir nodded with his mouth full.

Ganpat Suryavanshi seemed scared now. 'Please, why are you here? I have not done anything. I told everything to the police.'

Tanvir drank the last of the chai and wiped the khari crumbs away from his mouth, 'Don't worry, bhai, I know that you were not involved with them. I was just on my way back from there. The police and I were searching for something.' He got up to leave. Nodding at Ganpat's wife, he said, 'Thank you for your hospitality.'

A relieved Ganpat smiled. 'I'm just a small man. It was too much for me. But you are brave. I wish I could help. What are the police looking for now?'

Tanvir was in a hurry now and didn't really want to engage in a conversation. He walked towards the door, 'Oh, nothing really. Just a small marble-like glass bead. Anyway, take care of your boy. Salaam!' He exited before Ganpat could say anything further.

The night was cool outside. Tanvir started to wind his way out of the narrow maze-like gullies, in the direction from where he had brought the young boy home. As he came out from the Koliwada onto the main road, he heard a voice behind him. 'Wait!' He turned to see Ganpat Suryavanshi rushing down the winding path at a distance. A little irritated, Tanvir hung back, waiting for Ganpat to catch up with him. He wondered what the sentry wanted. Ganpat reached him, huffing and puffing away.

'What is it now?' Tanvir's impatience was now at its height as he waited for Ganpat to catch his breath. Ganpat opened his hand and extended it towards Tanvir. In his hand lay the evil eye pendant shining in the meagre streetlight. Tanvir's eyes lit up with excitement.

Ganpat panted, 'As I was leaving the godown tonight, I saw this lying at the corner of the gate post. I thought it was just a kid's marble, and so I picked it up and brought it home for my younger son to play with.'

Tanvir grabbed the bead and held it up. It didn't seem have a scratch on it. He guessed it must have come loose and rolled away towards the gate when he had torn open Rabia's burqa. Tanvir's happiness knew no bounds as he hugged the still-panting Ganpat.

◉

'Allied Computer Peripherals' proclaimed the signboard hung over the shut steel shutters of one of the wall-to-wall shops lined up on Lamington Road's wholesale electronics market.

The shop in question was owned and run by one Sarabjit Singh Sondhi, who was never likely to be lauded for his expertise as a homegrown Indian computer whiz, but was going to make a fortune through the cyber business, nevertheless. Through cyber crime, to be more specific.

Sarabjit and his small team of computer geniuses specialized in credit card fraud. He used his computer peripherals business to launder the money that he nibbled away from the credit cards of high net worth citizens. Sarabjit was also an iconoclast in other ways, in that he was married to Zulekha Siddiqui, his college sweetheart from Khalsa College. Not many people knew that Sarabjit and Zulekha's inter-caste marriage had been made possible only because Sarabjit had, in school, been friends with one Tanvir Khanzada. An upcoming young gangster, Tanvir had made sure that no hothead from either community challenged the two lovers as they bound themselves to each other in holy matrimony.

Now, as Tanvir rapped his fist on the steel shutters of the shop, he heard a familiar voice from inside, shouting, 'Fuck off, you bevda!'

'Your father is a bevda, and you are a chutiya,' retorted Tanvir, smiling. In a flash, the shutter was half-raised. The smell of stale food laced with rum floated out to Tanvir's nostrils. A grinning bearded and turbaned head popped out from under the shutter 'Oho, Eid ka chand, come in...come in.' Tanvir slid under the shutter into the dimly-lit shop. Sarabjit's grin widened as he gave Tanvir a warm hug. 'Sorry yaar, there's a drunkard who lands up here every time we're working nights. He keeps knocking and knocking, asking for a sip of our booze.'

Tanvir looked around the small shop. At a small workstation, two other Sikhs were sitting, working away on their laptops. A mass of jumbled cables, hard disks, USBs and connecters lay around them, intermingled with paper plates of half-eaten chicken tangdis and plastic glasses of half-sipped rum and Cokes. 'Tanvir, you remember my two kid brothers.' He turned to the engrossed Sikhs, 'Oye bhenchodon, pay your respects to Tanvir bhai.' The two Sikhs momentarily looked up at Tanvir and flashed him warm smiles, bobbing their heads in respect. 'Please forgive them, Tanvir, they are busy unloading some dollars from a fat Amriki tourist whose credit card we got today.'

Tanvir held out the nazar bead. 'I need to know what's on this.'

Sarabjit broke into a quizzical smile. 'Oh! So finally *teri goti kat ke tere haath me aa hi gayi?*'

Tanvir smiled at Sarabjit's bawdy joke. 'This marble has a chip camera inside it of the latest technology.'

Sarabjit's brothers, who had been busy on their laptops, stopped all of a sudden. Before Sarabjit could answer, one of them got up and grabbed the bead while the other brought out a torch and a toolbox.

Sarabjit smiled. 'You just said the magic words "latest technology".' He broke into a throaty laughter.

Within seconds, the two boys were busy dismantling the outer core of the bead. It didnt take them long to tweeze the tiny chip out of the bead.

'For these two, this is as exciting as finding an item girl's panties,' said Sarabjit, between guffaws.

One of the boys took out a super-small SIM-card-like object and shoved the chip inside. Sarabjit smiled and winked. 'That my friend, is our "Khulja SimSim" card. It converts any kind of coded information on any chip into the code that we have created.' His brothers coughed, trying to attract his attention. Sarabjit smiled and pointed at them, 'Correction. A code created by Santa and Banta here.' The two gave him a mock-dirty look.

The SIM card was now inserted into an iPad that was connected to a mass of wires. The iPad flickered into video mode and an image sprang on the screen. The image was of a serene-faced man who looked as non-threatening as a clerk in a nationalized bank. But what he said, made everyone's blood freeze. 'You may think I'm a bad man, but history will know me as a visionary who crossed the border to help his Islamic brethren in India. I want my brothers and sisters in India to get out of the poverty-stricken conditions that they have lived in for the past sixty-five years.' Tanvir realized that it was Aalamzeb talking to Rabia, while three other men, who had their faces covered, were wrapping something around Rabia. Tanvir guessed that it must be the bomb corset. He glanced at Sarabjit and his brothers and saw that they were staring at the screen, shell-shocked.

On the screen Aalamzeb continued, 'I want true vengeance for you, for all of Islam. The only way you can avenge your Muslim brothers is to tell the police that I will be hiding in the Bombay Stock Exchange building. Tell them to come and meet me on the roof, and all will be avenged.' Aalamzeb now took some plaster tape in his hand and began taping Rabia's mouth. 'But you can't actually tell the police that, can you? Because you are a bomb yourself, and bombs don't talk, they simply blow up.' Aalamzeb laughed a dry laugh that chilled Tanvir to the bone. Then he turned Rabia away from the camera, so that the camera now faced a wooden door.

After staring for a while at the image of the wooden door, Tanvir shot a glance towards the Sikhs. He saw that one of the younger brothers had fainted. Sarabjit sat, dumbstruck, all his jocularity was gone. Tanvir extracted the chip from the iPad, put it in his pocket and prepared to leave. Behind him, Sarabjit croaked, 'Are we all going to die?'

'Not if I can help it,' Tanvir replied.

◎

A hopping-mad ACP Hani, along with two of his men, helped Rabia into a taxi outside Dr Chitrekar's Lie-in Clinic. Standing next to them, Tanvir watched as Rabia settled down on the backseat.

On his way to the clinic, Tanvir had called the ACP and asked him to release Rabia in exchange for the camera. When ACP Hani had threatened him with dire consequences for his actions, he had laughed and reminded the ACP about the dire consequences of the ACP's actions. Tanvir had been clear that if he did not release Rabia, Tanvir would throw the camera chip into the sea. ACP Hani had reluctantly agreed, but only on the condition that Tanvir would not leave the city and would make himself available in case he was ever required again. Tanvir had given his word.

The taxi driver now started up the engine. Tanvir turned to ACP Hani and handed him the chip. 'It is the Stock Exchange Building,' Tanvir informed the stunned ACP as he slipped into the taxi next to Rabia.

The ACP and his team were already running to their vehicles as Tanvir's taxi drove away down the road.

◉

Chikal Wadi in Mumbai's Tardeo area is a small, predominantly middle-class Maharashtrian neighbourhood. Many a Chikal Wadi boy has dreamed of emulating its most famous son, cricketer Sunil Gavaskar. Throughout the day, one finds kids playing gully cricket in its many nooks and corners. In one such nook lay Tanvir Khanzada's small two-room tenement. He had acquired this home as a payment in kind from a cash-strapped builder whom he had helped by clearing an old suburban building off its reluctant-to-leave residents.

Tanvir used this place as a sanctuary. And that is exactly what he wanted for Rabia—a place where she could rest, safe and secure. Rabia was still in a semi-stupor and had been quite uncommunicative during the short taxi ride. Thankfully for Tanvir, she followed him up the wooden stairs of the century-old building without saying as much as a word. Tanvir opened the door of his tenement and led her in. The musty smell of a place lying unused and unopened for a long period of time almost made Rabia faint again. She clung to Tanvir as he led her to the single bed lying in one corner of the inner room. He propped up the pillows and helped her lie down. Then he busied himself in opening the windows to let some fresh air in. Satisfied with his ministrations, he sat down beside Rabia, only to discover that she had fallen into a deep slumber. Tanvir tucked her in as best he could. As he rose from the side of the bed, he heard Rabia mumbling incoherently in her sleep. 'Zohra...Aalamzeb...friend' was all he could make out clearly, before Rabia went back into a steady and silent sleep. Tanvir got up and exited the tenement, making sure that he locked it behind him.

◉

At that early pre-dawn hour, the taxi ride from Tardeo to Khetwadi Lane No. 10 didn't take more than ten minutes. It took another minute for Tanvir to run up the three floors of Friendship Lodge. He could have shaved off a few seconds, had it not been for the sleeping gentry on each floor landing. He had to literally hop, skip and jump over the huddled figures still stretched out on the floor, trying to catch the only bit of undisturbed sleep that they could afford, since their jobs involved working through the nights as support staff to the various prostitutes housed on every floor.

Now, as he stood panting outside the two-room 'suite' that Rabia shared with Zohra, his heart beat fast, not so much because of the run up the stairs, but because the semi-open front door signalled something ominous inside. Tanvir took a deep breath and pushed the door open a little further. There was an eerie silence. A faint blue light from the inner room that Zohra inhabited fell on the cheap vinyl-tiled floor, giving it the familiar otherworldly feel. The dark sky outside didn't help matters much. Tanvir tiptoed inside, trying his best to leave everything undisturbed.

Yet he need not have taken so much care, because Zohra's room was in shambles. A large steel trunk that usually functioned as a makeshift 'diwan' lay open and empty at the corner of the room. Zohra herself was lying on the floor in another corner of the small room. A dark pool of blood around her indicated why she had chosen the floor as a resting place. Tanvir rushed up to her and in the meagre light of the bedside lamp, he could make out that she had been stabbed in the stomach, not very long ago. Although Zohra had been left for dead, there still seemed to be some life left in her. She stirred at Tanvir's touch; her lips parted and tried to form words. Tanvir noticed that her right hand was clutching a wooden sindoor box tightly. She shoved the sindoor box into Tanvir's hands. Tanvir was a little nonplussed at receiving a wedding gift from a dying person. But then, Zohra pulled at his collar and using all her strength, brought his ear next to her mouth. She whispered for a couple of seconds. Tanvir strained to hear what Zohra was saying, but 'Zaveri Bazaar' were the only two words he could decipher as she died with a sigh.

◉

The Phiroze Jeejeebhoy Towers, popularly known as the Bombay Stock Exchange Building, is a twenty-nine-storey iconic structure in South Mumbai. It stands proud at the intersection of the famous Dalal Street, the Bombay Samachar Marg and Hammam Street in Mumbai's Fort area. Historically an open-outcry floor trading exchange, the Bombay Stock Exchange switched to an electronic trading system in 1995. Since then, the number of people going in and out of the building has significantly reduced. However, the symbolic significance of the building has not reduced one bit. It is the single landmark that immediately communicates Mumbai's status as India's financial capital to all.

At pre-dawn, the tower had never seen this kind of activity in and around it. Mumbai police had surrounded the building, while the bomb squad was conducting a painstaking search, floor by floor. By now, every senior police officer had seen the footage on the camera chip and had rushed their men to the

Stock Exchange, each hoping to grab a piece of credit for saving the day. ACP Hani did not welcome the unnecessary help from the other departments. Despite the pressure from the local police bosses, the NSG and even the army, he was not ready to step aside and give up the chase so easily. For the past two hours, he had helped conduct the search, combing through each and every room in the building, along with his chosen men.

While poking about in a toilet on the eleventh floor, the ACP received Tanvir's phone call. Casting an irritated glance at the caller ID, he nevertheless took the call. However, Tanvir's opening line got his undivided attention.

'We have been tricked again by Aalamzeb.'

◉

The small Chikal Wadi street was still clutching the last slivers of sleep as the sky looked ready to welcome the morning. An exhausted Tanvir trudged up the stairs of his building. As he stood outside the door of his tenement, he noticed that the door (which he had locked) was bereft of the lock. In fact, it was ajar. Tanvir shook off a sense of déjà vu as he kicked the door in and saw three smiling men, dressed in grey mechanic-like overalls, sitting inside. The man he had come to recognize as Aalamzeb was holding an automatic pistol to a petrified Rabia's right temple. Tanvir sighed and walked inside without a word. One of the men, with a constipated expression on his face, got up and shut the door behind him. The smiling Aalamzeb finally broke the silence.

'Welcome, Tanvir. We meet for the first time, but I feel as though I know you well.'

Tanvir's lip curled in a sneer. 'I don't think you know me well enough, Aalamzeb.'

Aalamzeb continued to smile 'Of course, of course, I don't know your deep inner thoughts, but I know you well enough to have been playing you like a mouth organ for the past three months.'

The other men laughed. For the first time, Tanvir noticed the third one, a rat-faced teenager who stuck close to Aalamzeb. Rabia half-rose from the bed, saying 'Tanvir, please forgive me...' but Aalamzeb reached out and pushed her down again. Tanvir moved to stop him, but Aalamzeb turned the pistol towards him, stopping him in his tracks. Aalamzeb smiled and spoke again, 'Thank you, Tanvir, for your hospitality. I knew I'd done the right thing by not killing you in the beginning. I've used you well. Even now, I'm using you. No one is looking for us in your house.'

Tanvir cursed under his breath. Aalamzeb continued to pour forth, like a man who was dying to be complimented for his intelligence. He only stopped when his mobile phone rang. He picked it up and listened to the voice on the other side. 'Okay' was all he said as he disconnected. He flashed his sarcastic smile once again at Tanvir. 'Thanks to you, in the next few minutes, the police will have emptied the Stock Exchange Building and gone off to Zaveri Bazaar.' Tanvir clenched his fists in impotent anger. Aalamzeb now got up and smoothed his clothes, as if headed for an important meeting. The other two Pakistanis took this as a signal and picked up the large duffel bags lying in the corner. Tanvir had not noticed them earlier. Aalamzeb unzipped the last duffel bag and took out another grey overall. He threw it towards Tanvir, indicating that he should wear it. Then he zipped up the duffel bag, picked it up and said, 'And now, Tanvir, you are going to help us get into the Stock Exchange building. Rabia will remain here as a guarantee against you trying anything funny, which you will not even dream of because, if you will notice, your house is wired to explode with a remote timer.' As Tanvir put on the overalls, he spotted the wires running along the floors for the first time. Rabia's muted sobs called for his reassurance. He touched her face with an indescribable longing. Then, without a word, he left the house with the three Pakistani terrorists.

◉

It is said that mornings in Mumbai are akin to mornings in New York, in that they infuse the same charged-up feeling in every Mumbaikar, getting him ready to spring into the new day to decimate it.

Today, Mumbai was set to come even closer to New York, to become a victim of a massive terrorist attack that would take down a symbolic monument in its financial district.

Tanvir's grim thoughts sketched out this comparison as he sat in the taxi with the three Pakistanis. Since the traffic lights had not started functioning as yet, the taxi had chugged its way through the by-lanes that led to the Stock Exchange. For some reason, Aalamzeb had directed the taxi driver to loop around Flora Fountain and approach Dalal Street from behind. As the taxi neared Horniman Circle, Aalamzeb gave instructions and the taxi stopped. He paid the taxi driver, who drove off. It was only then that Tanvir realized why this circuitous route had been taken. A police sub-inspector stepped out of one of the small by-lanes and approached them. As he neared, Tanvir saw that it was the same man, with the hyena-grin, who had earlier been posing as a burqa-clad woman, and before that, as the stone thrower. Hyena sensed Tanvir's thoughts. 'It's so easy to disguise oneself in Mumbai—

everything is available off-the-shelf.' This time, his high-pitched laugh didn't bother Tanvir so much as he fell into step with the others and walked towards the Stock Exchange building. Aalamzeb raised a quizzical eyebrow at Hyena, who contained himself and said, 'The last of the policemen left about fifteen minutes back. I have told the Stock Exchange security people that I will be coming back shortly with engineers and remote-sensing equipment to be installed on the terrace for additional security. They are waiting impatiently for us.' He could not contain himself anymore and broke into his signature laugh. Aalamzeb graced him with an indulgent smile.

⊙

As the elevator started its upward journey to the terrace, Tanvir could not help but marvel at the Pakistani terrorists' detailed planning. They all had impeccable IDs from one of Mumbai's largest engineering firms. What had impressed him the most was that they had even had an ID for him. Now, as they roared up in the lift towards the terrace, he swallowed hard and prepared for what lay ahead.

As Aalamzeb and the three Pakistanis stepped onto the terrace of the building, they were completely surrounded by armed policemen. The element of surprise was absolute! Before they knew it, their duffel bags had been grabbed out of their hands and they were lying on the floor with police guns pointing at every inch of their bodies. In a reflex action, the Pakistanis raised the cylindrical pendants around their necks to their mouths and bit into them. But the police had soda bottles ready. The constables sprayed the soda on their faces to wash away the cyanide powder in the pendants. Unfortunately, the rat-faced one and the constipated one had already bitten into the pendants and were foaming at the mouth. Aalamzeb and Hyena were slower, and all the cyanide was washed out of the pendants before they could swallow it.

Aalamzeb tried to rise. But ACP Hani stepped forward and pushed him down with a booted foot. Aalamzeb blinked at the ACP. Then he began to smile, 'Mr ACP, you are not that smart. This is only part of the plan.' He began to laugh like a maniac. Hyena joined him in his laughter, and was even more hysterical. ACP Hani pulled out his pistol from its holster. Stepping forward, he pistol-whipped Hyena. As luck would have it, one of the blows cracked his skull, and without a word, he fell dead. Aalamzeb swore, 'You behenchods have no clue. In fact, you're so foolish, you thought me to be the leader. I wish I were! My leader is the one with the brains, the one who called all the shots in this operation. I'm envious of my leader, who will go to jannat, whilst we will have to suffer fools like you.'

The ACP didn't react. Aalamzeb seized the advantage. 'Here, call this number.' He gave a local Mumbai mobile number. 'Our leader wants to give you all a goodbye message.' An incredulous Tanvir took out his phone and dialled the number given by Aalamzeb.

Rabia answered the call. Hearing Tanvir's tentative 'Hello,' she spoke in a voice that seemed entirely alien, 'I am at Churchgate Station, I have forty kgs of RDX strapped on me—'

Tanvir interrupted her, 'Rabia! Please, I know you're not one of them. I love you! Tell me you're not their leader!'

'Of course I am,' Rabia's pat reply left him dazed.

Tanvir didn't stop, 'Rabia, please. You will die!'

Rabia broke into chilling laughter. 'Death is a small price to pay for immortality.'

◉

Behind Tanvir, Aalamzeb added, 'You fool, when I was visiting Rabia, I wasn't sleeping with her but delivering RDX from its hiding place in Mumbra, one kg at a time. As soon as you appeared, we figured out that you must be in league with the cops. So we decided to play out this whole charade to understand your every step, and used you to throw the police off track.'

Tanvir's expression was one of rage mixed with disappointment. Leering at him, Aalamzeb continued with his sarcastic laugh, 'She was even ready to marry this fool to convince everyone of her innocence.'

Tanvir looked at the pistol in ACP Hani's hand. Without warning, he grabbed the ACP's hand, turned it towards Aalamzeb and squeezed the ACP's finger, which was resting on the trigger. Aalamzeb was shot through the head. Everybody stood still in shock. Then, almost simultaneously, everybody turned in the direction of Churchgate station, waiting to hear a distant blast.

But there was no explosion. All they heard was Rabia's cry of disbelief as she cursed aloud on the phone line.

Tanvir cut the line, smiled ruefully and said, 'The RDX detonator pins are all in my pocket. Zohra gave them to me in a sindoor box.'

◉

At Churchgate station, Rabia kept trying to pull the detonator in desperation, but nothing happened. Before she knew it, a police party rushed towards her, bringing her down to the ground in a matter of moments.

Rabia Bano, the rising star of the Lashkar Women Brigade, a woman who had trained shoulder-to-shoulder with her jihadi brothers at the Shawai Nullah Camp in Muzaffarabad, Pakistan Occupied Kashmir. A ruthless woman who had outperformed most men during the hard training, Rabia had finally been outdone by the only friend she had ever had. Zohra, the simple village girl who grew up just fifty miles away, across the border in Kupwara. Zohra, the prostitute, who managed to preserve the inherent goodness inside her, even though she spent a childhood among guns, grenades and RDX.

◉

ACP Hani was sitting on the parapet ledge of the terrace of the Stock Exchange Building, watching the rising sun. Tanvir was standing by, watching the policemen take photographs of the crime scene. He noticed the solitary ACP and walked towards him.

'You didn't tell me about the sindoor box?' quizzed the ACP, as Tanvir neared.

In the morning light, Tanvir answered, off-colour, 'When Zohra whispered "Zaveri Bazaar" in my ear, I had only one thought, to call and tell you about it…later, I wondered why a Muslim woman would give me a sindoor box. Only then did I look inside the box…'

ACP Hani broke in, 'When you called me about Zohra, I was stumped for a bit, but then I guessed that it was a double con that they were trying to pull. First, by leading us to the Stock Exchange building, then disappointing us with nothing there. Then pointing us towards Zaveri Bazaar, so that they could come peacefully to the Stock Exchange, while we stupid policemen would have believed that we had already checked the Stock Exchange and left it unguarded.'

Tanvir nodded. 'Rabia must have started hiding the RDX and the detonators in her room after I came along. Zohra probably discovered the RDX hidden in the trunk earlier today, after the Chira Bazaar incident. I guess she knew that they would not spare her when they came to get the RDX and thinking quick, she removed the firing pins. Poor Zohra, they stabbed her and left her with the false information of bombing Zaveri Bazaar to pass on to me. But she was smart enough to get her own back.'

The ACP didn't say anything. Tanvir shook his head in disgust, more at his own self than anyone else. 'Now that I look back at all that happened, I realize that Rabia had fooled me right from the beginning…and I never realized the deviousness of their plan.'

The ACP gave Tanvir a sympathetic look. 'I know it's very little solace, but let me tell you, I was as fooled by her as you. I should have conducted a double check on her background, but I could never imagine a fundamentalist jihadi female ever working as a prostitute, even as a member of a sleeper cell. She threw me off again when she had Aalamzeb strap her with RDX and make her go out in the cemetery. She never intended to get blown up there. She bet on the fact that my vigilant eye would spot the bombs on her, and I would save her somehow. She just wanted me to see the video on the nazar bead camera.'

'But I jumped to her rescue and...' Tanvir's voice trailed away. He shook his head again, disgusted. The ACP let him be.

Finally, Tanvir looked at the ACP and asked 'So now what?'

ACP Hani looked away into the sky. He sighed, 'Now the experts interrogate Rabia. While I go to Mumbra and search every house, every nook and corner for the rest of the RDX. Hopefully I'll find it before it…' He stopped mid-sentence and looked at Tanvir for a few seconds. Then he added, 'But, like I said earlier, you...are a free man.'

◉

On every street of Mumbai, the loud, pulsating throb of the unravelling day could be heard. The shop fronts, the bus stops, the local train stations—transformed from a rest house to the homeless to a temple of business, rapidly filling up with scores of devotees who would partake of its offering, en route to their daily battle for survival.

In the end, it was just another day in Mumbai. Mumbai's descent into mayhem had been avoided. Yet the average Mumbaikar, if there could ever be such a being, had no clue of the colossal danger that had been averted. The one man who had fought a battle for Mumbai walked unsung among the crowds in the Fort area. Office goers brushed past around him, unmindful of their saviour walking amongst them.

Tanvir stopped and stared at his face, reflected off a glass shop front. A haunted man with black stones for eyes stared back at him,. Tanvir felt his shoulders droop, his head sink a few inches below his shoulders. Standing right in the middle of the rush of the city, Tanvir felt alone, defeated.

With a jerk, he straightened himself to his full height. He shot a glance at the man in the mirror. His eyes were now shining bright.

Inside his mind, a fleeting thought had transformed itself into an idea.

◉

The rushing Mumbai office goers didn't even notice the heavily guarded police van threading its way through the morning traffic.

On its way to the Arthur Road Jail, the police van was flanked by two armoured attack vehicles. They were led from the front and followed at the back by police jeeps laden with policemen armed to the teeth. Right in the front of the motorcade was a white Ambassador car with a red light atop.

As the motorcade stopped at a busy traffic intersection, a nondescript Maruti 800 drew up along side. Tanvir disembarked from the Maruti and walked up to the Ambassador. He knocked at the window. A surprised ACP Hani opened the door. Before the ACP could say anything, Tanvir got into the Ambassador. The signal turned green and the motorcade started onwards.

The driver of the van behind received a wireless message from the ACP's Ambassador, telling him to park his van on one side of the road.

The confused driver looked up at the wireless, then at the red light atop the Ambassador and did what he was told. By this time, of course, the policemen in the jeeps and in the armoured vehicles had all jumped out and surrounded the van.

The ACP emerged from the Ambassador with a revolver at his temple. Tanvir, who was holding the revolver, announced, 'Give her to me, right now.' The senior inspector in charge of the motorcade stepped forward. He knew how important the ACP was. Just a few minutes back, he had been speaking to his friend at headquarters and had heard that the ACP was being recommended to receive the president's Medal of Gallantry for his role in averting the terror attack. He ordered the armed policemen to stand aside and asked one of the policemen to open the door of the police van.

Rabia emerged, looking very much like the meek and

demure woman that she had made everyone believe she was.

Tanvir's grim face didn't alter an inch. He held Rabia by the arm and led her to the Maruti 800. He opened the door and Rabia got in. Tanvir ordered the ACP to drive, then got in next to him. As a parting shot, Tanvir spat out a threat, 'If anyone follows us, the ACP will die.'

The door closed behind them. The Maruti swung away into the traffic.

The Maruti had long disappeared by the time the senior inspector got on to the wireless about the daring daylight kidnap.

◉

Excel Godown that morning was the most desolate piece of real estate one could find in the entire city. It had been abandoned after a thorough search the previous night, as if its role in the whole dramatic turn of events had been too insignificant to be worthy of a second look.

Rabia regained consciousness. She sat up and looked around through the haze that her mind was trying to clear itself out of. She realized that she was lying alone inside Excel Godown, sitting at almost the same point where she had stood with Aalamzeb the previous night, while giving him instructions.

A few silent minutes later, the wooden door behind her groaned open. Rabia turned to see who it was. Tanvir.

Rabia remembered that he had not spoken a word after he had got into the car along with her. In fact, he had ordered the ACP to keep driving till he felt that the police was no longer chasing him. Then, without wasting time, Tanvir had asked him to stop in a small dirty by-lane in a nondescript locality that she didn't recognize. He had doused a handkerchief drenched in some liquid—chloroform, she believed—and had held it to the ACP's nose. Once the officer had become unconscious, Tanvir had unceremoniously dumped him in the lane. She was just about to ask him where they were when he had held the same handkerchief to her nose, making everything lapse into blackness.

Now, as Tanvir advanced towards her, she registered the anguish on his face. It only heightened as he neared her.

'Why me?' he whispered. Rabia waited till he had reached her and then slowly rose to her feet.

Looking him in the eye, she hissed, 'Because you are a small price to pay for the cause.' Tanvir clenched his teeth. He whipped out an automatic pistol, levelled the gun at Rabia's heart and readied to squeeze the trigger.

Rabia stared silently at Tanvir, as if daring him on.

Tanvir yelled, 'You think I will not shoot, Rabia?'

Rabia continued to stare, her expression placid. For a while the two, who had not so long ago made passionate love and uttered sweet promises of eternal togetherness, simply stared at each other without a word.

'I am a soldier. A true soldier never fears death.' Rabia finally broke the silence. Tanvir's finger curled to squeeze the trigger. Rabia's expression remained frozen.

Tanvir's hand dropped to his side. He was overcome and fell down, sobbing. Rabia did not say anything. He reached out and handed the gun to her. 'Shoot me. Kill me. Before I become…like you,' he said in a shattered voice.

Rabia shivered.

The expression on her face was indecipherable.

She took the gun from Tanvir's limp grasp. A single tear rolled down her eye.

'I ask for your forgiveness,' she said

'I can only give you my love. Only Allah can forgive you.'

⊚

Outside Excel Godown, ACP Hani was pulled out of his thoughts by a loud 'Bang!' He leapt forward and opened the wooden door.

The gunshot still echoed inside the large godown. Tanvir was standing in front of Rabia's lifeless body. Her small hands still clutched the automatic pistol with which she had blown her brains out.

Tanvir's hollow voice boomed over the gunshot echo, 'She told me. The RDX is hidden in a sand barge in Mumbra harbour.'

The ACP walked up to Tanvir. 'Your plan worked, Tanvir.' He patted the young man's shoulder. Tanvir looked at the police officer with a hardened gaze. 'We got her with her own tactics,' he said.

The ACP nodded grimly. 'Yes, we did.'

ACP Hani bent down and pried the gun out of Rabia's lifeless hand. He half-lifted her body, dragging it on the godown's dirty floor, and pushing it into the waiting Maruti outside. Tanvir stood, silent, as the ACP got into the car and revved up the engine. He watched till the car receded and disappeared, turning a corner.

'But she did really love me,' Tanvir's broken voice said to no one in particular.

Injectionwala

The man sighed. Shut his eyes. Died.

Porus detached the syringe needle from the man's listless throat. Trembling ever so slightly, he let go of the man's limp body. The body slumped on the cheap cushions lining the sofa.

Porus scanned the body with his sharp, sparkling eyes. Searching for any last shivers. Looking for any indication that there still might be some life left lurking in those limbs. Noticing none, he eased himself into the chair opposite the sofa.

All of a sudden, waves of fatigue lashed his brain. He wiped his brow. It was dry.

He fished out some chewing gum from his pocket and popped it into his mouth, to relax himself.

Outside the window, the Mumbai rush hour was rearing its ugly head. Horns honked, brakes screeched, voices vomited viciousness.

After rummaging through the black backpack lying on the floor, Porus took out a small plastic medical kit. He detached the used needle from the syringe. Putting both needle and syringe into small comfortable slots in the medical kit, he shoved it into the bottom of the backpack.

Dr Porus Udwadia, MBBS, was done for the day.

◉

Inspector Ramesh Virkar entered the room. A thirty-five-year-old lean swarthy man with a ramrod-straight posture, Virkar looked every inch a street fighter, ready to jump into a fight and come out the winner.

The body still lay on the sofa. Virkar's eyes took in the educated face, the prosperous potbelly, the sedentary lower limbs, and...a tiny, protesting red spot on the folds of the sun-deprived neck. A pinprick out of place in the otherwise smooth remains, reeking of affluence.

'Injection,' Virkar heard a voice say behind him. He turned around. Dr Kishore Sawant from the government hospital looked grim. 'He was killed by a deadly injection, saheb.'

Virkar pursed his lips and turned towards the body again. He bent down for a closer look at the injection prick. The tiny red dot sat silently, not revealing any secrets at all.

Virkar's eyes keenly surveyed the room. He walked up and stood in front of one of the large wall-to-wall bookshelves, loaded with medical tomes. He stared at the titles. This was definitely a doctor's office. The only thing missing was a collection of large glass medical jars with body organs preserved inside—a common motif in movies.

There was a single door for entry and exit. Another door, set in the corner, seemed like the entrance to a bathroom. Virkar opened the door and entered. It *was* a bathroom: huge, as big as Virkar's one-room tenement.

Laid with ancient, white-tile flooring it had a cast-iron bathtub in a dark corner. There was also a porcelain washbasin with iron taps, which went out of stock in the middle of the last century. A modern, full-length mirror on a blank wall seemed the only thing out of place. Virkar walked up to the mirror and stared at his own image. Tiring quickly of his reflection, his attention now got directed towards the mirror itself. It was a little longer that a grown man's height, and wide enough for two people to be reflected together, if they stood side by side. Where it touched the floor, a few brown stains spattered its otherwise spotless surface. Virkar bent down and scraped one of the stains with his thumbnail. The dry powdery substance came off on to his nail.

Finally, some blood, even though dry.

His fingers touched the edges of the mirror, running up and down the entire length. He tugged at the mirror, trying to get it off the wall. Nothing happened. Then Virkar applied pressure, pushing against the mirror. Again, it didn't budge.

Virkar walked outside the bathroom, all the way to the corridor. There, he signalled to a paan-chewing constable. The constable picked up his moth-eaten rifle and shuffled behind his boss, irritated. Virkar led him back into the bathroom and pointed at the mirror. The constable made a grumbling sound, then picked up his rifle with both his hands and tapped the full-length mirror with the butt. Virkar expressed his annoyance: 'All your energy goes into chewing paan.'

The constable answered by smashing the butt of the SLR on the mirror. Dr Sawant rushed in on hearing the loud crash of cracking glass. Behind the space emptied by the mirror, a wooden door was revealed. The constable stepped back, surprised. All of a sudden, he was overtaken by a burst of energy. He started smashing away at the glass, taking care that none of the pieces flew back to cut him. Soon after, a tiny wooden door that had hidden itself behind the glass stood totally exposed. A catch-lever, at the left bottom corner of the broken mirror, revealed the actual mechanism for the door to swing open.

Virkar finally stepped forward and pushed his brown

leather shoe against the catch. The door swung open inwards. Sawant, Virkar and the constable stood looking at each other, a little wary of what they might find inside. Virkar drew himself to his full height and entered.

The first thing that hit him was the smell. Powerful. Medicinal.

His fingers tapped the wall for a switch. He found a modern switch set in the rough colonial wall and flipped it on.

The bright light bouncing off the stainless steel operating table in front of him hurt his eyes. On one side was a rack laden with medical operating tools. Oxygen tanks stood on the other side. An extendable domed light hung ominously from the ceiling.

Sawant pushed himself into the room behind Virkar. Words finally escaped his dry lips, 'Operation Theatre'.

Virkar didn't react to this superfluous information. His eyes were fixed on the far corner of the room. He had finally found what he had missed outside. A wall-to-ground shelf on the far side was loaded with scores of sealed glass medical jars. Virkar inched closer and stared at them. Floating in the preserving liquid in each jar was a single body organ.

Behind him, a bewildered Sawant whispered, 'Human kidneys.'

Doctor Murdered, Suspected to be Leader of Human Organ Trafficking Racket

The body of Dr Animesh Jetha, MD, FRCS (Edinburgh), winner of the Governor's Medal for Renal Research, dean of the prestigious Johnson Medical College, Mumbai, was found yesterday in his office chambers. Police have registered a case of murder. He is believed to have been poisoned by a deadly injection.

Sources have also confirmed the discovery of a secret operation theatre inside Dr Jetha's private office at Johnson Medical College. It has been alleged that Dr Jetha was running an illegal kidney transplant racket. Doctors at the hospital say that they never got wind of any such operations. 'Dr Jetha was an extremely respected doctor, all his patients will vouch for him,' a doctor, who wishes to remain anonymous, told us. 'We can't believe that he was part of such a racket.'

Mumbai Crime Branch officials suspect the involvement of more doctors at the college. It is believed that up to 500 kidneys have been sold over the last seven years.

◉

'Crime Branch? Wasn't I handling the investigation well?' Virkar asked Kapse.

Senior Inspector Ravindra Kapse got up from his chair and laid a hand on Virkar's shoulder. He sighed, as if speaking to a child. 'Virkar, Virkar, the case is too complicated. Too big! Why should we bother our little police station with such big cases? Let the Crime Branch handle all the shit. You have been assigned Law& Order duty. You have to take care of bandobasts. Don't dabble in criminal investigations.'

'But I was the one who found the operation theatre...'

'That is only because our station's PI Crime is on leave. That's why you were sent to the incident spot.'

Kapse's large frame, with the generous bulges that had succumbed to gravity long ago, was shaking uncontrollably. He was not used to standing for too long, and went back to his favourite sitting position, at the largest desk in the small police station's inner office.

Virkar's voice got harder, 'You don't know my abilities, saheb'.

Kapse's tone changed to a mixture of sarcasm and irritation. 'Yes, yes, I know! Everybody in the police station knows the "famous" Inspector Virkar, who fought Maoists in the jungles of Gadchiroli. Winner of the President's Gallantry Award, blah, blah, blah. But you know this is not Gadchiroli, this is Mumbai. This is not a small pond, this is the sea, where the big fish eat the small fish.'

Virkar's voice was a mixture of strain and patience. 'Sir, I know that I am a small fish, but sometimes, the small fish are the biggest catch.'

Kapse broke into derisive laughter. Bubbles formed at the corner of his corpulent mouth. 'Is that some profound saying by your fishermen ancestors?'

Virkar flinched. Kapse shook his head, as if trying to control his laughter. Then, serious again, he snapped, 'Go to the duty desk and report for today's VIP security duty. The Crime Branch will take care of the investigation and we will hear about it through the newspapers.'

Virkar didn't budge. Kapse picked up his phone and raised a quizzical eyebrow at him. 'Do you want to take me on, Virkar?' After a long silent stare, Virkar strode out of the office room without another word.

◉

Being given the short end of the stick was not something new to Virkar. He belonged to the Koli community, that's amongst the oldest inhabitants of Mumbai. A community of fishermen that has, over time, been eroded, and now exists only in small pockets along the Mumbai shoreline. A community whose rights have been disregarded by all and sundry when it comes to land and ownership. A community that is dwindling at an alarming pace, its traditional means of fishing fast becoming outmoded.

The scion of a line of Koli fishermen who adopted the title of Virkar ('worshipper of the ancestors'), Virkar grew up in the shanties of the Macchhimar Nagar area in Colaba. As a child, living and breathing in the shadows of the tall buildings of the upmarket Cuffe Parade, disparity stared him in the face everyday. But, his 'convent' education at the nearby Holy Mary High School gave him the English language skills and confidence to go up to the rich Cuffe Parade kids and play hide 'n' seek with them in their building compounds. However, as he grew up, dividing his time between keeping up with his schoolwork, helping his father fish and his feisty mother sell the daily catch, he knew that one day, he would have to face the prejudices that make the world an ugly place.

Although he passed his tenth standard board exams with flying colours and enrolled in the science stream at Elphinstone College, he switched to psychology after his dreams of joining an engineering college were shattered for want of two precious marks. After securing a first-class Bachelor of Arts degree, he had wanted to pursue a MBA, but there, too, the serpent of favouritism swallowed up his dreams. A chance reply to a Maharashtra Public Service Commission recruitment advertisement led to him joining the police service. For the first time, he felt at peace, as he had been selected on merit. But as he worked hard at the Maharashtra Police Academy in Nashik, a new kind of prejudice dogged his footsteps.

A reverse prejudice. His being the only English-speaking boy from Mumbai became a millstone around his neck. The cadets and teachers who hailed from rural and interior Maharashtra couldn't stand him.

One day, the inevitable happened. The somewhat naïve Virkar rose to the bait laid out by one of his jealous batchmates and made the cardinal mistake of correcting the pronunciation of an instructor. From that day on, Virkar was a marked man. And sure enough, as soon as the class graduated from the academy, he was handed a posting otherwise reserved as punishment for serious offenders within the police department, to a far-flung, Naxalite and Maoist infested war-zone called Gadchiroli. A place with a name he couldn't even pronounce at first. A place where death stared him in the face everyday.

◉

They made ferocious love. Specially-made-for-release love. Tension-expelling love.

As she lay savouring the throes of her orgasm, Porus spoke for the first time that evening.. 'I killed your father,' he said.

The four words spun around the room at lightning speed and exploded inside her head like an atom bomb.

Dr Saakshi Jetha lay dumbstruck. Tears crept into her doe-shaped eyes. The dusky beauty had been away, attending a seminar at the Army Medical College, Pune, when her father, Dr Animesh Jetha, was killed. The investigation had started even before she could reach Mumbai And she had come home only to be faced with interrogation about her father and his associates. She had been questioned about her own movements, too, and was only allowed to claim and cremate her father's body after a full forty-eight hours.

Sensing her emotional paralysis, Porus Udwadia spoke again. 'For seven years, your father's murder was my single-minded goal. Everyday, I would envision your father's death by my hands. In my head, I would play and replay how I would kill him, again and again.' His words continued to strip her already shattered mind, tearing through her tattered thoughts like shrapnel.

Saakshi still didn't move or speak; her limbs seemed welded into the mattress. Her lips were frozen stiff with the thought that her lover was her father's cold-blooded murderer. Her eyes, open but unseeing, visualized how her paramour must have taken the life out of her guardian and mentor, whom she had loved above all else.

Porus continued in an ominous tone. 'Your father killed my father. He didn't stick a knife in his chest or shoot him, but killed him by much more sinister means. My father was a small-time horse-trainer at the Mahalaxmi Race Course. Unfortunately, his horses lost too many races and he was reduced to a poor stable hand. But even during his days of penury, he held on to the dream that his studious son would one day become a doctor. Unfortunately, I didn't study hard enough. I fell short by a few marks and no respectable medical college would give me admission. And my father didn't have the money to pay capitation fees. So, through a horse-race bookie, he found his way to your father and pleaded with him to grant me admission in Johnson Medical College.' At this point Porus almost stopped breathing . His voice grew sharp. 'Your father was very accommodating. He gave me admission almost immediately. Of course, the only thing my father had to do was to give his left kidney to your father.'

Porus stopped to breathe, summoning up energy to carry

on with his monologue. 'It had to be the left kidney, because you see, the right kidney was damaged and would not last too long.'

Pain crept into his voice. 'My poor father gave up his one good kidney for my sake. He spent the next two years dying. Hiding his pain, he motivated me to continue my studies. Only after he collapsed in the stables and finally died one day, did I come to know his secret. My budding doctor's mind was shocked at the discovery of his scar, and I operated upon his body and discovered the true cause of his death'. Porus's words tumbled out, as if trying to escape from the painful memory. 'I broke down that day…I almost lost my mind, till the bookie who had sent my father to yours told me the entire story'. Sensing the end of the monologue, his body began to relax, 'As I watched the vultures circle over the Tower of Silence after my father's funeral, I swore that I would pay back his killer in the same coin.'

Porus fell silent and popped some chewing gum to relax.

For several minutes, the only sound heard in the room was the lazy clack-clack of the ceiling fan.

'Was getting me to fall in love with you a mere ploy to get to my father?' Saakshi finally broke the silence.

'Initially, yes, but as I got to know you, I fell totally in love with you. I know it sounds like a "filmy" dialogue, given the circumstances, but it is true,' Porus answered in an emotionless tone.

'Is it?' Saakshi's voice dripped with scorn.

'Yes, unfortunately, yes. Yes, I do love you. That's why I have told you everything. I wish I didn't have to kill the loved one of someone whom I love. But then that is the hell I have been ordained to suffer,' Porus said without hesitation.

Saakshi sighed. 'What do you want me to do now?'

'Hand me over to the police.' Porus's voice was calm. He popped a small gum-bubble.

Without warning, Saakshi turned and gave him a slap across his face. Tears sprung from her eyes. 'Do you want me to lose another man I love?'

She fell into his arms and they made love again. This time, the heat of their conflicted passion almost scorched the paint off the walls. Afterwards, they lay silent, staring at the high ceiling, watching the fan rotate at snail's pace. Saakshi broke into tears again.

Porus moved to comfort her. But she pushed him away.

'If you think it is you who is going through hell, can you imagine what I am going through?' she sobbed.

Porus whispered, 'Kill me, Saakshi. Once and for all, do away with the sickness that has afflicted your life.'

'The sickness runs too deep, Porus, and you are not the cure for it—I am,' a determined Saakshi said .

'What do you mean?' Porus asked, confused.

But Saakshi refused to elaborate. Instead, she spoke in measured tones. 'Porus, I would like you to leave now, I need some time to think'.

Porus got off the bed and dressed without protest. As he put on his shoes, he glanced at Saakshi. Her eyes were streaming with tears, but her face had frozen into an unreadable mask. For what seemed like eternity, Porus waited for her to say something. But she remained still. Tiring of the silence, he exited the apartment.

◉

Operation Organ—Police Get Some Results

The Crime Branch arrested 5 people in connection with the Operation Organ case on Tuesday . Two of them are doctors who served under Dr Jetha in his earlier posting in Pune and the other three are believed to be agents who would identify potential victims and establish contact with them. In a press conference today, the Crime Branch officials said that the accused broke down after interrogation and revealed certain startling facts.

The agents were employed by Dr Jetha to go out into the community and find potential donors. These agents, too, had sold their kidneys to the doctor. Migrant labourers, drawn to Mumbai from villages looking for work, were lured by these agents and taken to Dr Jetha with promises of employment, after which they were allegedly brainwashed into selling their kidneys. They were paid ₹50,000 for their organs, which were sold for 10 times the price to Jetha's rich clients.

Meanwhile, the police have made no headway into the investigation of Jetha's death. They suspect that it is the handiwork of a disgruntled member of the deceased doctor's network. 'Investigations are still on, and we will be making an announcement soon,' said an inspector on condition of anonymity.

◉

Saakshi sat by a large open window. Only now was she beginning to feel the grief of the sudden departure of her only parent. Like any other good Indian 'daddy's girl', Saakshi had idolized her powerful father and followed in his footsteps. After doing a course in medicine and an internship in the UK, she had come back to Mumbai. On her father's recommendation, she had joined the Johnson Medical College Hospital and quickly had become a popular figure within the small medical community there. Everybody would call her 'Saakshi didi' as she flitted along the corridors, going about her duties. Her highest ambition had been receiving a rare, appreciative smile from her father. For a while, it had seemed to everyone that Saakshi had dedicated herself to being a loyal foot soldier working under her colossus of a father, both of them single-mindedly dedicated to the cause of medicine.

But one fine day, at a medical convention, Saakshi ran into a young, handsome, fair-skinned doctor. And life changed completely. The young man had approached her at the lunch buffet counter and recommended the Andhra Crispy Karela. She had responded with the natural hesitation that everyone harbours towards the bitter vegetable, but out of politeness, she had taken a small helping, intending to leave it uneaten. However, while having lunch, she had caught the eye of the young doctor, who had been sitting diagonally across her. She noticed him looking at the untouched karela on her plate. A little embarrassed, she quickly ate a few pieces. To her surprise, she had found the dish to be quite tasty. When she had looked up again at the young doctor, he was grinning and had an 'I-told-you-so' expression. Saakshi returned his smile, blushing like a schoolgirl.

When she had bumped into him again at the dessert counter, she asked him, 'Have I met you before?'

The young doctor had smiled mischievously and said, 'No, but I have a feeling that you are going to meet me a lot in the future.' Saakshi's heart thumped against her chest as she heard his words.

Two weeks later, they slept together for the first time. Five months later, her father discovered the passionate secret affair. Two weeks after that, following a lot of cajoling, she received permission to introduce her Parsi lover, Porus, to her Gujarati father. Both of them had started bonding over a common language and life was just beginning to look perfect when, one week later, unbeknownst to Saakshi, her lover killed her father.

◉

A small knot of young Ukrainian students stood chanting slogans behind the police barricade in the open area opposite Taj Mahal Hotel. Virkar strode up to take the lead position, But the three constables already on duty just nodded at him, throwing him a lazy salute.

A student suddenly shouted, loud enough to be heard above the din, 'You policemen are dogs!'

Virkar's jaw set in a thin line and he looked ready to explode. He placed his hand on his holstered service revolver. Around him, the constables tensed, expecting action. But instead Virkar swivelled around, turning his back on the shouting Ukrainian students. Inside his head, he was cursing his situation, trying to block out the noise.

'How long are you going to take this, Virkar?' was the question he kept asking himself as the Russian foreign minister's entourage approached the hotel. He tried to distract himself and halt the train of dark thoughts.

As soon as the minister's car passed into the portals of the hotel, he turned his attention back to the ragtag bunch of students, who were now shouting throaty expletives, threatening, waving placards, as if challenging him again.

'But, what can I do? I am a dog,' muttered Virkar to himself. His body was still trembling with tension. A grey-haired senior constable saw his agitated state; he strolled up to Virkar and offered him a cigarette. Virkar declined, waving him away.

All of a sudden, from within the crowd, a Coke bottle was flung at the standing policemen. From the corner of his eye, Virkar saw the glass projectile hurtling towards them. Acting on pure instinct, he struck out at the bottle with the wooden riot baton in his hand. The baton connected with the bottle just as it was about to find its mark, the grey-haired constable's bare head. The bottle broke into pieces and fell into the empty space between the protesters and the police, without causing any harm. The policemen raised their batons, awaiting the order to lathi charge.

The senior constable, though shaken, laid a placatory hand on Virkar's arm and whispered, '*Jau diya, saheb*.' Virkar cooled down. He signalled the policemen to step back. The line of students, too, shrank back. By now, most of them had decided they'd had their fill of protesting and they quickly began dispersing.

The constable bent to touch Virkar's feet in grateful servility, 'Thank you for saving my life, saheb.'

Virkar was a little embarrassed. 'It was just sheer luck.'

The constable smiled, 'It was not just luck, it was the hand of God working through you. I am a God-fearing man, saheb. Your Goddess, Ekveera Devi, will not spare me if I don't pay you back in some way.'

Virkar shrugged. The old constable continued to protest. 'You are a good man, Virkar saheb. You are just caught in the wrong situation. I will help you change it.' Virkar looked at him, a little confused. The old constable lowered his voice to a whisper. 'Let me tell you a secret...'

◉

Behind its old iron gate, Cursetjee Castle seemed to stare at Saakshi in its entire stony, lost splendor. Its grandiose name was in sharp contrast to the rather ordinary architecture. Although at first, it had been one large house, the two-storeys now housed four separate apartments, carved out of the single structure. Three belonged to various descendants of the late Mr Darashah Cursetjee, a Parsi gentleman and ex-Indian Civil Service officer, who had served his British masters well enough to be awarded the plot on which Cursetjee Castle currently stood. The descendants, though, like many wealthy Parsi progeny, all lived abroad, and had locked up these apartments, using them more as godowns. The fourth apartment, situated at the back, however, was inhabited.

Saakshi asked her cab to wait as she entered the cavernous entrance of Cursetjee Castle. She walked up the stone stairs, through the dark unlit corridor, to this apartment.

Standing outside the old teakwood doors of the apartment, she took a deep breath and rattled the brass doorknocker under the nameplate 'Dr Porus Udwadia'.

The door opened instantly, giving Saakshi a start. As if Porus had been standing right by the door, awaiting her knock. Porus looked like he had not slept the previous night. He pulled her in without a word and led her in gently by the hand, past the large rooms, generally bare, except for some old, wooden furniture. Inside his bedroom, he sat her down on an old settee. His eyes searched her face, as if trying to read what was in her mind. Saakshi laid her soft hand on his unshaven cheek. Porus relaxed a little. Finally, she broke the silence. 'My father's not the only one involved in the racket, there are others. I have come to know that some people who are not doctors are the real brains behind the scam. They ensnared my father, used him for their evil purposes and made it seem as if he was the mastermind.'

She now looked deep into his eyes, as if speaking to his soul. 'I need your help.'

Porus swallowed, but his throat was aching, dry. 'What do you want me to do?' he asked in a soft voice.

Saakshi took in a deep breath. 'I want you to kill them, too,' she said with a determined look.

Hearing the strength in her voice, Porus felt fatigue creep into his body. He mopped his sweaty brow and looked around for some chewing gum. There was none.

Saakshi's face was inscrutable as she continued, 'You have to take revenge on them too. Kill them. Like they killed your father...like they killed my father, everyday...bit by bit...' her voiced trailed, waiting for Porus to say something.

He got up from the settee and walked around, trying to calm himself. After much deliberation, a hollow voice from within him spoke, 'Just let me confess to the police, instead.'

Saakshi got up and went to him, trying to stop his rapid pacing. She led him back to the settee and sat him down. 'You have cast the first stone, now I, too, seek revenge. Not on you. But on the others who coerced my father into joining them. Will you help me?' Porus was silent.

Saakshi rose from the settee with a cushion in her hand. She plonked the cushion down and knelt before Porus, with her knees on the cushion, and unzipped his pants. Porus shivered with excitement. She tugged at his underwear. Porus He raised his buttocks ever so slightly and the garment slid off him. Without a word, Saakshi buried her face in his lap.

'I will, I will.' The words tumbled out of Porus's lips almost like a sigh of relief.

◉

Policeman Involved in Organ Racket.

In a shocking development, the Mumbai police arrested a senior policeman on Wednesday in the fallout of 'Operation Organ'. Senior Inspector Ravindra Kapse allegedly accepted a bribe of Rs 40 lakh from murdered kidney kingpin Dr Animesh Jetha to cover up his involvement in an earlier incident of kidney sale at a private clinic run inside a small Colaba 'Guest House', Hotel Walton. The owner of the guesthouse, Sriram Shetty, was arrested, but fled the country on receiving bail, and Dr Jetha's involvement had remained a secret, until now. Police sources have said that the Crime Branch, on receiving an anonymous tip-off, investigated and found enough evidence regarding Kapse's involvement. A case was registered against him and six other constables for accepting bribes from Jetha and Angre. They were allegedly bribed by an as yet unidentified key associate of Jetha's.

Additional Chief Metropolitan Magistrate D. P. Rane remanded Senior Inspector Kapse to fourteen days' judicial custody. Inspector Ramesh Virkar, from the same police station, has been given temporary charge of Senior Inspector Kapse's duties.

◉

Virkar rode his Bullet motorcycle up the Western Express Highway. The 'dhak-dhak-dhak' sound of his Bullet was, as always, music to his ears. The almost empty highway felt like a runway under his wheels. Virkar hummed the tune of his favourite Koli song as he sped northwards: '*Mee Dolkara/ Dolkar Darya Cha Raja…*'

After almost a year of anguish, Virkar felt alive. 'Big fish make good fish-fry,' he remembered the joke from his childhood. He laughed to himself, inwardly thanking the grey-haired constable for passing on the crucial information on Kapse. Virkar was convinced that Kapse was, at that moment, being fried in a vat of hot oil and was soon going to be eaten alive by the Crime Branch. 'I just helped stir the curry a little,' Virkar snickered. 'But I should take every step carefully.'

Just before Vakola Junction, Virkar turned to the right under the flyover and headed off the highway. A little further up the road, Virkar stopped the Bullet in front of a large, white, four-storey building. The sign outside said 'Directorate of Forensic Science Laboratories'.

Virkar parked outside and walked up to a side gate. He shook the sleeping watchman's shoulder. The watchman didn't stir. Virkar jumped over the side gate and walked into the main building. The indoors were dark, with just a narrow ray of light streaming in through a small corridor on the far right. The sign above the corridor pointed to the toxicology department. Virkar made his way towards the source of light and stood before the open door of a lab. He pushed the swivel door and stepped inside.

Inside, the sole occupant, Dr Girish Gite, a boyish man, beamed as Virkar approached him. He bent down and touched Virkar's feet. 'Arre, what are you doing?' Virkar stepped back, a little embarrassed.

Dr Gite replied, 'Just showing my respect, saheb. I haven't seen you for so many years.'

Virkar returned his smile and hugged the young doctor. 'How are you, Giriya?' he enquired. 'I am okay, saheb, as you can see.' Dr Gite gestured towards his surroundings, still smiling.

Virkar's thoughts went back to the teenaged Giriya from Aheri village in Gadchiroli, the young boy who had performed exceedingly well in academics at school. So well that the local Naxalite dalam had identified him as a potential soldier for their militant cause. Giriya had, in fact, flirted with Naxalism, joining their Sangam Cultural Front and going from village to village performing street plays with coded messages of revolution. It was after one such performance that the young Sub-Inspector Virkar had arrested him. Virkar, however, was quick to understand that Giriya was just a young boy who needed an intellectual outlet. The sympathetic Virkar had recommended his application to the Nagpur Medical College. On securing his admission, Giriya and his family had declared their indebtedness to Virkar's kind act. Virkar simply asked them to spread Giriya's story among the nearby villages. The story had caught people's imagination and the local Naxalite sangam group had gradually lost its teeth. Virkar had been hailed as a policeman with a heart.

Dr Gite's serious tone cut through Virkar's thoughts. 'It is

Tributame. An animal euthanasia drug generally used to put horses to sleep.'

Pulled out of his reverie, Virkar was a little confused at this information. 'Animal euthanasia...horses... I don't understand.'

Dr Gite explained, 'Euthanasia or mercy killing methods are designed to cause minimal pain and distress while putting animals to death. Dogs, and sometimes, larger animals, like horses, are almost always euthanized through intravenous injection.

'And what is this Tribut...but...' Virkar struggled.

Dr Gite replied, 'Tributame is basically a mixture of three drugs—embutramide, chloroquine phosphate and lidocaine—and has become popular because it causes death with even a lower volume of injection. Unconsciousness and cardiac arrest follow rapidly, one after the other. Usually within thirty seconds.'

Virkar held up his hand to stop the information onslaught. Realization dawned on him. 'You mean to say Dr Jetha was killed by an animal poison?'

Dr Gite nodded in all seriousness. 'Yes. The killer obviously had access to veterinary drugs and knew how to use them.'

Virkar half-turned towards him. 'Will you share this information with others?'

Dr Gite replied with a straight face, 'If someone asks, yes. But then, nobody ever asks me anything...'

Virkar didn't say anything. He patted Giriya on his shoulder and walked away. As he neared the door, Dr Gite said, 'Hope you get him, saheb.'

Virkar nodded at Giriya, and exited the lab, shutting the door behind him.

◉

The rotund white-haired man in the rumpled grey safari suit was called 'Wagh Mama' by all and sundry. He was sitting with his customary morning cutting chai on a rickety wooden bench on the footpath next to Shyamlal's cart, outside the main gate of Johnson Medical College Hostel. This daily morning ritual had been repeated so many times over the years that the students who passed in and out of the gate did not as much as give Wagh Mama a second glance. Save for one ex-student, sitting in the Light of Persia restaurant across the street, gazing at him through uncertain eyes.

Porus's attentive eyes were following Wagh Mama's every action, but his thoughts were clouded with confusion. Wagh Mama was an institution by himself. He had been the head night watchman at Johnson College for years, some said forever. Every hosteller knew that if he or she needed to get in or out post curfew, Wagh Mama needed to be kept in good humour. Which was easy enough, as Wagh Mama was prone to paroxysms of laughter at the slightest hint of jocularity. Indeed, the old man was a stereotype of the good-natured watchman of the share-a-joke-bum-a-smoke variety. His popularity among the students was such that his morning tea, that he so enjoyed after his regular night duty, was funded by a special students' 'account' at Shyamlal's cart. Every student contributed ₹10 a month towards his morning 'cutting'.

After duty hours, Wagh Mama would head straight to Shyamlal's cart, quickly down the half-full chai 'gilass' and head for the bus stop to catch a bus to wherever he lived. No one knew any details of that part of his life, except for the fact that he had no family and lived alone. Watching him gulp down the chai, Porus couldn't bring himself to believe that this jolly old man was part of the kidney racket.

Saakshi had been insistent that he 'take care' of Wagh Mama, but Porus had balked at the task, not only because he wasn't really a hardened killer, but also because he had shared many a joke with Wagh Mama during his student days and had fond memories of the man.

In the midst of the conflicting emotions invading his mind, Porus noticed that Wagh Mama had got up from the bench and was helping a tired-looking man up from his seat. The man had obviously been recently discharged after treatment and was not fully fit yet. He was wearing a red T-shirt with a yellow 'Being Human' logo. Wagh Mama, in his usual, gregarious way, was also being human. Porus watched as he led the dazed man to the bus stop. A bus approached, Wagh Mama helped the man into it and followed him inside. 'He is a good Samaritan, not a kidney-stealing killer,' Porus thought as the bus left the stop for its onward journey.

Porus paid his bill and left the Light of Persia restaurant, cursing the situation he was in. Once again, he thought of heading towards a police station, but gave up the thought as soon as an image of Saakshi's angry face flashed in his mind. He knew he would be deprived of their soul-satisfying lovemaking sessions if he didn't think of a convincing excuse for not 'taking care' of Wagh Mama. By force of habit, Porus popped some gum into his mouth as he began to work on his story.

◉

Body Found in Drain

A decomposed and badly injured body of an unidentified man was found in a drain in Kandivli on Tuesday. Police suspect that the man is about 35 years old and had committed suicide. Sub-Inspector Sachin Ramteke told us, 'Around 5 p.m., a local resident informed us that a body had been spotted floating near a quarry in Vadarpada. The land, which is a prohibited area, belongs to the Mumbai Metropolitan Regional Development Authority. The drain is very deep and the spot is uninhabited. The nearest slums are about a kilometre away.'

The police have registered a case of accidental death. 'It appears that the victim might have jumped from the hill above the drain. The spot is inaccessible otherwise,' informed Ramteke.

Due to the advanced state of decomposition, identification of the body is difficult. However, the body has a recent surgical scar on the left side of his abdomen, extending from the back to the front, suggesting that the man had had a kidney related operation.

The police said the body was found in a red T-shirt with a yellow Being Human logo, black trousers, dirty white sports shoes and a brown leather belt. No wallet and no identification was found on the victim, but the police discovered a small 'chor' pocket in the man's pants. A fifty-rupee note, a small packet of tobacco and a passport-sized photograph (given above) were found in the chor pocket.

◉

Porus was cold. Not because of the weather, but because of the sensation that had crept down his spine. He had been staring at the Sunday paper for the past fifteen minutes. He was unable to tear away his eyes from the small passport-sized photograph printed above the innocuous crime report. Even though Porus had only had a fleeting glimpse of him, there was no mistaking that the photograph was of the same man he had seen Wagh Mama help into the bus.

Porus put down the paper. He had been mistaken. Saakshi had been right. Oh, how she had fought him when he had told her that Wagh Mama couldn't be a part of the operation. She had abused him to high heaven and nearly torn off his shirt in her agitated state of mind. She had only calmed down when he had promised that he would do something within the week. Although he had bought time from her, he had had no intentions of doing anything to Wagh Mama and had been looking for another excuse—until now, at least.

Now he was full of regret. He had committed the cardinal sin of letting emotions cloud his judgment. 'You fool! You could have saved this man's life. If only you had listened to Saakshi and not used your own, addled brain,' a voice inside his head screamed.

Porus got up from the coffee table in his living room and walked into his bedroom and. There he opened a small cupboard, which functioned as his private pharmacy. Bottles of pharmaceutical drugs were lined up in the cupboard. The different labels displayed a vast array of drugs for every occasion and purpose. He reached into the back and picked up two medium-sized brown bottles. He bent down and pulled out his black backpack, unzipped it and took out his medical kit. He walked into the living room with the medical kit and the bottles.

Sitting on the settee, he opened his medical kit, took out a fresh plastic syringe, broke open a pack of needles and screwed a needle onto the syringe. He filled the syringe with Pancuronium from one of the bottles, and then drew from the other bottle, marked Succinylcholine Chloride.

Soon after receiving the injection full of this lethal concoction, Wagh Mama would begin to feel numb and his breathing would become constricted, leading to his death.

◉

A sign painted on a rock outside Tulpulgonda, a small village deep inside the Bhamragarh forest in the remote Gadchiroli district of Maharashtra read 'Death to all Policemen'. Virkar jumped out of his jeep, his police-issue automatic pistol drawn. The four other constables with him were ready with their cocked SLRs. They were searching for Bhimrao Khetmange, a man who had given wrong information to the police. Information that caused the death of sixteen policemen in a landmine blast. The huts in the village were empty, but the exodus from this village seemed to have happened recently. Virkar and the four armed constables searched the huts, one by one. Some scattered belongings were lying on the rough, dry ground between the huts. It looked as if the villagers had left because they feared an attack. Who from, was the moot question that Virkar had come to find an answer to.

As he reached an open area in the centre of the village, gunshots rang out. Two of the constables fell. Virkar and the other two took cover and returned fire. Taking advantage of the hilly, thick, forested area surrounding Tulpulgonda, the Naxals had taken up positions on the treetops bordering the village. They had constructed morchas at vantage points on the trees. The policemen had no place to hide, as they were surrounded from all sides. Virkar and the two constables retaliated as best they could, but Virkar realized that they were massively outnumbered and exposed on the lower ground. There were at least nine or ten Naxalite guerillas attacking them. Virkar felt death advancing towards him. But he was not ready to strike an acquaintance with it yet.

He asked the two constables to scream loudly, as if they were shot, and then all three of them lay silently. After almost fifteen minutes, they saw dark shadows in green fatigues emerging from the trees lining the village. Seven of them coming towards the village clearing, in attack formation. Three on the left, three on the right, the leader in the centre. Virkar motioned his constables to get ready, and on his command, they fired. Virkar took out the leader in the centre with one single shot to his head. The crossfire confused the Naxals, and the policemen had quickly managed to eliminate all seven. It had happened fast, but the few Naxals in the trees started firing indiscriminately, making it increasingly difficult to continue in the positions that Virkar and the two constables were maintaining. By then, the policemen were almost out of ammunition. There seemed to be no way out...

A mobile phone rang. Virkar woke up with a start. It was early morning, only a few hours after he had returned from the police station. He had spent the previous twenty-four hours trying to find a link between Dr Jetha and Tributame, and had come up with nothing. Irritated with himself, he had drowned the rest of the night in his favourite Godfather beer. Somewhere between the fourth and the fifth bottle, he had fallen asleep, only to have the one dream that he was trying his best to get away from. To purge from his system.

He picked up the call after the sixth ring. The voice on the other side spoke in a hurried manner. Virkar's expression changed to one of excitement. Controlling himself, he said, 'Okay, now do exactly as I tell you.'

◉

Porus was chewing gum as usual, waiting patiently at the Light of Persia restaurant. He had come in early to get the window seat that would look over the entire front of Johnson College Hostel. It was a vantage point from where he could see Wagh Mama make his way out of the premises for his morning chai, and track his movements thereafter. Porus had planned to follow Wagh Mama on to his bus, till he reached home. 'Let the old man get comfortable, and then I'll strike,' Porus thought.

Wagh Mama emerged from the hostel gates, bleary-eyed after a long night's vigil. A creature of habit, he sat down on the same part of the wooden bench at Shyamlal's stall as always. But today, there were already two men sitting there. Their manner and body language suggested that they were probably night watchmen at one of the super-elite gated towers that had sprung up in the area.

In his usual, good-natured manner, Wagh Mama requested the men to move further up the bench to accommodate him. Seeing his bulk and the silver in his hair, one of them got up and offered him a seat. Wagh Mama sat down, but before he could get comfortable, the other man slipped a pair of handcuffs on him.

Wagh Mama looked at him in shock and confusion, but the man was expressionless. The man lifted his shirt seam a little and showed Wagh Mama a gun tucked in his belt. Before anyone could say anything, a police Gypsy drew up out of nowhere. Wagh Mama was bundled into the Gypsy, which took off, as if on cue. The whole operation lasted for only a couple of minutes.

Porus reeled with shock, but then his eyes fell on Shyamlal, who was watching the Gypsy recede into the traffic. From Shyamlal's expression, Porus realized that here was another man who had recognized the photograph in the newspaper.

Porus stepped outside the restaurant and ran around the corner to where he had parked his 1983 Rajdoot Yamaha RD 350. His father had owned an RD in better days and had taken little Porus for many a joyride on it. Afterwards, he had had to sell it to fuel Porus's education. Porus had bought one exactly like his father's, as soon as he could afford it, as a fond memory of his childhood, and had named his bike 'Rapid Death'.

Porus put on his helmet and gunned his RD to a roar. Those who have experienced the raw power and pure adrenalin rush from the legendary RD's throttle will know that none of the modern-day Indian performance bikes can even touch 150 km/hr. Porus had tinkered long enough with his bike to make it capable of hitting 165 km/hr in sixth gear.

Before the police Gypsy had reached the busy intersection under the Parel flyover, Porus was but three vehicle lengths away. Falling behind a large milk truck to keep himself sufficiently covered, Porus peeked out and saw that Wagh Mama had fainted and was slumping on the left side in the backseat. The two policemen had left him there and were seated on the right, deep in conversation.

The intersection, as usual, was crowded and the wait looked long. Porus rode his bike forward and quickly brought himself parallel to the Gypsy. Wagh Mama's neck was resting against the open sliding window. The policeman sitting in the left front seat of the Gypsy was nodding off. The people in other vehicles around were too busy concentrating on how they would get out of the jammed intersection as soon as the signal turned green. As cool as ever, Porus took out the syringe from his inner jacket pocket. Cupping the syringe in his hand, Porus angled the syringe till only the needle protruded from between his leather-gloved fingers. Pretending to steady his bike, he raised his arm to rest against the Gypsy's open window. As soon as his fingers reached the open window grill, he thrust his fingers to the base of Wagh Mama's skull; the needle found a vein and broke into it. No one could see that the bottom of Porus's palm was pressing down upon the plunger of the syringe, emptying its contents into Wagh Mama's spinal cord.

A few seconds later, Porus had moved away from the Gypsy and merged into the traffic. The signal turned green and the Gypsy continued its journey to the police station. Porus turned west towards Byculla and drove his RD into the small garage-cum-workshop tucked away in the overgrown backyard of Cursetjee Castle.

◉

'Injectionwala'—Killer or Hero?

The past few weeks have seen two killings carried out by the mysterious Injectionwala, who murders his victims by injecting a poisonous substance into their bodies. But here's the catch— his victims were both involved in the 'Operation Organ' exposed by Mumbai Crime Branch recently.

The last 'injection killing' of the alleged supplier-cum-agent of the organ racket, Bhimrao Wagh, head watchman of Johnson Medical College and Hostel took place in broad daylight. The police are still trying to ascertain when and where did the Injectionwala poison Wagh. It was only after the Injectionwala's phone call announced that Wagh had been his target that the police got to know that Wagh, too, had been injected by a deadly drug. Until then, they had thought that Wagh had had a massive heart attack. The phone call has been traced to a phone booth run by a blind man in Colaba. To their credit, the police have been able to determine that Injectionwala is male, between the ages of twenty-five and forty, and that he seems to be well educated with a good knowledge of medical drugs and procedures.

But, the big question is whether the two people who have been killed by Injectionwala got their just deserts.

Unlike the usual outrage, the silence in the media in this case seems to suggest that they silently support the Injectionwala's brand of justice. What drives our silent acceptance of this dark Robin Hood? Do Injectionwala's actions mirror our deep disgust of and desire to stick it to the corrupt and the depraved? Is the Injectionwala a vigilante who has avenged the murdered and saved countless innocents from Dr Jetha's organ trafficking racket?

The time has come for us to be true with ourselves in the media: we like Injectionwala

If we did not like him, we would put pressure on the police to immediately catch him. Instead we sit back and wait silently wishing that Injectionwala strikes again.

This sentiment is not limited to the media alone. A senior policeman, speaking on condition of anonymity, told this correspondent, 'We may have a messiah out there.'

◉

Virkar stood in front of Additional Commisioner of Police (Crime) Abhinav Kumar, DCP (Crime) Ramesh Hemdev, South Zone, and ACP Pitle, South Zone, revealing the results of his investigation. As he spoke, Abhinav Kumar listened to him intently, wondering whether he had made the wrong decision to have Virkar transferred to Mumbai from Gadchiroli. Although Virkar had used his investigative skills well in the case at hand, he had also interfered with the Crime Branch investigation and a crucial suspect had been killed due to his intervention, creating a public relations mess of gigantic proportions. Perhaps Virkar was a fish out of water in Mumbai. Kumar was concerned not because he feared the wrath of the politicians or the media but because Virkar had not shared his findings with him before behaving like a bull in a china shop. Kumar would now have to step in and do some political machinations if he wanted to save Virkar.

As Virkar finished his statement, Kumar turned towards DCP Hemdev and ACP Pitle. 'What is your opinion?' he asked his tone stern.

DCP Hemdev exploded, 'Who cares about this Tribut… whatever! The Crime Branch has a solid lead on the Injectionwala. We are close to cracking the case.'

ACP Pitle fell back on the familiar course of action. 'Sir, let us send him back to Gadchiroli. A few more years there will clear all the charbi from his brain.'

Kumar didn't react; he turned towards Virkar and said, 'Virkar, you've really created a big mess. I've no choice but to suspend you till further notice. Do you have anything to say to this?'

Virkar saluted and turned to leave. 'Where are you going?' Kumar called out to him. Virkar turned back, a little surprised. 'I want to have a separate word with you Virkar, please wait.' Saying this, Kumar turned to the two senior officers, 'Gentlemen, let's hope that this matter can be closed. Thank you very much, that's all for now.' The two officers left.

As soon as they were out of the room, Kumar looked directly at Virkar. 'Virkar, what is it that you're trying to achieve?' While serving as the superintendent of police in Gadchiroli, Kumar had identified Virkar as a dogged investigator. In local terminology, Virkar had been nicknamed Ghorpad, or monitor lizard. It is rumoured that a ghorpad's claws can cling fast to any surface. The Maratha leader Shivaji's general, Tanaji, had used them to good effect to win the battle of Sinhagadh. A number of Tanaji's soldiers had scaled a vertical cliff with the help of a rope, one end of which was tied to a thick-skinned ghorpad, clinging to the top of the cliff. Virkar, like the ghorpad, would not let go of anything he latched on to. And today, he had shown that same tenacious quality. But in the process, he had also stepped on too many toes.

Virkar managed a nonplussed expression, 'I don't know what you mean, sir.'

Kumar raised an eyebrow, 'Do you think that you can fool me, Virkar? I watched you operate all those years in Gadchiroli and saw how you handled tricky situations between the tribals, the politicians and the Maoists, without letting any fingers be pointed at the police department's functioning. And now you go and create such a big ruckus here...'

Virkar stood expressionless, staring at Kumar. 'Sir, I respect you too much to get you involved. So I will not say anything but that my quest is for justice. True justice.'

For a couple of minutes, Kumar held his gaze and then a frown broke out on his forehead. 'I don't want to lose a good officer.'

Virkar's face remained inscrutable. 'I won't let all that you've taught me go to waste, sir.' Abhinav Kumar nodded.

This time, Virkar clicked his heels and saluted, conveying his deepest respect towards his mentor.

◉

'There is a man named Athavle, he claims to be a real estate agent. I had seen him having late-night meetings with my father. Every time he would call, my father would get tense. I always wondered about the hold he had over my father, and now I know the reason.'

Saakshi had earlier congratulated him on a job well done in the only way that Porus seemed to like, by making passionate, searing love. Porus was now energized and the pall of remorse that he had carried around his shoulders earlier had disappeared.

Porus, who had been staring outside his window, stopped Saakshi from saying anything further. 'Is this Athavle slightly dark and stocky, with a thick moustache?' he asked.

Saakshi looked at him, surprised. 'You know him?'

Porus whispered through ragged breath, 'No, but I have a feeling I will get to know him. He is standing in the compound below.'

Saakshi walked up to where Porus was standing and followed his gaze. She saw the man, Athavle, standing, as Porus had said, in the dusty compound of Cursetjee Castle. Athavle was trying to peer through Porus's window. The old, dust-caked glass in the windows, as well as the plants in the balcony, had kept Porus and Saakshi hidden from his view. As they watched, he gave up looking and entered the building. Saakshi was about to say something when Porus displayed surprising efficiency. He put a finger on her lips and signalled to her to stay where she was. He rushed into a small storeroom on the far corner, emerging with a large heavy bone-china vase. He hefted the large vase in his hands, to give Saakshi an idea of his plan, then went into his kitchen and exited the house from the servant's entrance.

Entering the corridor, he tiptoed upstairs to the second floor. Standing at the banisters, he then positioned the large flower vase in his hands above the gap of the stairwell, that extended till the ground floor. Athavle emerged on the ground floor, trying to walk without making any sound. Porus let go of the flower vase. The falling vase hit Athavle's head with a mighty thump. Athavle let out a slight gurgling sound and collapsed on the floor, unconscious. Saakshi came rushing out of Porus's apartment. She leaned over the banister and looked down at Athavle's prone body. Both she and Porus rushed down to the ground floor. She checked Athavle's pulse, while Porus examined the gash on the man's head. 'He is still alive,' Saakshi said, breathing heavily.

Porus nodded. 'You'd better go. I'll take care of him.'

Saakshi looked confused, 'No…but…he might say something.'

'I said I'd take care of him. I don't want you to get involved. Leave now.' His voice had a sharp commanding tone.

Saakshi started walking towards the gate.

Before she left, she said, 'Don't let him regain consciousness. Kill him right away.' At the gate, she turned and looked back at Porus. He waved her away into the fast gathering shadows. She exited the gate, closing it behind her with a metallic clang.

◉

In a small backroom of the stables of the Mahalaxmi Race Course, a bunch of syces were sitting on rickety wooden chairs across an equally rickety wooden table. They were in the middle of a round of mendicot, a popular Mumbai card game. Virkar stood in the doorway, but nobody seemed to notice him, amidst all the shouting and thumping of the table. After a few minutes, he smiled, cleared his throat and called out, 'Are outsiders allowed to play?'

The players stopped their noisy game and turned towards him, surprised.

No one spoke till a bright-eyed, grizzled old man, who was clutching some cards in his hands, replied, 'Only if they are ready to lose their shirt.'

Virkar, smiled even more broadly, approached the table and pulled out an empty wooden chair. 'I have played it enough to know that I am better than any old man, even though he may have taught me.' He gave the old man a friendly thump. 'How are you, Uncle Moses?'

The old man smiled through his tobacco-stained teeth, 'So, Ramya, I see you after twenty years and the first thing you do is challenge my skill at mendicot?' He puffed up his chest and added loftily, 'Get ready to face the champion of Mahalaxmi Race Course Stable No. 1 backroom'. The other young syces burst into laughter. Virkar couldn't help but join in the infectious mirth around him.

A prolonged card game ensued, with money changing hands and many syces losing their month's salary. More syces joined in, bringing with them quarter bottles of rum and whisky to aid their losing streak. Moses Koli was, indeed, a champion. He wiped out everybody at the table, grinning away all the time, his tobacco-stained smile adding injury to the insult. Virkar lost all the money he had. In a desperate last attempt to win back all his losses, his rum-addled mind finally added the keys of his Bullet to the lot. Unfortunately, Virkar lost this game, too, and could do nothing but look at Moses helplessly as the latter gleefully hefted the Bullet's keys in his hands, all the while flashing Virkar his trademark grin. Then Moses got up and called it a night. The groaning syces complained their way out of the room, promising to win back everything the next month. Moses smiled and waited for everyone to depart, then gestured to the inebriated Virkar to follow him.

Moses led Virkar through the stables into the now-deserted dark parking area. His old eyes scanned and spotted Virkar's Bullet parked at a distance. He walked with the stumbling Virkar up to the Bullet, started the bike and asked the policeman to sit behind him. Virkar obeyed. Moses rode the bike out of the parking area through the gate towards Haji Ali, with the woozy Virkar holding on to him. He stopped the Bullet outside the Haji Ali Juice Centre and ordered the eager waiters to bring two glasses of fresh mosambi juice and two grilled cheese sandwiches. Moses Koli stood on the parapet facing the Arabian Sea. His eyes rested upon the wondrous Haji Ali dargah, perched on a mini islet in the midst of the sea. He sighed, 'Praise the Lord!'

Thanks to the citric shock of the juice and the cheesy bread soaking up the alcohol inside him, Virkar started to come back to his senses. Moses burped, and handed back the Bullet's keys to Virkar. Leaning against the parapet, he picked at the small bits of cheese and bread lodged between his tobacco-stained teeth. 'So, Ramya, how's your police career shaping up?' He asked.

'What career? I got suspended from my job today,' slurred Virkar.

Moses looked at him, surprised. 'But I'd heard you were doing well?'

Virkar continued blubbering, 'That was in Gadchiroli. Here, in Mumbai, I, the son of a fisherman, have become a small fish myself and now, this fish has been eaten up by the system.'

Moses steadied Virkar, who was rocking on his feet. 'Ramya, what happened? Tell me?'

'I had just been appointed acting in-charge of my police station. My lucky break, I thought. Then I sent two plain clothes men from my police station to arrest someone after we received an urgent tip, but the man they arrested was killed on the way. Someone had to be the scapegoat. It turned out that I hadn't done the necessary paperwork before I sent my men. So here I am, suspended, pending an inquiry.'

Moses looked philosophical. 'Sometimes, when the Lord closes one door on us, he opens another one.'

Virkar's addled thoughts went back to the time when Moses was a fisherman, famous in the Colaba Machhimar colony as the man who could bring in a good catch even during the monsoon months. This reputation, along with his devil-may-care attitude, led to his undoing one rainy day, when the boat that Moses had sailed out on capsized. It was Virkar's father's boat, and Moses had been forewarned not to sail. The boat sank off the Mumbai shores. Luckily, Moses was rescued by a passing merchant ship. Virkar's father, however, lost his source of livelihood that day, even as Moses saw his rescue as a miracle and rediscovered Jesus. He decided to give up fishing and start a new life. Through a friend's connections, he joined the stables at the race course and metamorphosed into Moses, the syces. But Virkar's father never forgave Moses for taking out the boat without his permission, and did not say a word to him till his dying day.

Virkar, by now more clear-headed, said, 'Uncle Moses, I want to know if you can tell me anything about an animal drug called Tributame?'

Moses looked at him in surprise, 'Tribhoot, we call it Tribhoot, but how do you know about it?'

Virkar perked up at this. 'It was used to kill a man. I want to find out who did it.'

Moses' face grew serious. 'Who was the man...the one who was killed?'

Virkar replied, 'A famous doctor, the dean of Johnson Medical College'.

'Johnson Medical...dean...isn't he the man involved in the kidney racket?' enquired Moses. Virkar nodded. Moses's face grew dark and thoughtful.

Virkar studied the old man's face. When Moses didn't speak for a long time, Virkar prodded him. 'What happened, Uncle?'

Moses's voice was laden with mixed emotions. 'I think...I know who might be involved.'

'Who?' Virkar exclaimed.

Moses continued in a grave tone. 'There was a man, a syce. Well, actually, he was a trainer who was unfortunate with the races, and became a syce like me.'

'But what is the connection?'

'His son was a student in Johnson Medical College.'

'Where is this syce now?'

Moses shook his head. 'He died five years back'.

Virkar was about to lose interest, till he heard the rest of Moses's sentence

'The syce died of kidney failure.'

◉

A black stray dog scurried through the small compound of Cursetjee Castle. The dog's nose twitched in the direction of the stairs. The nape of its neck was taut with tension as it bounded into the stairwell. A low whimper escaped its mouth at the sight of broken bone china and its eyes finally spotted what it had been so aroused by—a small congealed puddle of blood. The blood, mixed with shards of bone china, was spread in a lazy circle on the ground, soaking into the old stone tile. The dog nosed his way into this bloody splash, questioning its presence. A loud howl of confusion escaped its throat.

Upstairs, in the living room of Porus's apartment, Athavle sputtered to consciousness hearing the howl. His eyes opened and glazed over, confused at his situation. Porus, taking this opportunity to revive him fully, poured a saucepan full of water on his face.

Satisfied with his work, Porus went back to the settee and sat down. He began to chew on a fresh stick of gum while he waited for Athavle to gain a little more focus. He shot out a stream of questions as he began his interrogation: 'How many kidneys did you trade? How many people did you cheat? How many lives did you and Dr Jetha ruin?'

Athavle grimaced, still in pain.

'It was just a business…' he said after several minutes.

'Bastard! You took people's body parts and sold them. Is that what you call a business?' Porus shouted.

Athavle's face was a mask. 'Yes, it was just a business, a normal, everyday Indian "cheating" business. Like cheating on government contracts for making roads, taking bribes at a police station, overcharging on real estate, overcharging at hospitals, as in your case…just plain, simple cheating. We were just innovative in our approach. Nothing else.'

Porus went into one of the rooms and emerged with a small tape-based Dictaphone. He tested it for clarity, then rolled the tape back to the start mark. All this time, Athavle eyed him with a dark expression.

Porus thrust the Dictaphone near Athavle's face. He pressed the record button and barked, 'Now please repeat what you just told me'. Athavle shook his head and smiled. A smile that dripped pure slime.

Porus flashed him a good-natured smile in return. 'I have been quite naïve in my judgment of you. However, I am also equipped with enough intelligence to remedy it'.

Porus kept the Dictaphone on the settee and walked back into his room. He came out with a syringe full of a golden-hued liquid.

Athavle had been watching him with growing fear. When Porus tapped the needle and pressed the plunger to squirt a couple of test drops, Athavle couldn't take it any more. He screamed, 'Don't kill me…don't kill me!'

Porus smiled. 'It's interesting how your manner has changed so quickly…people are always scared of injections.' He walked towards Athavle, bearing the syringe in his hand.

Athavle pleaded. 'Please, I don't want to die.'

This time, Porus gave a dry laugh. 'Don't worry, Mr Athavle, this is just Scopolamine, the long-forgotten truth serum. Did you know it was the favourite drug of the KGB? It is, in fact, the original narco-analysis drug.'

Athavle screamed. Porus spoke in his soothing doctor's manner. 'Oh, don't worry, it will just put you into a state known as "twilight sleep", helping you to confess everything, even the naughty pranks you played as a little boy! The best part is that you will remember nothing after you regain consciousness, as this friendly drug has the added quality of blocking out recent events.'

In one jerk, Porus tore off Athavle's left shirtsleeve. Athavle tried to shake him away, but Porus held his arm down, looking for a vein. He quickly plunged the syringe into the vein and injected the serum. Then he walked back to the settee and turned the Dictaphone on. He pulled a chair close to Athavle and sat down. Athavle was already going into a trance-like state. Porus slapped his cheeks lightly to gain his attention. 'Now, Mr Athavle, please tell me all you know about the kidney racket,' he said.

All of a sudden, Athavle's eyes rolled back in his head. A spurt of blood escaped his nostrils and spattered onto the Dictaphone. Porus was surprised. He laid the Dictaphone on to the ground and pushed up Athavle's rapidly flickering eyelids. Athavle's body was shaking. Porus quickly checked Athalve's heartbeat; it was racing. He got up and ran back into the inner room, took out a bottle from his drug cabinet, and ran back into the living room. He picked up the syringe and quickly drew up some liquid from the new bottle, but by the time he reached Athavle, the man had lost consciousness. Porus checked for a pulse. Finding none, he let go of Athalve's hand. A mixture of disappointment and regret appeared on his face. He stared at the lifeless Athavle and let out a sigh. 'What I neglected to tell you, Mr Athavle, is that, in one case out of a hundred, Scopolamine induces massive cardiac arrest.'

◉

A bespectacled man with a heavy moustache was sitting at his table, his manner aggressive, as he spoke to a thin, earnest-sounding young boy. The man said, 'How dare you suggest such a thing?'

The boy pleaded, 'Sir, please, my entire future depends on these two marks, if you could, sir, just please help me, sir.'

The man was incensed. 'You people think that you can bring your sob stories to your professors and they will give you the marks, just like that. You are lucky that I'm not taking your case to the Board authorities, otherwise you will be rusticated and marked zero, forget the two extra marks.'

The young boy started crying. 'Sir, please, my father is a poor fisherman, all he wants is that I should go to an engineering college. I studied really hard, sir, but I also have to help him in his work, sir, I am helping support our family, sir, I am just two marks short of the percentage needed for getting into an engineering college. Please help me, sir, it will not make any difference to you, but my family position will change, sir.'

The man shouted, 'You cheater! Get out of my room, or I will report you to the police.'

Virkar woke up with a start. Dryness tickled his throat as his glazed eyes instinctively began to focus on the cheap plastic wall clock. It was 3 a.m. He had slept for three hours straight after coming home from his evening with Moses. By now, the effect of the alcohol had worn off. But he felt drained even while lying on his bed. Moses's words went through his mind again. The heart-wrenching story of Udwadia, the syce, and his ambitions for his son Porus had touched a raw nerve. There could be no other explanation for the sudden, vivid resurgence of his long-forgotten memory. He wanted to get up, wash the sweat off his body and, hopefully, the memory off his mind. But he realized that he would have to go through the entire painful process till the memory washed itself away. There was no escape.

Two days after his meeting with the professor, Virkar's father had returned from a fishing expedition with his usual meagre catch. At home, all his father could do was complain, complain, and complain about how the mechanized trawlers were clearing out the oceans, leaving nothing for his poor dhow. Virkar's mother, as usual, had tried to focus on the bright side of things. She had applied the salve of the young Virkar's impending engineering degree as the way out of troubled waters. His father had perked up and the joy on his face had chilled young Virkar's heart. His father had looked at him and proudly proclaimed, 'Ramesh Ramdeo Virkar, the first engineer from Colaba Machhimaar colony. My biggest catch!'

Standing in front of the engineering college gates, anger was the only emotion that had embraced him. The warmth of that embrace set his heart on fire.

His mind had been burning, too, as he walked through the narrow gullies of Colaba Machhimaar colony later. Vengeance was what young Virkar had demanded. Vengeance was the only way to douse the fire.

Three months later, while standing at a bus stop near the Regal Cinema, the mustachioed professor had been beaten up by three street youth, over a senseless argument about taking up too much space at the crowded bus stop. The professor had sustained a hairline crack in the skull and had spent the better part of six months in a hospital. The three youth were never caught. No one ever got to know that they were a certain

Ramesh Ramdeo Virkar's cousins from far-off Versova.

Virkar was restless as the memory filled him with shame. He walked to the tiny washbasin in the corner of the tenement and turned on the tap. The gentle trickle of water was soothing. He splashed some water on his face. Feeling slightly better, he glanced at the cheap plastic wall clock again. 3.15 a.m.

Virkar reached out for his pant and shirt that were hanging from a hook in the wall. He exited his tenement and walked into the narrow streets of Bhoiwada that were, at this time of the morning, devoid of their usual hustle and bustle.

Virkar's mind went over the directions given by Moses. The directions that he hoped would lead him to the man he had been hunting.

◉

4 a.m. on a Mumbai morning is the darkest, quietest time anyone can imagine in this bustling city. It is said that at this time even burglars rest in the city that pretends never to sleep. Only a rare car passes through local neighbourhood streets. Otherwise, the streets in most neighbourhoods are uninhabited, except for a stray dog or two.

It was one such dog, standing under a streetlamp, that caught Virkar's attention as he stood in the shadows opposite Cursetjee Castle. He noticed a wet, glistening blackness on the dog's snout. He searched his pockets for something to offer the dog, but found nothing. He whistled softly. The dog twitched its tail and glanced at him; a little confused whether he was friend or foe. Deciding that Virkar was harmless, it bounded towards him, wagging its tail in friendship.

Virkar patted its head and rubbed its back, his eyes fixed on the dog's mouth. The dog playfully licked his hand.

Virkar took this as an opportunity to rub his hand against the dog's snout. The dog growled a little and backed away. Virkar raised his hand and examined the slimy substance under the dim glow of the streetlight. It was what he had thought, blood. Thick, blackish blood. The dog growl turned low and throaty.

Virkar took a step towards the dog but it yelped and bolted into the night. He bent down and picked up a piece of paper lying on the ground, scraped off the blood from his hand with the paper, and folded it. Preserving it as evidence in his pocket. His hand went to his hip and he realized the biggest disadvantage of being a policeman on suspension. His gun was lying safely in its holster, secure in a Godrej steel cupboard, inside his police station.

He turned his attention back towards Cursetjee Castle. His eyes scanned the black, two-storey structure, as if trying to bore a hole through the stone walls to find the source of the blood. He decided to take a closer look and was about to cross the street to get closer to Cursetjee Castle, when he heard a scraping sound coming from that direction. He hid himself deeper in the shadows. He strained to figure out the source of the scraping sound. His curiosity soon got the better of him, and he crouched and tiptoed towards the compound wall bordering Cursetjee Castle. Upon reaching a dark patch on the compound wall, he raised himself to try and get a view inside, but the wall was too high. He then clasped the top of the wall. Using all his strength, he managed to raise himself parallel to the wall, enough for him to take in the dark compound and the goings on within. Like a precariously balanced gymnast, Virkar hung in his suspended position, his tense body struggling against gravity. The scraping had grown louder and Virkar could now decipher it as the sound of a heavy object being dragged on dry mud.

Suddenly, he caught a movement in the darkness. His eyes focused on what looked like a man struggling with a large gunnysack, heading towards the silhouette of a car standing at the far end of the compound. He calculated that the man would take at least a minute to reach the car at his current pace. Lowering himself back on to the ground, he allowed himself a quick chance to relax before getting back into position. His heart thumped as he began to understand what was happening on the other side of the wall. After he had rested for about forty-five seconds, he hoisted himself back into the same position and his eyes searched again for the man. He saw that the man had reached the car. A sliver of moonlight bounced off metal, and Virkar could make out that the boot was open. The man was now hoisting the gunnysack into the boot. Struggling with its heavy proportions, he somehow managed to overturn it in. As the gunnysack disappeared inside the tight space with a low thump, the man relaxed, catching his breath. He shut the boot door as quietly as possible. Virkar then heard the car door open and moments later, the sound of the engine starting. But the headlights didn't come on.

Virkar quickly jumped back off the compound wall, onto the footpath, and scurried back across the street, merging himself into the shadows once more. Just then, he heard the car at the compound gate. He saw the dark shape of a man get out of the car and open the metal gates. The man got back into the car and drove away, down the street, turning right at the first by-lane.

As soon as the car had disappeared from sight, Virkar sprang out of the shadows and ran towards his Bullet that he had earlier parked under a building midway down the street. He sprang onto the motorcycle and took off in the direction of the car. Turning into the by-lane that the car had taken, he saw the car at quite a distance from him. The car took a turn on to the main Mazagaon road. Virkar followed at a discreet distance. Luckily for him, the driver had turned on the lights after hitting the main road. He spotted the car again at a distance, turning towards Byculla. The car headed through Byculla and reached Gloria Church, where it looped across Sir JJ Marg towards 'S' Bridge.

The car and the motorcycle wound on and on through the black roads. Virkar wondered where they were headed, as the car had almost reached Nana Chowk. He watched as it turned right into a lane just after Gamdevi Police Station. On an impulse, Virkar stopped the bike on the main road and parked it behind a couple of other cars on the side of the road. He walked into the lane on foot. Using the parked cars in the street for cover, he walked down the lane. He saw the car, parked in a gully opposite a garbage bin. Virkar realized that the bin was directly behind the Gamdevi police station, except that it was hidden from sight because of the high compound wall. The boot of the car was open and the man was lifting the gunnysack out of the car. Virkar watched in silence. The man dragged the gunnysack across the street to the garbage bin and propped it against the side of the bin. The man hurried back across the street and started the car. As quietly as possible, he reversed out of the dark gully and drove off in the opposite direction.

Virkar waited for the car to disappear, then emerged from the shadows and walked towards the gunnysack. He approached it with some amount of trepidation, fearing what he may find inside. He poked at the rough fabric and felt something soft and pulpy. A sinking feeling started growing in the pit of his stomach. He quickly undid the knot at the top and let the gunnysack fall over to the side. Out spilled the body of a recently dead man. What surprised Virkar was that he recognized the man. A small-time real-estate broker called Athavle, who had connections with the underworld. Athavle had, on many occasions, been an informer for the police and was quite the favourite with the erstwhile 'encounter specialists'.

A neatly folded crisp white paper popped out of Athavle's pocket. Virkar reached for the paper, but stopped himself at the last minute. He took out a handkerchief and wrapped it around his hand like a glove. He then extricated the note. He opened the note and strained to read the scrawled lettering under the dull moonlight.

> 'This man's name is Athavle. He was an associate of Dr Animesh Jetha and had helped him in the kidney racket. I have killed him. People like him, who prey on the poor, need to be removed from this earth. I will not rest until all the members of this organ racket have been brought to justice by me. My justice is their death.'

The note was unsigned, but Virkar already knew who had written it. He stood silent. He wanted to go after Porus, but strangely, held himself back. He had no real answer for this hesitance. The only answer that sprung to his mind was that somehow, Porus's actions had opened up a locked door within him. A hidden door that led to the darkest part of his soul. To a visceral understanding of Porus's motive. To the revelation that perhaps, he himself was not very different from Dr Porus Udwadia.

Around him, the chirping of birds began to fill the air. The night was dying, giving way to a new day. After what seemed a lifetime, Virkar recovered his wits.

He folded the note, placed it back in Athavle's pocket and shoved the lifeless man back into the sack. Quickly, he tied the sack up again and left it next to the garbage bin. He then melted into the grey Mumbai dawn.

◉

The Bullet cruised past the still unawakened Metro Cinema Junction and slid between the Kayani and Bastani Bakeries. Passing the next traffic signal without any hindrance, it turned right onto an arterial road leading right into the heart of Kalbadevi.

Virkar's eyes scanned the shop signboards and finally rested on the one proclaiming: 'Elite Estate Agency, Proprietor— B. K. Athavle'.

Maakad Nakwa shifted on the pillion seat, reminding Virkar of his presence.

Virkar gestured towards the signboard. Maakad nodded back. Virkar rode the Bullet into a narrow by-lane and stopped near a parked car. Maakad said, 'So what do you want me to look for, some land deal papers?'

Virkar replied, 'No, I want you to get me anything that looks as if it is connected to doctors or the medical profession.'

Maakad raised an eyebrow in surprise but held his tongue.

Maakad Nakwa was perhaps the single most capable cat burglar left in Mumbai. Born and brought up in the Colaba Machhimar Colony, he had shown no interest in following the footsteps of his fisherman father. Instead, he had had an early inclination towards his current trade. As a child, he would slide up the mast of his father's old fishing boat, curl himself into a ball, and hide in the smallest of places. His first name was Ravi, but he had been named Maakad (monkey) because of his ability to jump from roof to roof of the neighbouring huts, without making a sound, or denting the corrugated aluminum roof sheets. As an adolescent, Maakad's talents were utilized by the Sundre Gang to enter the old houses of Colaba, by making him scale pipes and use his body compacting skills to gain entry through gaps in window grills barely large enough to let a small animal through. The spate of new construction brought in new apartments with smaller grill gaps and, therefore, less possibility of entering through the windows. Maakad was the only member of the Sundre Gang who survived the wave of arrests in the 1990s that put most of the gang behind bars. To keep in step with the changing times, Maakad surreptitiously trained at a locksmith's shop in the Fort area. He then went solo and travelled from Colaba all the way to Bandra, breaking locks and entering apartments in swanky bungalows. He stole enough to create a steady income for himself. Occasionally he would venture towards burglarizing a house in Colaba. After Virkar had been posted to the Colaba police station, he warned his old friend Maakad to stop operating in Colaba. Maakad did not heed his warning and had robbed a jewelry cache from a rich businessman's house. Virkar arrested him, although he was kind enough not to pressurize him to return the stolen goods. Six months later, Maakad was out. After having spent his first stint in jail, he had decided to go straight. Finally taking up the profession that almost all his family members had wanted him to be a part of, in the first place, he bought himself a mechanized fishing trawler by selling off the stolen jewellery.

Now it was time for Maakad to return the favour. He stood

at the side entrance of Elite Estate Agency. The door was set inside an old, almost condemned, Kalbadevi building. On it was an old Godrej padlock. With the flick of a long fingernail on his right little finger, he slid out a large metal bobby pin hidden within the seam of his shirt. He inserted the bobby pin into the padlock and turned and twisted it, feeling his way to the catch lever. Finding the touch point, he pressed the bobby pin with full force and the padlock snapped open. In one smooth movement, Maakad took off the padlock, opened the door and entered the room.

In the side street, Virkar sat on his Bullet going through the events of the previous night in his head. The soft, rising sun was brightening up the street, but Virkar's mood remained dark. In his mind, Porus's face was flashing over and over again. Virkar was searching for any signs of cruelty, but all he could remember was a placid, matter-of-fact expression.

Maakad's sudden return jolted Virkar out of his reverie. Maakad shrugged. 'There were only real estate papers there, sale deeds, etc. The only remotely medical-looking thing that I found was this.' He handed over a colour photograph.

'It was the only thing kept inside a safe, so I presumed it must be important, somehow'.

Virkar took one look at the photograph and put it inside his pocket without a word. He gunned the Bullet engine and started to ride off.

The surprised Maakad shouted out behind him, 'Hey! How am I am going to get home'?

Without turning, Virkar said 'Take a taxi, you can afford it'. He rode out of the lane into the early morning traffic of Kalbadevi.

◎

Injectionwala Strikes Again

The Injectionwala found another victim on Tuesday night. This time it is a fixer, B. K. Athavle. He is alleged to have given several bribes on behalf of Dr Jetha so that Jetha could continue his heinous activities unchallenged. Police sources say that Athavle was the man who bribed Senior Inspector Rajendra Kapse, too. It is yet to be ascertained whether Athavle was Man Friday to Dr Jetha or was he the leader of the ring.

In a note left with the body, Injectionwala has said that killing is his brand of justice for the wrongdoers in our society.

In an online opinion poll we ran yesterday, we asked people whether they wanted Injectionwala to continue killing, or to be brought to justice. This is what some respondents had to say: Aditya, 24: 'I hope Injectionwala keeps killing. We have plenty of worthless, corrupt people to bring to justice... He has become a local hero of sorts.'

Zainub, 50: 'Why don't you imagine a person in your family in the same situation as the victims of the kidney racket?'

Karamdeep, 21: Injectionwala going to jail won't bring the world to peace, it won't make the victims come back to life. It would be better if he never gets caught.

Bharti, 28: 'Injectionwala is the first good thing that has happened to this city in a long time. He should go after all the corrupt people in our society.'

Ravi, 46: 'There's an Injectionwala inside all of us.'

◉

Maskati Cloth Mills in Byculla was one among the numerous mills whose machines had fallen silent in 1982 due to the mill-workers' strike. Its operations were too small to survive the prolonged standoff. The owner, who had hoped to earn some big bucks by giving it for redevelopment, had locked it up, preferring instead to concentrate on his other businesses. Presently, the crumbling building was lying unused, inhabited by a few disinterested security guards.

Today, however, its dilapidated main building was finally being used. Inspector Virkar was standing behind a dust-encrusted arch on the second floor, looking through binoculars at the equally dilapidated back façade of the neighbouring Cursetjee Castle, about twenty feet away.

Virkar had found this vantage point after discreetly circling the area a few times. A flash of his ID card had gained him a quick entry into the mill premises, no questions asked. Now his eyes were glued to the only window that had light emanating from within.

Inside the room, a stark-naked Saakshi was facing the window while straddling an equally naked Porus, who was tied to a cast-iron four-poster bed. Saakshi was riding him like a cowgirl, and below her, Porus was writhing in the throes of ecstasy. Although the scene was exciting enough to distract any normal individual, Virkar was focused on Saakshi's face.

Porus let out a loud yelp and sank back into the bed, spent. Saakshi smiled and rolled off him. Porus reached out for her and they both went into a lip lock that, to Virkar, seemed to last forever. Virkar stepped back into the shadows as if he, too, was done. But the wheels inside his mind were whirring.

◉

Porus rose from the bed. He padded towards his cupboard and took out a pair of jeans. Saakshi, who had been lolling till now, propped herself up on the pillows, Where do you think you're going?'

'To kill that bastard Khorche,' Porus replied.

Saakshi raised an eyebrow. 'Who, that municipal corporator who was in the news sometime back for inciting a riot?'

'Yes, that same motherfucker.'

'But I've got nothing against him.'

Porus shook his head. 'He's corrupt to the core. He took money from some builders and, because of him, many people died.'

Saakshi persisted, 'But, Porus he's not part of the racket...'

Porus burst out, 'Saakshi, don't you understand? It's not about you, or your father, or the organ racket anymore. It's about justice. It's about punishing the corrupt.'

Saakshi was worried now. 'Porus, please, hold on a minute. When did it become about all that?'

Porus said in a lofty manner, 'Look around you, read the papers, switch on the TV. They are praising my work; they want me to go on. I am their hero.'

'No, Porus, they are all just venting their frustration. You are the flavour of the season; tomorrow, they'll be talking about someone else.'

Porus threw her a petulant sneer. 'You are just jealous that I'm getting all this attention in the media.'

Saakshi got up, walked towards him and put her arms around him. 'Porus, you have to stop thinking like that. I love you.'

'You just want my work to go unnoticed.' Porus disengaged himself from her.

Saakshi said, angrily, 'Porus, it's over. The people who deserved to die are dead. You have to call it quits.'

Porus began to laugh. 'Call it off! Now? This is just the beginning.'

Saakshi fell silent. Porus was expecting her to say something. But she just kept staring at him. After what seemed like aeons, she spoke. 'Porus, I want you to come to the hospital for a checkup. You are getting delusional.'

'I will not go to any hospital-shospital. I'm a doctor. I can take care of myself,' Porus snapped.

Without another word, Saakshi held his hand and led him back to the bed. Holding him by the shoulders she pulled him on top of her. Porus stopped being petulant and busied himself between her legs. But, just when he was about to climax, she abruptly shook him off. 'Will you come to the hospital?' she asked.

Porus's eyes wore a glazed expression. He looked as if his favourite toy had been snatched away. Saakshi began to get up from the bed.

Porus he grabbed her hand. 'Okay, okay, I will. I promise,' he said, pulling her back to him. She smiled and climbed back on top of him.

This time, Virkar's eyes stayed on the couple. He couldn't help but watch the twisted moment play out.

◉

Dressed and smiling, Saakshi headed for the door. Porus shuffled behind her.

Saakshi turned, a little irritated. 'Come on, hurry up, we'll get late. I have to report for duty.'

Porus's voice was firm. 'Look, I feel fine now. I just had a temporary lapse of reason.'

Saakshi knew that she'd lost her advantage, now that he'd got what he wanted. She decided to change her tack. 'I'll give you a couple of hours to think about it. As far as I'm concerned, if you don't show up at the hospital within two hours, I will consider our relationship over.'

Porus immediately changed his tack, too. 'It's not that I don't want to do what you say, Saakshi. Just think of my reputation. I'm a doctor from another hospital. How will people at my hospital feel if I went to yours for treatment?'

'Hmm…you do have a point there. We'll just pretend you had an attack of indigestion and had to rush to the closest hospital.'

Porus realized that she was not going to take no for an answer. He shrugged his shoulders. 'Okay, give me a couple of hours and I'll be there.' Saakshi gave him a long look. He seemed resigned to his fate. Reassured, she made her way towards the main gate. Porus walked beside her. He grabbed her hand. 'Saakshi, I love you a lot. Thank you for looking out for my well being.'

Saakshi gave him a smile and a loving pat on his cheek. She hailed a passing cab. Porus waved until her cab had disappeared into the traffic.

He turned and headed back to his apartment. As he neared the door, he noticed something lying on the ground. He went closer, only to realize that it was a large, brown-paper envelope. He whipped around. Cursetjee Castle was silent. He picked up the envelope. It was unsealed. He opened it. What he saw inside made him freeze.

◉

Injectionwala Caught

In a stunning breakthrough, Mumbai Crime Branch has nabbed serial killer 'Injectionwala'—a final year medical student from Johnson College, Rakesh Awasthi.

Awasthi's arrest was set in motion a week earlier, when a reporter from a leading English newspaper received an anonymous email praising a story profiling the murdered Johnson Medical College watchman, Bhimrao Wagh. Attached to the mail was a map of Antop Hill with a spot marked with an 'X'. The email claimed that another body would be found at that location.

After finding the body of a ragpicker at that location, the Cyber Crime Cell of the Crime Branch focused on the source of the email.

Experts from the Cyber Crime Cell provided the investigating team with the evidence that the mail had originated from a fake IP address using a proxy server. Ethical hackers spent over two days tracing the name of the server that issued the IP address. Finally the source was traced to a cyber café in Bhandup.

Crime Branch sleuths were able to identify the customer through CCTV footage maintained by the cyber cafe.

Then followed an extended search and surveillance operation that led to Rakesh Awasthi. At first the Crime Branch suspected that Awasthi might be a part of the organ racket and may have other associates.

After it was finally deduced that he was acting on his own, the police team swooped down on the Johnson College Hostel late last night and arrested Awasthi, who was, at the time, surfing pornographic websites.

Awasthi will soon undergo a narco-analysis test.

◉

Virkar was laughing to himself while reading the late morning edition. "'Rakesh Awasthi, Cyber Scapegoat" is the next headline, I am going to read,' he thought. He raised the newspaper to cover his face, and shuffled behind a rack inside the shop across from Cursetjee Castle. Porus, dressed in a pair of blue jeans and a stylish black leather jacket, had just emerged, pushing his RD through the iron gates. He shut the gates with a gloved hand and kicked his RD to a start. Virkar noticed the long black riding boots Porus had on. Porus put on a fashionable black-helmet and rode towards the main road. From behind the shop, Virkar's Bullet, too, rolled out slowly towards the path Porus had taken.

Porus was already a speck in the distance. Virkar smiled to himself. 'I'll show him what a Bullet can do.' He revved and the bike responded with a mighty roar. The Bullet went from casual to race speed. Porus drew closer as the Bullet hungrily ate up the road, reducing the gap.

Heading south, Porus powered along the road under the JJ Flyover. Just when he was nearing CST, he abruptly took a U-Turn. So sudden was the turn that Virkar realized it only when he saw Porus on the other side of the road, passing him by. Cursing under his breath, Virkar kept his eyes on Porus through his rearview mirror. At the last minute, he saw Porus swing into the JJ College of Arts campus.

Losing precious minutes in the jammed traffic, Virkar swung his Bullet towards JJ College, still cursing himself and hoping that Porus had not parked his bike and gone inside the building. By the time Virkar reached the gate, he saw

Porus on his RD, emerging from the exit gate a little further down the road. Virkar quickly fell behind keeping a vigilant eye on Porus this time.

Porus went on towards Dhobi Talao, swinging past the police commissioner's office. Virkar kept on his tail, hoping that no one would spot him as he rode past the commissioner's office. 'What is he up to? He can't be taking joy rides in the day.' Virkar had an uneasy feeling as he watched Porus's back a few cars away. Nevertheless, he kept up as Porus rode towards Churchgate. 'He's going to either go in the Fort area or towards Colaba,' thought Virkar.

'*Aicha gho*! The bawa has made me a chutiya!' Virkar suddenly registered that Porus was not wearing black leather riding boots. His boots were of black leather, but of a different type. He couldn't have changed the boots in the time that Virkar had taken to reach the JJ College gates. That was not Porus. Virkar shook his head, disgusted with himself. He revved his bike, closing the distance between the RD and himself. Drawing up alongside, he flashed his police ID card signalling the rider to stop. The rider drew up on the side of the road a little ahead. As he took off the helmet, Virkar noticed that there was some resemblance between the rider and Porus.

'Whose bike is this?' Virkar asked.

The rider was confused. 'My cousin Porus's. But he gave it to me.'

Virkar knew the answer, but had to ask, 'When did he give it to you?'

'Is there a problem, sir?'

'Just answer the question.'

The rider was now a little scared. 'He gave it to me just ten minutes back. He had called me earlier, saying he was going away, and wanted to gift me his bike and riding gear.' The rider patted the black jacket and helmet. 'He told me to take the bike for a long ride, by myself. He was in a hurry to be somewhere. I offered to drop him, but he declined.'

Virkar sighed, because he already knew where Porus had gone. He quickly kickstarted his bike, hoping that he would get there in time.

◉

Porus stared at the old colonial British building in front of him. Knots of people were milling around the entrance, under the large peeling sign that said 'Johnson Medical College'. He strode through the murmuring crowd and entered the foyer. He climbed up the wooden staircase, his long strides in the black leather boots making a loud booming sound on the centuries' old teakwood stair panels. He threw an admiring glance at the symmetrical black stone blocks that made the walls of the corridors.

At the end of the corridor sat Joshi, the peon. Nonchalant as always, Joshi was going through his customary paan-spitting ritual. Red spittle against black stone, as if challenging the long-gone British authority.

On seeing Porus, Joshi straightened perhaps just an inch. Porus gave him his usual please-respect-public-property look, to no effect. Joshi tilted his head slightly towards the open door on the right. 'Doctor Madam is inside.' Porus gave him a stony stare. Joshi swallowed slightly and grudgingly added, 'Doctor Saheb.' He spat out the last word as if it was an irritating piece of supari in his paan.

Porus entered the room. Saakshi was sitting across a large wooden table, talking to a student. On seeing him, Saakshi gestured to the student to leave. Porus sank into the chair, silent.

'What's the matter?' Saakshi asked softly.

'He is going to kill me.'

Saakshi looked doubtful, 'Who?'

Porus burst out, 'The Motorcycle Man.'

'Is he here?'

'No, I managed to shake him off on the way.'

Saakshi fell silent.

'He sent me a message.'

'Who?'

'The Motorcycle Man.'

'What message?'

'That I have to kill one more time.'

'Who do you have to kill?'

'He didn't say. I have to guess that.'

'Who is this Motorcycle Man?'

'I don't know.'

Saakshi fell silent again. After a while she said, 'Porus, these are early signs of paranoid schizophrenia.'

Porus looked at her, irritated. 'I'm telling the truth.'

'You know that the early symptoms are delusions of persecution, usually accompanied by hallucinations and mood disturbances.'

Porus's eyes jumped all around the room. His body language was still extremely agitated.

Saakshi looked concerned. 'You are having an anxiety attack. Calm down, Porus. Where's your chewing gum?'

Porus stared at her. 'Why are you not believing me?'

Saakshi sighed. 'People with paranoid schizophrenia may have mistaken beliefs or delusions that one or more people are plotting against them,' she spoke with obvious authority. 'It is difficult or impossible for others to convince them that they are not the target of a plot. Whatever you see or hear from now on should be suspect. Don't believe anything.'

Porus's eyes finally focused on Saakshi's. 'Should I believe you, Saakshi?'

Saakshi looked a little surprised. 'Of course, you should.'

'Why?' A soft smile played on his lips.

'Because I'm the only one in this world who loves you, Porus,' she half-whispered.

Porus smiled. 'Then I'm ready to die for you. Do what you want with me.'

Saakshi stared at him, a little concerned. Porus wore his quiet smile. Saakshi broke her gaze, 'Okay, let's go to the observation ward.' She got up from the chair and patted Porus gently on his shoulder. Porus took out a stick of chewing gum and offered it to her, but she refused. He popped it into his mouth and followed her out through the corridor into a smallish ward.

Saakshi motioned to Porus to lie down. He obeyed. She took off his riding boots. 'Porus, I'm putting you under observation for twenty-four hours. I need you to relax,' she said.

Porus smiled and meekly said, 'Yes, doctor.'

Saakshi giggled.

'Come here, give me a kiss.' Porus pulled her towards him.

She went into his arms and slowly rubbed herself all over his body. Sensing his arousal, she started giving him a deep, wet kiss. In a few seconds, she broke away. '*Chee*! Porus, your mouth smells foul!'

Porus looked apologetic.

'Sorry, what am I doing? I'm supposed to be calming you down,' she said in mock anger. She patted Porus's cheek and left the room.

'I'll send the sister with some Alprazolam,' she called out from the door.

Porus nodded. 'Yes, that will help me relax.'

◉

The nurse had left a minute back. The sister had fussed around him, asking him to change out of his clothes into a hospital gown, which he had politely refused. However, he had lain down and let the sister administer an injection. Now he was lying relaxed, his eyes shut.

Virkar entered the observation room, and walked to his bedside. Porus half-opened his eyes.

'Are you the one who left the envelope?' Porus came to the point.

Virkar nodded.

Porus reached inside his pant pocket and extracted the envelope.

'Here it is. I don't know whether to curse you or to thank you.'

Virkar took the envelope.

'I think you actually did me a favour. I had lost my way,' said Porus.

'So?' Porus sighed. 'So goodbye, my friend.'

Virkar looked nonplussed.

Porus smiled, 'The Injectionwala has been given a deadly injection.'

Virkar burst out in agitation,

'But can't we do anything? An antidote perhaps... something? You are in a hospital, Godammit!'

Porus continued to smile. 'Don't worry! Thanks to you, I was prepared.' He winked.

Virkar stood looking at him. The smile remained on Porus's face, the eyes still held Virkar's gaze, but all movement slowly stopped.

Virkar stayed there for a few minutes, hoping to see some signs of life appear miraculously. He felt that although Porus's limbs were frozen, he was still conscious and aware of his surroundings. Porus let out a weak shudder and shut his eyes.

Virkar then shook himself out of his trance. The envelope slipped from his grasp. He picked it up and opened it. It had a photograph inside. It was a candid picture of Dr Jetha inside his secret operation theatre, extracting a kidney from the body of an unconscious man. What was more interesting was the fact that he was being assisted in the operation by none other than his loyal daughter, Dr Saakshi Jetha.

◉

Dr Saakshi Jetha sat on her chair in her office room, absolutely still. Yet, if someone could read her mind, they would realize that she was desperately trying to reach the call bell to summon Joshi, the peon. But her limbs would not obey her brain. She decided to topple herself off the chair, in the hope that the noise would attract Joshi's attention. But her legs didn't seem to exist at all. She could see them, but she couldn't feel them. Her brain wanted to scream out, 'Joshi!' But her tongue was frozen. In any case, she realized that it was of no use. Joshi was, as usual, out for his chai break at this time.

Slowly, her third-year toxicology professor's voice began to play in her mind, like an old, extra-stretched tape. The professor was explaining, 'The poison has a strong, fetid odour. You can't miss its foul smell! After ingestion, symptoms of paralysis occur within half an hour. The central nervous system is not affected and the person remains conscious and aware for a while, until respiratory paralysis results in cessation of breathing. After some time, breathing becomes very slow and then stops. Lips go blue and then the fingers and toes also turn blue. The skin colour becomes pallid. The brain will be starved of oxygen and death will follow soon.'

Slowly, every sound faded away. Only one line kept repeating in her brain, 'Porus's kiss...Porus's kiss...Porus's kiss...'

◉

Twist in the Injectionwala Tale

In a new and bizarre twist to the Injectionwala case, a young doctor, Dr Porus Udwadia, was found dead in a ward in Johnson Medical College. Moments later, another doctor, Dr Saakshi Jetha's body was discovered in her office. Dr Saakshi was the daughter of murder victim Dr Animesh Jetha, the brains behind the sensational kidney racket.

A piece of chewing gum in Dr Porus Udwadia's mouth was found to contain coniine. Historically, coniine, popularly known as hemlock, is the poison that killed the Greek philosopher, Socrates.

However, on further examination, traces of Alprazolam were also found in Dr Udwadia's system. According to experts, Alprazolam is a drug commonly used to handle anxiety attacks, but it is administered only in the form of tablets. An injection of this drug is especially dangerous because, when crushed in water, it does not fully dissolve, causing severe damage to the arteries and a fatal overdose.

On interrogation, the staff nurse confessed that she was specifically instructed to administer the injection by Dr Saakshi Jetha.

After examining Dr Saakshi Jetha's stomach contents, it was found that she, too, had been poisoned with coniine, although it is unclear how the poison was administered to her.

Sources allege that Dr Saakshi Jetha, may have been involved in her father's racket.

It is not known whether the alleged Injectionwala, Rakesh Awasthi, knew either of these victims. Police are still searching for any possible connection between Dr Porus Udwadia and the Injectionwala case.

◉

As he entered Cursetjee Castle, Maakad Nakwa in tow, Virkar's mind was set. 'They may conjecture all they want, but they will never be able to prove it. Porus suffered enough.'

It took Maakad the better part of three minutes to get them inside Porus's apartment.

It took Virkar fifteen minutes to remove every trace of connection between Dr Porus Udwadia and the Injectionwala.

Justice had been served. Virkar style.

◉

Coma Man

*N*aked. Beautiful. Uninhibited.

Standing on the first-floor balcony of their cottage, she looked every inch an ethereal goddess who had descended on earth to please one man alone. Him. Samir Khanna.

Her long hair fluttered in the wind blowing in from the sea. The setting sun unleashed an orange sunbeam that seeped through the tiny gap between the buildings opposite the cottage, and lit up the contours of her body.

'So, what are you giving me for my birthday?' The cheeky, dimpled pout on Bahaar's face made her look so much more endearing.

It was then that she noticed the velvet box he was holding in his hands. An excited shiver ran through her body as she sprang towards the box. She opened it, instantly going into paroxysms of delight on seeing its contents.

She pulled out the diamond necklace from the box and clasped it around her slender neck. Shining gallant in the rapidly dipping sunlight, the necklace seemed to salute her allure. She smiled, the twinkle in her eyes matching the gleam of the diamonds.

Samir's body resonated with desire as she walked into his arms.

◉

'Today is my wife's birthday, too,' he said, as he rose from the bed he had been occupying for almost twenty years.

The sound of his voice startled Sister Sandra, she turned to look at the only other person present in the small special room tucked away at the back of the Bhonsale Medical Trust Hospital in CBD Belapur, Navi Mumbai.

Coma Man, as he had come to be referred to by the few who knew about his existence in the hospital, was sitting upright in his bed. Shocked, she dropped the dirty clothes and sponge pan she was carrying. She had just finished her daily ritual of shaving Coma Man's stubble, sponging him, dressing him in fresh white pajamas and half-sleeved shirt and then laying him back in a position that applied the least amount of pressure on his bedsores. Over the years, Coma Man had gone from young to middle-aged and yet, his features remained ruggedly handsome. Although his limbs had been prone, his muscles had not atrophied. 'Because of myostatin suppression, due to some kind of brain chemical imbalance,' a doctor had explained to her long back.

Often, she would gaze at his immobile face and wish that she had such a good-looking man in her life. As was her practice, she would chatter away about some inane topic or the other, which she believed would put Coma Man in a good mood. Today, she had been talking about the birthday party that she was going to attend that evening on the terrace of her friend's building. She had expressed her fear that rain may spoil the party, since it was already 15 June. The sharp jerk of his head had given her a start, even though she had keenly monitored his extraordinary progress since he had started coming out of his coma, almost eight weeks ago. Although he had shown rapid improvement and gained some amount of motor function in his limbs, he had never made this kind of sudden movement. She looked into his eyes. The eyes that had worn a glazed look for the last nineteen years seemed sharp today, almost as if he had a secret he was bursting to share. Sister Sandra had wondered what was going on in Coma Man's mind. Now, she knew.

Sister Sandra nearly fell on her knees as he took his first firm step off the bed. After nursing his prone body for so many years, hearing him speak and seeing him walk was nothing short of a miracle. Coma Man seemed unaware of the amazing feat he was putting up as he took slow, yet steady, steps towards her.

'I'm going home,' he said. 'It's my wife's birthday.' Sister Sandra was unsure of what she should do. Like everyone else in the hospital, she had no idea who Coma Man really was.

'Do you know where your home is?' She finally found her voice.

'No, but I will find out,' Coma Man continued, albeit confused. The Sister now remembered that it was her duty not to let patients leave the hospital, unaccompanied. She stood blocking Coma Man's path to the door. But his pleading look was enough to melt her. If ever there was a man in love, here he was. Something inside her told her to put aside hospital rules. This is God's will, she thought. She directed him towards the back door, which opened on to the unguarded back gate of the hospital. He gave her a smile that seemed to make all the years spent tending to him worth it.

'Before you go, won't you tell me your name?' she called out. He didn't stop, but replied over his shoulder, 'My name is Samir Khanna.'

◉

Madhukar Bhonsale, the chief trustee of the Bhonsale Medical Trust Hospital, had just got up after a long night of drinking alone in his penthouse in Kharghar, Navi Mumbai. He had still not recovered from his massive hangover when his chief medical officer called to give him the information that Coma Man was missing from the hospital.

Madhukar had been camped in Kharghar for the past six weeks after he had heard the news from the CMO about Coma Man coming out of his coma. The CMO had been working at the hospital only for the past eight years and didn't know much about Coma Man, except that he was supposed to be kept in the small special ward at the back of the hospital and was to be provided all the medical care that only VIP patients received. Being a non-interfering, let-me-keep-my-job type, the CMO had quietly kept sanctioning all the facilities that were required for Coma Man. In fact, when the patient had suddenly come out of his coma, he had had no idea what to do. Luckily, the CMO had called Madhukar before his eager deputy had gone to the local press to announce this almost miraculous happening. Madhukar had instructed the CMO to clamp down on any news. He wanted no mention of Coma Man even within hospital premises. The CMO had duly complied.

But now, Madhukar's fingers trembled as he disconnected his mobile. He knew that his dark secret was about to come to light.

As he pulled on his clothes, his thoughts went back to that fateful night nineteen years ago, in 1993. He had been young and full of daredevilry. After having downed one whisky peg too many, he had decided to drive down to Pune to meet an ex-girlfriend for a drunken romp. He had been driving on the Mumbai–Pune highway when, somewhere near Panvel, he had passed by a truck accident that had just taken place. The truck was smashed against a tree by the highway. Madhukar had been drunk and didn't want to get involved, so he had driven past without stopping to help. A little further up the road, his conscience had got the better of him and he had decided to go back. As he swung back, he heard a thump against his car. He stopped the car and sprang out. Outside, he saw a young man lying on the side of the road, unconscious, but not dead. The man had apparently been hit by his car. Madhukar, who was scared that he may be slapped with a case of drunken and rash driving, rushed the man to the then spanking new Bhonsale Medical Trust Hospital at CBD Belapur, started by his father, Dr Ganpatrao Bhonsale, a renowned surgeon. The man didn't have any identification on him, and was bleeding from a head wound. But since Madhukar himself had brought the man in, his father had not informed the police and had personally taken the man into treatment. Dr Bhonsale had operated upon the man, who had had multiple fractures, apart from severe brain trauma, and still had managed to save the man's life. But the man had slipped into a coma. The doctor had wanted to inform the police, but had been emotionally blackmailed by Madhukar's mother to keep the whole incident a secret, because she felt that the future of her beloved son was at stake. Dr Bhonsale kept scanning the papers for reports of missing people, but apart from the usual reports of rioting in Mumbai and sundry crimes, there was none. One small, insignificant report of a truck accident off Panvel had appeared, though, where a truck, laden with leather goods, had swung off the highway. Its driver had been killed on the spot. But there was no mention of a missing man.

Finally, under Dr Bhonsale's reluctant orders, the man was

quietly moved to a small room at the back of the hospital, and assigned a special nurse and doctor to care for him. This, though, was not before Dr Bhonsale made Madhukar swear in front of all the deities in their pooja room that should the man come out of his coma, Madhukar would confess all to the police.

Fifteen years had passed since. Dr Bhonsale had died, but Coma Man had just been lying there, breathing, but otherwise as good as dead. Many a times, Madhukar had wanted to pull the plug on the man, but was bound by the word he had given to his dead father, in front of God. Madhukar prayed that the man would die on his own, putting an end to the story, but Coma Man continued to cling defiantly to his vegetative existence.

Over the years, the doctors had predicted that he would never recover. Then, one day, eight weeks ago, Coma Man had twitched a finger just a fraction, almost giving a heart attack to the doctor on duty. Over a three-day 'awakening period', he had started coming out of his coma. Over the next few weeks, Coma Man had slowly also regained his motor functions. The doctors were clueless as to how this had happened. Using brain imaging, they built a hypothesis that Coma Man's brain had reconnected the neurons which had remained intact, and formed new connections to circumvent the damaged areas. The new connections seemed to have grown around the back of the brain, forming structures that do not normally exist in human brains. Soon, Coma Man had gained the ability to control some parts of his body. The doctors had believed that Coma Man might regain consciousness, but his speech and memory functions would remain incapacitated. Obviously, they were wrong. Coma Man had not only spoken to his nurse, he had remembered his name, and his wife's birthday, too.

And now, he had vanished, turning Madhukar's world upside down. Madhukar shuddered, wondering what the man would remember about that fateful January night of 1993.

With utmost reluctance, he decided fulfill his promise to his late father.

◉

'Samir Khanna…his name is Samir Khanna,' the still-slightly-inebriated Madhukar said into the phone.

'Yes…yes, I understood his name, but what crime has he committed?' asked Sub-Inspector Tirke at the CBD Belapur police station.

'I told you…he has left the hospital!'

'Was he a patient there or an employee?'

'Well…he was a patient.'

'So, if a patient leaves, what is the problem?' Tirke snapped.

'He…he was not an ordinary patient…he was involved in an accident.'

'Oh, it's an accident case… Accha…where was the accident?' Tirke cleaned his ear with his little finger.

'On the highway near Panvel… I…'

'Panvel…then you have to call Panvel police station, na. This is not in our jurisdiction.'

'Look. Let me explain again…the accident took place nineteen years ago—'

'So what? See, baba, if the accident was in Panvel…you call Panvel.' Tirke dragged his words, as if speaking to a child.

'But he was getting treated here, in Navi Mumbai.' Madhukar's voice rose a decibel.

'So? Did any accident take place here? Any crime?'

'Well, I didn't tell anyone about the accident. And now he's gone...' Madhukar sank into his sofa and sighed.

'Has he recovered?' Tirke asked.

'Hmmm...yes...and no.'

'If he has left the hospital on his own, that means he has recovered. Boss, you are lucky.'

'I guess I am... But I still want to register the accident...'

'Look, if you want to register an accident that took place nineteen years ago, go ahead and waste the time of the Panvel police station. I have bigger cases pending.'

Hearing the phone click at the other end, Madhukar flinched. 'Idiot,' he muttered.

At the police station, Tirke was about to go back to his chai when he heard the familiar booming voice from the inner office: 'Tirke!'

He cursed under his breath, took a quick sip of his chai and hurried inside.

Senior Inspector Pandian was having his customary morning bun-maska and chai. 'How many times have I told you, Tirke, this is not Dharavi. This is a posh area. Here, you have to be polite to the callers. All these people are well connected.'

Tirke bit his tongue, making a 'please-excuse-me' face. 'Sorry, saheb. This man was drunk and wasting my time. He was making a complaint about an accident that took place nineteen years ago.' Tirke started guffawing as he pulled up a chair and sat down with his boss.

Senior Inspector Pandian joined in his junior's mirth.

'Who was the victim?' asked Pandian.

'Someone called Samir Khanna.'

'Samir...Khanna...did you say?' Pandian grew pensive.

'Why? Does the name sound familiar?' asked Tirke.

'But why was this man calling now?' Pandian asked in turn.

'Because this victim—this Samir Khanna—has suddenly left Bhonsale Hospital.'

Pandian nodded, still thoughtful. His fingers drummed the table.

Tirke continued, 'Arre, I kept asking him, if the victim has left on his own, if the victim is not making a complaint, what is your problem? You are lucky!' He laughed again.

Pandian merely smiled.

'Okay, Pandian saheb, I'm going back to duty. Hope I don't get any more such cases.' He let loose a last rumble of laughter as he left.

A serious expression settled on Pandian's face.

He dialled a number.

◉

Raghu Nadar, the young and dynamic municipal councillor from Vashi, Navi Mumbai, was sitting in his office, shell-shocked.

He had just got a call from Senior Inspector Pandian of the Kharghar police station. Pandian was a man from his Tamil Nadar community and a family friend.

As always, Raghu had started his day early. He was in his office to meet the constituents of his ward, who trooped in everyday to discuss their civic problems. 'The door of Raghu Nadar's office is always open' was what was said about him. Today, too, there was a long line of people outside his office. In fact, the throng was bigger today and everybody seemed to be in a celebratory mood.

Raghu got up and walked up to his office door.

Much to the surprise of his staff, supporters and constituents, he closed the door on them for the first time. He wanted privacy.

Alone, Raghu sat down at his table and took a deep breath. Today was the defining day of his life—a day that he had been awaiting since the death of his father, when he was a child. A day that would lift him out of the lower-middle-class morass that he had been clawing at throughout his short life, and catapult him into the big league.

After arriving in the newly-formed suburb of Navi Mumbai one fine day as a fatherless eight-year-old with only an illiterate mother as a caregiver, Raghu had motivated himself and risen to the challenges of adjusting to a new life and a new community. Right from his schooldays, he had charmed his way into people's hearts through his tireless acts of social service. Ever-ready to do a favour for a person in need, Raghu had gained the respect and adulation, first of the people of his neighbourhood and then of those in his municipal ward, who had urged him to contest the municipal elections as an independent candidate. Raghu had won by a thumping majority, reflecting the people's faith in his abilities to get the job done. Indeed, he was not a man who did things in half-measures. And he was not afraid to show his ambitions to the world. Even his worst critic admired his doggedness. And it was this perseverance that had caught the attention of the ruling party. Although he had been an independent councillor for the past three years, during the last six months, he had been wooed by the ruling party to join forces with them. The canny Raghu had hammered out a dream deal.

Today, Raghu would be welcomed personally into the ruling party by the party president, who was flying in from

Delhi to address the public and party volunteers at a large gathering in Mumbai's Azad Maidan. With this formal induction, the party president would declare Raghu Nadar the official ruling party candidate for the Vashi assembly seat.

The Vashi seat was a stronghold of the ruling party, but had fallen empty recently, due to the death of the three-time sitting MLA. The party now wanted to field only candidates with clean records, especially in urban areas. It was unfortunate, however, that every other potential candidate had a tainted past, automatically disqualifying them in the eyes of the party high command. None of the party's junior workers matched the dynamism and clean image of the independent people's choice—Corporator Raghu Nadar. So, he became the right choice for the party, which was also seeking to expand its base at the grassroots. In fact, Raghu had also wangled a nod for a junior minister's berth after his sure-shot victory.

Raghu looked at a framed photograph hanging on the wall with a fresh garland hanging across it. The stern-faced, dark-complexioned man in the photograph bore a striking resemblance to him.

He opened a drawer in his desk, took out a large file and started leafing through it urgently, till he spotted a newspaper cutting. It was a report about the Fortune Leather Factory fire incident that had transpired during the bloody 1993 Mumbai riots. Raghu scrutinized the photos of the victims printed on the page. The first photograph was that of Samir Khanna, taken in his younger days.

The news report stated that eight Muslim workers had been killed at the Fortune Leather Factory in Dharavi by a mob of Hindus. Their bodies had been found charred beyond recognition. Samir Khanna, the owner of Fortune Leather

Factory, had tried to save them, but had got trapped under a fallen beam and had himself been charred to death. The mastermind behind the attack was said to be one N. Selvaraj, the factory in-charge. According to the report, Selvaraj had incited a mob of Hindus against his Muslim co-workers and fled the place, fearing police action against him. He was never traced, despite the police's best efforts. At the bottom of the report was a photograph of Selvaraj. The same one that hung on Raghu Nadar's wall.

Raghu was thoughtful. He dialled a number on his mobile. At the other end, his mother picked up.

'How are you, Amma?' asked Raghu softly.

'Raghu…what is wrong?'

Raghu realized that his mother had caught his mood. He tried to cover up. 'Nothing really, Amma, I was just remembering Appa.'

His mother's eyes grew moist. 'I think of him everyday and pray that he will come back to me. If only I knew what had happened to him that night….' Then she steadied her voice. 'But what am I saying? Let it go, Raghu. Every time you think of your father, you have an emotional breakdown. I can't see you go through that pain again.'

'Amma, that was when I was a boy,' Raghu replied in a placating manner. 'I have grown up now. I can control my emotions.'

His mother smiled to herself. 'You will always remain a little boy when it comes to this.'

Raghu inhaled and pulled himself up on his seat. 'Amma, please give me your blessings.'

'You always have my blessings. But is something the matter? I can hear a restlessness in your voice…'

'Nothing, Amma. Okay, I have to go now. I will call later.'

'Please be careful,' were his mother's parting words as Raghu put down the phone. He shook his head and thought, Mothers! How do they always know?

Raghu's mother, although illiterate, possessed a native intelligence so sharp, she had figured out Raghu's restlessness during his early college days. Unfortunately, her actions, that rose out of an instinct to protect him, had backfired. She had sent him to his native village in Sirumalai, Tamil Nadu, to visit his ailing grandfather, hoping that the old man would have a calming effect on him. Instead, to her horror, Raghu had disappeared from his grandfather's home. She had looked for him high and low, but there was no sign of him, only rumours that he had teamed up with a group of youngsters who wanted to join the war for Tamil Eelam in Sri Lanka. A year later, Raghu had returned to Navi Mumbai out of the blue and resumed his college studies as if nothing had happened. The restlessness was gone and he seemed totally calm and in control. He had never spoken about his whereabouts during the previous year. His mother, who had just been thankful that he had returned, chose never to question him, and referred to that period in his life only obliquely. But Raghu always felt that she knew each and every dark deed of his.

Raghu took another deep breath. He took out a key from his pocket and went into an inner room. He opened a small Godrej safe and took out an iron box. He ran his fingers over a cloth-wrapped package. Then he unwrapped it and took out an Austrian-made 9mm Mini Glock pistol.

Raghu loaded the pistol.

◉

Samir Khanna's legs supported him well as he made his way round the back of the Bhonsale Medical Trust Hospital. He could feel a dull throb of pain in his limbs sometimes, but a swirling energy flow resonating from his brain to the rest of his body, kept him surging forward.

His luck had been good, as he weaved through a small dirty gully that opened into the large ground of an adjoining yoga centre. Among the yoga enthusiasts, his white pajama and shirt went unnoticed. He avoided all eye contact and instinctively walked westwards. He entered a large maidan, where the first groups of morning exercisers were flexing their muscles. A couple of them looked curiously at the barefoot Samir. Then they got on with their routine, assuming him to be one of those who followed his own quirky exercise regimen.

At the western end of the maidan, Samir came across a small, almost deserted road. He crossed it and entered a school ground. Because of the school holidays, the playground was empty at that morning hour. He then made his way through the grounds to the Sion-Panvel Highway that bordered the school on the west.

He stumbled for the first time as he stood by the highway. Not because his legs gave way under him, but because he was struck dumb by the number of cars whizzing past him at an alarming speed.

As the morning traffic screamed its way into his ears, he felt disoriented. It was as if the ambient noise levels had risen by many quantum decibels in the past nineteen years. Voices seemed to be louder, cars seemed to be noisier and tempers seemed to be shorter as he stood surveying the sputter and flow of the vehicles in front of him.

Finally he composed himself and took a tentative step to

cross the highway. The throaty protest from a passing truck sent him scurrying back to the safety of the edge of the road.

Fearing that he would be run over, he gave up his attempt to cross, and started walking along the highway without knowing where he was going. Still in his patient's uniform pyjama and half-shirt, walking bare foot, he was quite a sight. But to his surprise, no one paid him any attention as they drove past like speed bullets.

A loud, hollow honk just behind him made him jump. An air-conditioned BEST bus, emblazoned with advertisements for a fairness cream, brushed past him. Instinctively, he jumped aside, straight towards a bush lining the highway. Not being able to control his balance, he fell. The bush broke his fall. Luckily for him, it was not thorny and was able to cushion him from getting hurt. He straightened up to see that the bus had stopped by the side of the road, a little ahead of him. The bus conductor was leaning out, looking at him. Samir quickened his pace, trying to reach the bus. The conductor threw a disgusted glance at him and walked back into the bus. The automatic doors closed and the bus starting moving.

A surprised Samir broke into a run and, with some effort, was able to grab the back door handle and haul himself on the footboard. But instead of stopping, the bus gathered more speed. Samir frantically banged on the plexi-glass door of the bus. The passengers sitting inside took their noses out of their newspapers and looked at him and threw quizzical glances at each other. The bus stopped with a jerk. Samir almost fell off, but somehow managed to keep clinging on. The angry bus conductor gestured to him to get off. But Samir persisted. 'Let me in. Let me in,' he begged. Finally, with an exasperated gesture, the conductor signalled to the driver to close the door. With a loud 'whoosh' the door that Samir was clinging on to started swinging to the side. Samir was swept off his feet by the hydraulic strength of the door's opening mechanism, and he lost his balance and fell on the roadside, landing on his back. The bus doors shut unceremoniously and the bus started its onward journey. Samir stared silently at it. The conductor shrugged, raised his right forefinger to his temple and twisted it. 'Pagal,' he said.

The passengers nodded, exchanging knowing smiles and resumed reading their newspapers.

◉

The Glock was doing its job. Madhukar Bhonsale and the CMO were scared out of their wits. Raghu Nadar had stormed into the Bhonsale Medical Trust Hospital half an hour ago and demanded to meet the doctor in charge. Unfortunately, the doctor in charge had had no clue of what had happened and flatly denied any knowledge of a coma patient. Samir Khanna's presence in the hospital was a fact known only to a handful of employees. But when Raghu had raised his voice a few decibels, the doctor had scurried to the CMO's office and summoned him to face Raghu's wrath. The CMO, in turn, had quickly placed a call to Madhukar and requested his presence to face the irate municipal councillor who was threatening to introduce a motion to close down the hospital in the next session of the municipal council.

Madhukar, at first, tried to lie through his teeth about Samir, but when he discovered that Raghu had the details of his drunken phone call to the police station, he had no option but to own up. And when Raghu drew out the Glock and kept it on the table in front of him, Madhukar's tongue gave up its reluctance and rattled off the full story of Samir's long stay at the hospital, every minute development included.

As Madhukar concluded his story, Raghu's face grew grim. Madhukar and the CMO watched as he picked up the Glock, 'Now, tell me, what is this Samir Khanna's current situation? Is he is absolutely fine, out of danger?' Raghu asked, brandishing the gun with just enough menace to cause a large *lump of fear* to mushroom in their chest.

A creature of habit, the CMO assumed his practised doctor's tone, 'Well, Coma Man…uh…Samir's case, is unique. As yet, medical science has encountered only a few cases of people who have recovered fully after such a prolonged coma. Then, too, not many have regained motor functions to the extent that Samir has. A kind of freak energy is keeping him going, but then again his limbs have not been used for many years. They are bound to give away soon…' The CMO stopped mid-sentence. Raghu's Glock was a few inches away from his face.

'Doctor, I am not interested in a lecture,' Raghu hissed. 'I am simply asking, will he be able to remember events from the past or not?'

The CMO dabbed the sweat on his brow with a handkerchief. 'He is just recovering and as yet, he has not fully regained his memory.'

'What can be done to help Samir Khanna regain his memory fully?' Raghu asked.

'Sometimes, if the patient undergoes a harrowing or scary experience, it triggers a memory recovery. But he might get confused between his real memories and what he may be told. So, it's best to let him recover at his own pace.'

'Now one last thing… Where did he go?'

The CMO seemed clueless, but Madhukar quickly

intervened. 'The nurse who was tending to him said that he went out towards the back gate, which means that he could have gone towards the highway. That's all we know.'

Raghu hissed, 'It will be best if you keep your mouths shut about the whole thing.' The implication of the municipal councillor's thinly-veiled threat was not lost on either Madhukar or the CMO, as he stormed out of the room.

◉

The sleek Japanese motorbike weaved its way through the traffic snarl on the highway. The besotted young couple astride the motorbike were lost to the world, and were attracting the attention of others on the highway. The lovelorn girl on the backseat, clad in a diaphanous T-shirt and denim shorts, had her breasts squashed against the rider's back and her arms firmly linked across his muscular bare chest. She was whispering something in his ear that made him grin. As he swerved between the vehicles, he arched his back, as if to derive maximum pleasure from the girl's body.

Samir Khanna stood on one side of the highway snarl, near the junction of Uran Road and the Sion-Panvel Highway, watching the couple on the motorbike. The rising heat of the morning and the barefoot walk along the highway had finally got to him, and he had stopped to catch his breath. A faint memory entered his mind. Although his eyes seemed to be looking at the young lovers, his mind was travelling into an inner space that had been locked away for a long time.

◉

'Faster!' Bahaar shouted, flushed with excitement. Her eyes had that familiar twinkle Samir found so endearing. They were on

their way to Goa in their brand-new Mercedes 500E. The car was winding its way slowly along the coastal road, but Bahaar wasn't happy. She was pestering Samir to speed up. She had the windows down and was craning her neck out to catch the wind on her face. She giggled, like a teenager sharing a naughty joke with a friend. 'Keep your head in. It's dangerous,' Samir cautioned.

Bahaar looked at Samir. The colour on her cheeks was the rosy flush he normally noticed during the first moments of sexual excitement. 'I love danger,' she whispered, reaching for the seam of her T-shirt. In one smooth movement, she peeled it off her body. She wasn't wearing anything underneath. He felt the first stirs of excitement.

She gestured to him to keep his eyes on the road as she slid towards him. Samir complied. Bahaar splayed a leg across his lap and Samir's grip on the steering wheel loosened. She slid into the space between the steering wheel and Samir's body, and faced him as she straddled his lap; her naked breasts pressed against his face.

For a few seconds, Samir couldn't see the road. He panicked. But Bahaar arched her body at an angle that allowed him to keep his eyes on the road. She stroked his hair with her soft fingers. He was finding it tough to focus on the road. Then she repeated the one word Samir was dreading: 'Faster!' He pressed his foot on the pedal and the Mercedes roared. The jerk made Bahaar's body arch forward. Her breasts were in Samir's face as he tried valiantly to keep driving. Finally, he succumbed to her offer, somehow managing to keep the vehicle going simlutaneously. God was smiling on them that day, as the Mercedes ate away the kilometres without meeting any accidents, allowing the lovers to reach the heights of ecstasy.

◉

The abrasive honk from a vehicle snapped Samir out of his reverie. He found himself still standing at the junction where the traffic had eased up a little bit.

The horn now almost blared into his eardrums. Samir swivelled and saw a white SUV parked beside him. He stepped backwards to get out of its path. But the front window on the driver's side slid down, and a gust of air-conditioned breeze wafted towards him. A dark-complexioned young man leaned out of the window and gestured towards the passenger seat.

Samir didn't think twice. His feet were hurting from the scorching sun and the effort of his walk. He slid into the passenger seat.

Samir was uncertain how to open a conversation with the man behind the wheel.

'Where are you going?' asked the man.

Samir realized that he didn't really have an answer to the question. He blurted out the only reply he could muster up, 'I'm going to my wife.'

'Where is your wife?'

'I don't know.'

'So you don't know where you are going?'

'Yes,' Samir gave in. 'She must be out there somewhere...'

The young man gave him a long look. Samir squirmed in his seat, a little uncomfortable with the direct gaze upon him. He wondered why the man was taking such a keen interest in him. The man continued to look into his eyes, as if searching for something lost in there.

For a while, they drove in silence. Samir's gaze wandered out of the moving SUV, and for the first time, he noticed that they had veered off the highway into a small, bush-lined by-road. The road seemed to be going up a hill, and sure enough, after a few hundred yards, he saw a sign that said 'Parsik Hill Road'. But then again, the SUV swerved off this road into what seemed like a nature trail. Soon, all signs of civilization disappeared and they were on a narrow path that led into a densely forested area. Samir turned to look at the young man, who was concentrating on the track ahead. Samir leaned back against the seat and wondered where they were headed.

Soon, the vegetation on the sides of the track became dense and dark, and the track opened into a small clearing. All of a sudden, the man braked and the SUV jerked to a halt. Without a word, he got out of the vehicle. Samir kept sitting, wondering what would happen next, till he noticed that the man was at his door. The man then opened the door and yanked Samir out of the SUV, pulling him by the collar. Samir fell on the muddy ground. Before he could react, he was dragged by the man to a clearing. The man then pointed a pistol at the shocked Samir and said, 'My name is Raghu Nadar, and I am the son of Selvaraj.'

An uncomprehending Samir stared at Raghu's grim face.

'Selvaraj...N. Selvaraj...you don't remember him?' Raghu's voice was raised now. Samir shook his head, his face was blank. Raghu rested the nose of the pistol on Samir's temple and tightened his grip on the weapon. Samir shivered.

'Tell me what happened that night?' Raghu snarled.

Samir's confusion increased. 'Which night?' he timidly asked. Raghu seemed infuriated at the question. He walked a few steps away and let out a scream of frustration. Samir started to scramble to his feet.

'Stay down!' Raghu barked.

Samir obeyed. Raghu again searched Samir's face. But Samir simply stared back with empty eyes.

'You really don't remember anything, do you?' said Raghu.

'I remember my name, and my wife's name and face. Today, 15 June, is her birthday. We live in a cottage somewhere between some tall buildings. I have a Mercedes 500E. That's all,' Samir said robotically.

Raghu walked a little distance away from Samir. This time, Samir made no attempt to get up.

Raghu stared at the trees in front of him. He was lost in thought over what Madhukar and the CMO had told him. So it is true, he thought. Samir, obviously, doesn't remember much.

But Raghu did take heart at the fact that Samir remembered a few details. He wondered if more memories would come back to him. He debated whether to show the old newspaper cutting to Samir, but then decided against it. He once again mulled over Madhukar and the CMO's conversation with him. Samir wouldn't have known what the newspapers had said. And even if he was shown the newspaper report, he might just play back what was written in the report as his memory, without attempting to remember what had actually transpired that day. But Raghu wanted the whole undiluted truth. And fast.

He pulled out his mobile and called a number as he walked a short distance away from Samir. 'I need a favour,' he spoke to the person on the other end in hushed tones.

Samir glanced in Raghu's direction. Raghu's voice drifted towards him in snatches; it looked like he was speaking to someone. Samir's eyes swiftly scanned his surroundings. He felt confused. He couldn't see anyone around, so who was Raghu talking to? It was clear that Raghu was disturbed by Samir's lack of memory. But who was he? Why did he have a gun? Was he some sort of criminal, a gangster? Samir wondered whether he himself had been involved in some sort of criminal activity in the past. He shivered at the thought.

Raghu finished his conversation and walked back towards Samir. The pistol was now tucked away in his pocket. 'C'mon, Uncle Sam. We have to go,' he said.

Samir felt uneasy all of a sudden; thoughts swirled in his head. 'That name...' he muttered under his breath. He tried reaching into the recesses of his mind, but shook his head when he drew a blank. Raghu shrugged and led Samir silently back to the SUV. He made Samir sit on the passenger's seat and then began the journey back down the dirt track.

◉

The sun started to beat down on Samir as he walked along a long empty stretch of Palm Beach Road, Navi Mumbai. He wondered where and what was in store for him ahead.

He had been dropped off along the six-lane road by a grim-faced Raghu. While Raghu had ignored him throughout their return journey downhill, Samir had observed Raghu with unabashed fascination as he spent the better part of the ride speaking on a mini-cordless instrument through a small device attached to his ear.

Samir felt sheepish about his naïvety. He now understood the secret of Raghu's conversation with himself in the woods. He had been amazed at the device and was itching to try it himself, but feared the wrath of the grim man with a gun. Raghu had been intently trying to explain to someone that he had not changed his mind and was a man of his word. Through the discussion, Samir had gathered that Raghu was a political figure of some importance, and he was supposed to be meeting a big leader that day for a life-altering event.

The people he was speaking to on the 'phone' wanted him to drop everything and join them, wherever they were. But Raghu had insisted he was very busy 'with some personal matter' and that he would be at the meeting as soon as he was done.

They had driven down Parsik Hill Road and had turned on to Palm Beach Road. Samir had been fascinated by the surroundings as they had driven past giant buildings and shiny colossal structures with huge multi-coloured signboards attached to them.

As the vehicular and human population thinned, Samir had turned his attention to the mangroves that lined the road on the other side.

Suddenly, Raghu had braked to a halt on a deserted patch of the road and told Samir to get off. A confused Samir had obeyed without argument. As he had stood by the SUV waiting for further instructions, the door had closed and Raghu had driven off, kicking up a small storm of dust, still engrossed in his chat on the amazing telephonic device.

For a while, Samir had stood rooted to the spot, wondering whether Raghu would be back, but after a while, he had given up hope and started walking in the direction that Raghu's vehicle had gone.

Samir's throat was dry. He looked around for something to quench his thirst with. Unfortunately, there seemed to be nothing. He stopped at one of the cement benches on the pavement and caught his breath. He wondered whether he would find his way to a shop and whether the shopkeeper would be kind enough to give him some water.

He was jolted out of his thoughts when a sleek silver-grey van drew up beside him. The door opened; there were two men sitting at the back. One of them, the stouter of the two, extended a plastic water bottle towards him. 'You look thirsty, bhai. Have some.'

Without any hesitation, Samir grabbed the bottle and drank in large gulps. He finished over two-thirds of the bottle before he stopped to catch his breath. The man who had given him water smiled. 'You seem to be low on energy, would you like some biscuits?'

Samir nodded without thinking. The man rummaged through his bag. The other man patted the space next to his seat. 'Please come and sit here. It's more comfortable.' Samir got into the van and sat down. The cushioned seat was, indeed, comfortable. The first man gave him some biscuits. 'Where are you going, bhaisaab?' he asked.

Samir was about to tell him everything, but checked himself. He stuffed some biscuits in his mouth to avoid further conversation. People were acting in strange ways around him! The man genially offered, 'We are going up to Chembur, we can drop you there.' Samir nodded. The man shut the door, and the van's driver started the engine. As they drove down the road, the two men started chatting with each other, leaving Samir in peace as he devoured the rest of the biscuits.

Speeding down Palm Beach Road, they didn't notice the white SUV parked behind a Road Building Authority shed.

In the SUV, Raghu Nadar dialled a number and read out the number of the silver grey van to the person at the other end.

◉

The van cruised along Palm Beach Road, unaware of a black Scorpio creeping up from behind. Before the van driver could react, the Scorpio had sped forward and overtaken him. The Scorpio came to an abrupt halt, bang in the middle of the deserted stretch of road, blocking the van's path. Caught off-guard, the van driver braked hard, transferring almost all his weight on to the small metallic brake lever at his feet. The van skidded almost 360 degrees before finally coming to a stop, facing the Scorpio. The passengers in the van were unharmed, save for their thudding heartbeats.

As if on cue, all four doors of the Scorpio swung open together. Approximately seven to eight men sprang out from within, and in a flash, surrounded the van. All the men had some sort of weapon in their hands, ranging from AK-47s to automatic pistols to revolvers. The men grabbed every door handle of the van and tried to force the doors open. When they discovered that the doors were locked they began shouting, 'Kholo!' Some of them broke into expletives, 'Behenchod!' 'Maadarchod!'

Samir Khanna had been a mute spectator to this turn of events. His heartbeat had somewhat stabilized, but he was still in a state of shock. The two men sitting with him in the van were cowering. All the sophisticated sheen had disappeared from their manner, replaced by a naked fear for their lives.

One of the men outside shouted, 'If you don't open the door, we will shoot through the windows.'

Inside the van, the driver, who had been crouching under his seat, slowly tried to open his door. The fat man who had offered Samir the water and biscuits finally made a move from his frozen spot. He grabbed the driver's hair and pulled him, with surprising strength, on to the backseat. Seeing this, the other man punched the driver in the face. The driver fell unconscious.

'We were just on our way to make some deliveries...' said the fat man.

'We know. Don't worry, come out, there will be no encounter,' shouted the man outside.

The two men exchanged looks. Samir swallowed hard as he listened to the bizarre discussion that followed.

'What is the guarantee that you will not kill us?' said the fat man.

'Look, if we wanted to kill you, we would have shot through the glass, we just want the maal,' said the man outside in a softer voice.

The fat man was not ready to give up yet. He lifted the backseat and extracted a small automatic machine-gun from the cavity beneath. Without any warning, he placed the muzzle against a stunned Samir's temple. 'I have a hostage with me. If you don't let us go, I will kill him,' he snarled.

The armed men outside peered through the van's tinted windows, to make sure whether the fat man was telling the truth. Seeing Samir being held at gunpoint inside, they lowered their weapons. Emboldened, the fat man shouted, ' Allow us to drive away, or I will shoot this man. I will count up to three. One... Two...'

A shot rang out. Samir lost consciousness.

◉

A roaring fire was engulfing the signboard that proclaimed, 'Fortune Leather Factory'. The men surrounding the signboard were whooping with rabid joy, behaving as if they had brought a mighty devil to his knees. The flaming kerosene-soaked bamboo-and-cloth torches that they held in their hands now demanded more victims. Sensing each other's murderous thoughts, the men turned as one and entered the portals of the factory, seeking their next prey.

Samir ran into the factory behind the mob, shouting, screaming, begging for mercy. As he entered the main door, he heard screams louder than his, coming from deep within the workshop section. These screams were not of the mob, but of a scared group of men huddled together. Men fearing for their lives. Men staring at the face of death.

Samir dashed in the direction of the screams but tripped and stumbled. Something had obstructed his path and he landed with a thud on the factory floor. The wind was knocked out of him. His mind swam through a murky blackness that threatened to envelop him. He lay there on the ground, trying to focus on a torchlight floating towards him. As he tried to gather his wits, something hit him on the back of his head, and the room swayed before him. But before he lost total consciousness, he felt a mildly perfumed cloth being shoved into his mouth. 'Handkerchief' was the last word that his semi-conscious mind threw up from within the black haze that now totally engulfed him.

◉

A seagull soared in the air, making its way across the blue cloudless sky. Samir was lying flat on his back, staring at the open sky above, slowly regaining his senses. He rolled on his side and saw that he was lying on soft ground, surrounded by dense green mangroves. With some effort, he heaved himself off the ground and looked around. He found himself in a man-made clearing inside a mangrove swamp. The ground beneath him had been filled with mud to give it a semi-hardened texture. As he turned his head to one side of the clearing, he saw the men who had attacked the van standing at a distance around a heap on the ground. With a shock, Samir realized that they were staring at the bullet-ridden dead bodies of the two men in the van. An involuntary cry escaped his lips. The men standing around the dead bodies looked in his direction. A swarthy, heavyset man in a fawn shirt and black trousers walked up to Samir, who tried to keep his initial shock at bay by falling silent. The man's face was impassive, but his voice had a hint of concern. 'You are lucky that I am a sharpshooter, otherwise, he would have killed you.'

Samir reacted in the only manner that a confused man would. 'Who are you? What is happening? Why did you kill those people…?'

The man put up his hand, silencing Samir. 'We are policemen. The two men you were with are—were—wanted hardcore killers and drug smugglers. We got a tip-off about their movements and trailed their van. Luckily, we were also told that they had picked you up from Palm Beach Road.'

'What nonsense! Drug smugglers? Those two nice men?' Samir scoffed, shaking his head.

The self-proclaimed policeman standing in front of Samir gave a small smile, while the others tittered from a distance. 'Both of them had many pending murder cases against them.'

Samir now stood up, shaking. 'But if they were the men that you say they were, why would they offer me a lift?'

The policeman shrugged his shoulders, 'I don't know why, my informer just told me that he spotted them when they opened their van door and asked you to sit inside.'

The policeman now placed his hand on Samir's shoulder and pointed towards a small path that led out of the clearing. He gestured to Samir to follow him as he walked up the path. After casting a last glance towards the dead men, Samir followed the policeman. He walked about a few hundred steps, and to his surprise, found himself back on Palm Beach Road.

The policeman now led him to the same van parked by the side of the road. Samir noticed a single bullet-hole in the window where he had sat.

'I shot the man who had his pistol on you,' the policeman said, in a matter-of-fact tone.

'And how did you kill the other man?' Samir wondered aloud.

The policeman shot him a sharp look. 'The other man jumped out and tried to escape into the mangroves. While running, he shot at us. My men returned fire in self-defence. They are obviously better shooters than him...otherwise...'

'You shot him in cold blood, didn't you?' Samir cut him short.

The policeman's voice rose a decibel. 'What's your problem, bhai? I saved your life.'

'By taking the law into your hands,' Samir shot back.

The policeman's face darkened in anger. 'Don't teach *me* about law and order. Look...' He slid open the van's side door and showed Samir the blood-soaked interiors. He tugged at one of the seats, raising the seat to reveal packets of white, powdery substance neatly arranged in the cavity below. 'Mr Law-abiding Citizen, there is enough cocaine here to last Mumbai's drug users for months.'

Samir fell silent. The policeman let the seat drop into place. 'What do you do to criminals like these? Catch them and put them in jail? But they'll be out in no time. Spreading their poison on the streets again.' Samir just shook his head, not knowing what to say.

'What do you want to do now? Can we drop you somewhere?' The policeman sounded tired.

Samir shook his head. 'You are a killer, even though you claim to be a policeman. I can't even dream of going anywhere with you.'

'Behenchod, you are lucky that Raghu Nadar was the one who called, otherwise...' the policeman hissed.

Samir was stunned. 'Raghu... Did you say Raghu Nadar?'

The policeman realized that he had said more than he should have. He pointed up the path. 'Just keep walking away from here, and don't talk about this to anyone. Go now.' The policeman walked back into the mangroves. Samir stood looking at his receding back for a few minutes before venturing on to Palm Beach Road once again.

◉

'Thank you, Inspector. I owe you one,' said Raghu into the phone.

'He seems to be a man of principles,' said the inspector.

Raghu's face tightened. 'Unfortunately, he doesn't realize that the age of principles is long gone. Thank you, once again.' He cut the call and steered his SUV back on to Palm Beach Road.

Samir had been walking for about fifteen minutes and sweat had begun to stream down his forehead when Raghu's white SUV drove up alongside him. 'Where are you headed to now, Mr Khanna?' Raghu smiled from the driver's seat.

Samir stopped and gave him a hard stare. 'It's none of your business.' He continued walking.

'If it wasn't for me...'

'If it wasn't for you, I wouldn't have been put in such a dangerous situation,' Samir said, his tone vehement. 'You... you asked those two to pick me up, didn't you?' He glared at Raghu.

Raghu shook his head. 'You were never in danger, the inspector is an expert.'

'And the drug smugglers... What about them?' Samir shot back.

'Those chutiyas had it coming. They thought they would get a safe passage up to Mumbai by doing me a favour.' He spat in disgust.

Samir stopped short in his tracks. 'But why did you put me in that situation?' Samir screamed. 'Who are you?'

'I'm someone who knows about your situation. The doctor at the hospital told me that if you have a scary or dangerous experience, it might trigger a memory recovery,' Raghu, now sombre, said.

Samir fell silent.

Raghu quirked an eyebrow. 'Well, did it?'

Samir just kept staring at Raghu for a long few minutes, then he got in beside him in the SUV and banged the door shut. 'Dharavi,' he said, looking at the road ahead.

◎

Raghu did not like to go back to Dharavi. As he drove Samir to his destination, the Muslim-dominated Nawab Nagar area of Dharavi, the silence that Samir had lapsed into made Raghu confront the uncomfortable memories he had not let enter his head for over a decade now. His thoughts wandered back to his childhood in the adjoining Naya Chawl, the Hindu Tamil-dominated area, to how his father had disappeared one night never to be found. The Muslims and the Hindu Tamils could never go back to the pre-riot harmony they had shared. Six months after the riots ended, Raghu and his mother had left

Dharavi for Navi Mumbai, along with a majority of the Hindu Tamils.

Today, Dharavi seemed to be almost a different country. The roads, although crowded, had at least the minimal level of organization required to make them drivable. Not that one could drive very deep into Dharavi's womb. Raghu finally had to park his SUV at one point to proceed further into the teeming maw. Samir stepped out of the SUV, feeling lost. Raghu sensed his confusion, but didn't say anything. He let Samir walk through the gullies, looking here and there, at the signboards and at the never-ending stream of passers-by. Finally, Samir turned to Raghu and asked, 'Fortune Leather Factory?' Raghu's heartbeat thumped as he heard those words said out loud. He reached out for Samir's wrist, and led him by the hand through a narrow dirt-encrusted lane. The muck and slush on the ground made Samir slip a couple of times, but he regained his balance to keep walking. Raghu quickened his pace and Samir stumbled on behind him.

The narrow path now led into a large, open area. Raghu stopped. Gesturing towards a plastic recycling unit, Raghu said, 'That is where it stood.'

A cloud passed over Samir's face. 'I don't remember much,' he said in a cracked voice. He broke away from Raghu and walked a few steps around the open area, his eyes scanning the place, as if trying to match the surroundings to a faded photograph hidden in his memory. But he drew a blank—till he passed a paan shop. The middle-aged paanwala with a lush moustache, who was folding the paans, glanced at Samir as he walked past and kept his gaze on him as he walked around the area. Samir retraced his steps and neared the paan shop again. He locked eyes with the paanwala. A spark of

recognition flashed on the paanwala's face. 'Samir bhaiya...
aap?' he gasped.

All of a sudden, Samir's legs gave way, and he fell on
the ground. The paanwala dropped the paan he was folding
and leapt towards him. He managed to grab Samir in his
arms and break his fall. He propped up Samir on a seat in
his paan shop.

Raghu watched the goings-on intently. He was about to
help Samir too, when his mobile phone rang. He glanced at
the caller ID and cursed under his breath. It was the Mumbai
City president of the ruling party. Raghu had no alternative
but to take the call.

The voice on the other side was flat and emotionless. '*Kai
zhalla, Raghu bhai*? Have you decided not to join our party?'

'No, Pachphute saheb, nothing like that. Just some personal
work...' Raghu quickly replied.

'I know...you have been saying that to all my people
since this morning, but please tell me the exact nature of this
"personal" work,' Panchphute cut in. Raghu sighed. He realized
that Panchphute could not be brushed off easily. Summoning
all his creativity, Raghu began spinning a long yarn.

Meanwhile, at the paan shop, Radheshyam, the paanwala,
overjoyed by Samir's appearance, hugged him again and again.
A slightly dazed Samir did not stop him. Radheshyam began to
apologize profusely for not being able to help him 'that night'.
Samir got a grip on himself to begin a line of questioning.

'Tell me what happened that night,' he got straight to the
point.

'Unfortunately, I was not here and you...you...were killed,'
the paanwala stuttered. 'I'm sorry...that is what we were led
to believe.' Radheshyam's face reddened.

Samir gave him a gentle smile. 'Yes, I was dead for almost twenty years. But now, I am alive and I want to know what happened.'

Radheshyam's face grew grim. 'A mob burnt down your factory, Samir bhaiya. It was believed that you were killed too...burnt alive...along with the seven others that night.'

'But who did it? Do you know?'

'They said Selvaraj did it. But I never believed that story. It was a mob. A crazed Hindu mob.'

'But why?' Samir continued to probe.

'Hindu versus Muslim riots. It was new then, but it's quite common nowadays.'

'But I am a Hindu.' Samir was confused. Radheshyam replied. 'I know, Samir bhaiya, but the mob was not local. And then...your workers were all Muslims...and apparently, somebody told them that your name was Samir Khan.'

Samir recoiled at this piece of information.

'Who?' he hissed. Radheshyam was nonplussed. 'No one knows. They never caught anyone from that mob.'

A frustrated sigh escaped Samir's lips. 'Did I live somewhere...here?' he asked.

Radheshyam looked at him in surprise. 'You didn't live here, Samir bhaiyya, you are a seth, your house is in Bandra... Sherly Village. I remember I had come to your house once to take a loan... You don't remember?'

Samir looked apologetic. 'No, unfortunately I don't. All I remember is that it's Bahaar...my wife's birthday today. Can you help me find my home? Find my wife?' Radheshyam looked at Samir's face for a long while.

'Come with me,' he said at last. He led Samir into his matchbox-sized paan shop. At the back of the shop, a door led into what looked like a small house. The house opened into a large back veranda bordering a thin, snaking lane. A surly-faced young man was cleaning a brand new motorcycle in the veranda. Radheshyam snapped his finger at the man. 'Mantu, go sit in the shop for a couple of hours.'

Mantu opened his mouth to protest, but held back when he saw that his father was clearly in no mood for an argument. He tossed the cleaning cloth and turned to go into the shop.

'Aye, Mantuwa, give me the keys,' Radheshyam called out. Mantu reluctantly handed the motorcycle keys to Radheshyam.

'Chaliye, Samir bhaiyya!' Radheshyam smiled at Samir. He started the motorcycle and gestured to Samir to take the pillion seat. Samir hesitated for only a fraction of a second, then got on. Off they went, swerving crazily away from the veranda, down the snaking path, into a labyrinth of gullies between the huts.

Meanwhile, Raghu had finished his long yarn. To his chagrin, Pachphute had not believed any of it. 'Raghu bhai, now that you are done with this filmy story, please tell me what is actually going on?'

Raghu realized that he should come clean. 'Okay. If you want the truth, I have finally found the man who holds the key to my father's death.'

There was a long silence on Panchphute's end. 'I hope you will not get involved in any criminal activity. Otherwise...' But by this time, Raghu had ceased to listen. His attention had now diverted to Radheshyam's paan shop. To his shock, he noticed that both Samir and Radheshyam had disappeared. In their place was a morose young man. Raghu sprinted towards the shop.

'Where is Samir?' he asked, breathless with the effort.

'Samir who?' asked Mantu.

'The man with the paanwala, who was just here?'

Mantu now lost interest in the conversation and began to apply chuna on a paan leaf. Raghu realized that his line of questioning would not get him any results. He took a deep breath and, with all his might, delivered a hard slap on Mantu's cheek. Mantu spun with the force of the blow, nearly falling off his seat.

'Where is he?' Raghu repeated, gritting his teeth.

The slap did the trick. 'He…he… left with my father on my motorcycle for…I don't know where…' a dazed Mantu replied.

Raghu realized that there was no time to be lost. He took out his mobile punched it to speaker phone mode, and handed it to Mantu. 'Dial your father's number.'

Mantu did as he was told, but all he got was an automated message that the number was unreachable.

Mantu shrank a little into the paan shop. 'Mobile phone signals are weak in Dharavi, saab.'

'Which direction did they go in?' Raghu asked.

The slap still ringing in his ears made Mantu extremely helpful. 'They were going up the gully from the back of our house and could be headed anywhere. But they have to anyway cross the Mahim level crossing. If you hurry, saab, you can catch them there, it's a long wait over there.'

Raghu grabbed Mantu's shirt and with one hard tug, pulled him out of the shop. Dragging Mantu along with him, Raghu ran in the direction of his SUV. 'If you are lying to me, you will be under the next train that passes along the tracks at the level crossing,' he snarled as he made his way through the slush-filled path.

Raghu reached his SUV in record time, considering that he had to contend with a slippery road and a reluctant companion who kept losing his footing every couple of steps. He pushed Mantu into the passenger seat and wove his SUV through the crowded streets, in the direction of the Mahim level crossing.

The vehicle was forced to come to a standstill at quite some distance from the level crossing itself, as a large number of vehicles were lined up on the road, waiting for the barrier to be raised. Raghu abandoned his SUV right in the middle of the traffic and, with a tearful Mantu in tow, ran between the parked vehicles, making his way towards the railway barrier. In the crush of traffic a short distance ahead of them, Raghu spotted two men on a motorcycle close to the crossing bar. The pillon rider was undoubtedly Samir in his distinguishable hospital attire. Raghu increased his pace. He took out his cell phone and re-dialled the number that had been keyed in by Mantu, but the signal was still weak. He quickened his pace further, but at that very moment, the signal turned green and the barrier was raised. The traffic sprang back to life again, pouring across the railway tracks to the other side. Raghu now literally dragged Mantu at full speed towards the motorcycle. The gap between them narrowed, till an impatient deliveryman with a hathgaadi blocked his way. Raghu tried to vault over the handcart in a desperate attempt to stop the motorcycle before it disappeared from sight, but his foot got jammed in the wheel and he fell headlong on the cart. Mantu's shirt ripped in two and slipped out of Raghu's grasp. Mantu ran back through the traffic before his captor could grab him again.

Raghu examined his injured foot. Luckily, it was only twisted, not broken. He hopped on one foot and tried to continue his chase, but realized that the motorbike carrying Samir had disappeared from sight.

◉

For Samir, the journey from Dharavi to Bandra was like travelling from a world steeped in sludge to another that seemed to have been transplanted from some first-world country. All around him, tall glass and concrete buildings were sprouting towards the sky, tearing upwards through dilapidated, older structures. The sleek unrecognizable landscape bore a mute testimony to the fact that Samir had been away for a long, long time.

Radheshyam now looked over his shoulder for the first time since they had started off on this journey. '*Bhaiya, Sherly Village aa gaya.*'

Samir glanced all around him and was even more taken aback. He had hoped that upon reaching Sherly Village, the sights and sounds would jog his memory further, but all he could see around him was...change.

Sherly Village in Bandra West is a curious mix of old-world charm and concrete jungle ugliness. The tall buildings are always under construction, and most of the small cottages, peeping through these concrete monsters, are continuously taking their last breath.

Radheshyam stopped the motorcycle in a by-lane off the main Sherly Rajan Road. He gestured at a modern, seven-storied building. 'Gladioli Apartments', a large board announced in elegant ornate letters. 'This building is where your house once was, Samir bhaiya,' he said. Samir looked at the building. He then searched the surroundings, hoping against hope that something would spark off a memory. Yet, nothing seemed familiar. His eyes rested on the names that were emblazoned on the gates of the other buildings around: 'White Rose Apartments', 'Sweet Mary', 'Charlotte Villa'. Nothing seemed to jog his memory. He would have continued to stare at the surroundings if it hadn't been for the sharp voice that called out to them, 'Please, no loitering near our building. There have been too many robberies recently, please go from here,' said a shrill voice.

Samir looked up at Gladioli Apartments. It was an old East Indian Catholic lady who was sitting on the first-floor balcony of the building. Before Samir could react, Radheshyam shouted: 'Do we look like chors to you, madam? This is Mr Samir Khanna, this building...the bungalow, which was here before the building, belonged to him... We are just here...'

But he stopped mid-sentence when the old lady rose from her seat in the balcony and shouted, 'Samir! Samir Khanna is dead. Who are you people?' Not content, she now shouted even more loudly, 'Watchman! Watchman!'

A world-weary man in a shabby uniform shuffled up to the gate and enquired, 'What is the matter?'

But Samir was in no mood to answer him, as his attention was now fully focused on the old lady. He shouted out to her, 'Please, madam, did you know me...I mean, Samir Khanna?'

The old lady was silent, looking thoughtful. The watchman advanced towards Samir and Radheshyam, 'Bhaisaheb, I don't care who both of you are, please go from here. These people don't want to speak to your types.'

'Our types? What do you mean our types, haan?' Radheshyam was now parking the bike, gearing up for a full-blooded fight, but Samir stopped him. 'No violence. Let us go from here.' He turned to Radheshyam and signalled to him to get on the bike.

Suddenly, the old lady called out, 'Please, gentlemen, can you come a little closer? My eyesight is bad nowadays.'

Radheshyam shot back, 'For what? So that you can insult us some more and get us beaten up by your watchdog?'

The old lady shook her head. 'No, no I want a closer look at this man.' She pointed to Samir. 'Your voice sounds familiar,' she said to him.

Samir quickly walked past the watchman into the gate and stood directly beneath the balcony staring up at her. 'Can you see me better now?'

She looked at his face, then took in a sharp breath. 'Samir... Is it really you? I'm not sure. Your hair is all grey?'

Samir smiled, relieved. 'Yes, it is me. Thank God you remember... Uh...I am sorry, I don't remember your name.'

The old lady broke into a crinkled smile, 'Gladys...Gladys Andrade...your landlady. Don't you remember?'

Samir shrugged sheepishly. The old lady smiled. 'Aunty Gladys will tell you everything, please come up.'

She called out to the watchman, 'Please show them the way up.'

Radheshyam, who had been watching the exchange between Gladys and Samir, butted in: 'Samir bhaiya, do you need me, or should I go back to Dharavi...to my types,' he sneered at the watchman, who saluted in apology.

Samir walked back to Radheshyam. Trying hard to contain his excitement, he said, 'Radheshyam bhai, I think I will take time here. So, thank you very much for your help.'

Radheshyam smiled. 'If you need my help, Samir bhaiyya, you know where I am...and I also have to pay back your loan...'

Samir hugged him, 'Consider the loan repaid... In any case, I don't even remember it.'

They laughed. Samir waved as Radheshyam zipped off on the bike. Then he entered Gladioli Apartments.

◎

'ACP saheb, it is very important for me, please help me,' Raghu Nadar pleaded into the phone. He had just asked for a favour from ACP Ranadive, head of the cyber cell, Mumbai Crime Branch. Raghu wanted the ACP to track the location of Radheshyam's mobile phone.

After losing Samir and Radheshyam at the Mahim level crossing, Raghu first thought that he would just wait till Radheshyam got out of Dharavi and then call him again, but then he thought better of it. He didn't want either Radheshyam or Samir to find out that he had been following them and put them on their guard. Moreover, since Radheshyam's son was no longer his captive, the paanwala would not feel compelled to return Samir back to Raghu, safe and sound.

Raghu clicked his tongue in disgust. That Mantu may have by now called his father and tipped him off about Raghu's search for Samir. Radheshyam could have done any number of things, including hiding Samir at some unknown location. But Raghu surmised that if he could track down the men through Radheshyam's mobile phone, he could easily spring a trap and get them.

ACP Ranadive was not a charitable person. Normally, his first reaction on receiving such a request would be to ask if the police force belonged to the callers' baap. But this time, it was Raghu Nadar calling, the man who had helped get the ACP's laggard son admission into a prestigious engineering college in Navi Mumbai, that too, without paying any 'capitation' fee.

ACP Ranadive sighed and called out to his deputy: 'Borkar!' In a few seconds, Inspector Borkar sauntered in. He then tore out the piece of paper on which he had written Radheshyam's mobile number and handed it to Borkar. 'I want all the movements of this mobile phone for the past two hours.'

Borkar took the paper slip and causally glanced at it. 'Whose number is it?'

'Your baap's!' ACP Ranadive exploded. 'Don't waste time, I want the full report within half an hour.'

◉

After the customary exclamations at Samir's troubles and the shedding of some tears, Aunty Gladys had laid out the red carpet for him. She had fed him chicken-and-spinach quiches and fresh Hungarian cake. Samir had initially protested, as he was anxious to know his past, but then, he realized that he had not eaten anything since the biscuits and water offered to him by the drug smugglers. He quickly gobbled up as much food as he could. Aunty Gladys made him wash down all the goodies with an ice-cold bottle of raspberry soda. Samir gladly drank the sweet, medicinal-tasting liquid and was grateful for the sugar kick it brought, along with its fizz.

Wiping his mouth and burping the last of the bubbles away, Samir was ready to hear his story. Gladys recalled how she had first met Samir, a newly married, young, up-and-coming leather goods entrepreneur. He had entered into an arrangement with her to rent the upper floor of Gladioli Cottage, the house that her dead husband had lovingly built for her. Samir had promised to restore the crumbling cottage to its former glory, and buy it in the future. Aunty Gladys had been happy, as she didn't want to sell the house to developers, who had been eyeing Sherly Village like a pack of hungry wolves. Samir and his pretty young wife, Bahaar, had moved in and brought a ray of sunshine into the widowed Aunty Gladys's lonely life.

Aunty Gladys had especially taken to Bahaar, Samir's young nymph-like wife. Bahaar had come into Samir's life on one of his business trips to Delhi. As a sales girl at a five-star boutique, she had sold Samir a designer tie, then a shirt and a suit. She would have sold him the entire shop, were it not for good sense prevailing on him at the last minute. Samir had asked her out on a date then and there. The initial spark between them had turned into a raging fire that could only be doused by marriage. For a while, after marriage, they had lived a quiet and happy life in Gladioli Cottage. The only disturbance that Aunty Gladys suffered due to them was the sounds of their incessant lovemaking.

And then, Babri Masjid was demolished. The secular foundations of Mumbai were rocked, riots erupted and chaos ruled.

One night, Samir had been summoned urgently to his factory in Dharavi to address some worker-related issues. He wouldn't have gone, had it not been for the large order of leather gloves that had to be executed for an American client. He ventured to his factory that night, never to return again... till this day.

Everyone had thought he was dead. Burnt alive. Bahaar had been heartbroken. She had mourned him intensely, refusing to go out of the house for months. Then she had told Aunty Gladys that she could not bear Samir's absence anymore. She had decided to go away as she couldn't live in Gladioli Cottage without Samir any longer. The home they had built together reminded her too much of him. Aunty Gladys had understood, had wished her well when she left. It had been almost nineteen years since then and Aunty Gladys had never heard from, or seen her, again.

Aunty Gladys paused in her story and wiped her eyes. A stunned Samir took a sip of water. She then picked up where she had left off.

Ten years later, she had succumbed to the machinations of a developer and Gladioli Cottage had turned into Gladioli Apartments. She had been relegated to her first-floor apartment, whose only respite was the balcony, where she spent most of her day. As for Bahaar, no one knew where she lived. However, a few years ago, Gladys's younger son, who was visiting from Canada, had bumped into Bahaar in Colaba one day. She had told him that she lived close by but didn't give her address. Samir's business partner, Rishi, who lived in Delhi and used to visit him and Bahaar every now and then, had also called on the phone once to check for some mail, but had not left any number to call back on.

◎

Dense grey smoke. Orange flames licking at his feet. Through the black haze beyond, a face appeared. Rishi. He seemed tense. Scared. 'Let me help you,' he said. He grabbed Samir by the shirt collars and dragged him through the blackness.

Outside, there was a cool wind blowing. Breathing would have been easier were it not for the cloth stuffed inside Samir's mouth. A hanndkerchief! He tried to spit it out, but couldn't. He drew in as much fresh air as he could through his nostrils.

Rishi looked back at the factory. He looked around. There was no one else. But there were voices coming from inside the factory. Angry. Violent. Ready to kill. Rishi suddenly noticed a truck parked nearby.

He dragged Samir to the truck, heaving him into the dark empty back of the truck. Samir lay flat on the vehicle's cold metallic floor.

Blackness. Blackness. Blackness.

The truck started moving. Samir opened his mouth to shout but no sound came out. He opened his eyes wide. Weak. Blackness again. Samir had rolled to one side of the moving truck. He grabbed at the canvas siding of the truck and pulled himself up. Through the peephole of the driver's cabin, he could see the driver concentrating on the black road. Samir tried shouting again but no sound emanated from his mouth. The handkerchief. Samir pulled out the hanky and...screamed.

The driver heard him. Shocked, he spun around. Through the peephole, he saw Samir's bleeding face and was aghast. The truck swerved. The driver had lost control. It spun off the road and Samir was violently thrown out of the truck. Blackness again.

◉

'Rishi...Rishi saved my life,' said Samir, coming out of his thoughts.

Aunty Gladys was staring at him, a glass of water ready in her hands.

'Thank God you're fine. I thought you were having a stroke.' She handed the glass to him. He drank till the last drop.

'Sorry...my memory comes back in flashes.'

Aunty Gladys smiled benevolently. 'Would you like to eat something more, son?'

Samir shook his head.

'Where can I find Rishi, Aunty?' he asked.

Aunty Gladys shrugged. 'I wish I could help you, Samir, but, like I said, I have no contact at all.'

Samir nodded, a little dismayed. 'I have to find Bahaar. Today is her birthday.'

Aunty Gladys smiled. 'You'll have to go and search in Colaba. Wait.' She walked into an inner room.

She emerged a few minutes later and handed Samir a thousand-rupee note and some change. Samir started to wave away the money, but she pressed the notes into his hands.

'This is all I have right now. Please take it. I wish I could come with you, but I haven't gone out of the house for months now. I am scared. The world has changed'.

'If you are scared, think how I might be feeling,' said Samir, pokerfaced. 'I've not been out for nineteen years,' he laughed, a hint of mischief in his eyes. Aunty Gladys looked at him, serious for a few seconds, then burst into laughter. Samir glanced at the cash in his hand and studied the thousand-rupee currency note. 'One thousand rupees in one note? Wow! India has really progressed.'

Aunty Gladys was rueful. 'It will buy you as much as a hundred-rupee in 1993.'

Samir made his way to the door.

'Aunty Gladys, thank you for your kindness. Its value is greater than ever today.'

◉

Raghu's SUV turned off Carter Road and entered the Sherly Village area. He held a computer printout in one hand, with track points showing the movement of Radheshyam's mobile phone over the past few hours. Raghu was looking for the last point that Radheshyam had stopped at in Bandra. He stopped his SUV right in front of Gladioli Apartments, got out and stood in the middle of the road, looking at all the buildings around, wondering which one Samir and Radheshyam had gone into. A curious watchman called out from behind a closed gate, 'Saab, please don't park in front of our gate.' Raghu gestured to him to come out, but the watchman was hesitant. Raghu walked towards him and fished out a brand new hundred-rupee note from his wallet. He flashed it in front of the watchman.

'Did two men on a motorcycle come here a couple of hours before? One man was in a white hospital uniform.'

The watchman gulped, his eyes shining. He quickly reached out and pocketed the hundred-rupee note. 'Yes, saab. I tried to stop them, but Gladys madam called the one in the hospital uniform to her place. The other one left on the motorcycle. *Saala lafanga.*'

Raghu was excited.'Who is this Gladys? Where is the man? Is he still with her?'

The watchman eyed Raghu's wallet. Raghu sighed, pulled out another hundred-rupee note and handed it to the watchman. 'He left about an hour ago for Bandra station, saab. I know, because I got the autorickshaw for him from the naka,' said the watchman.

Though disappointed, Raghu was not ready to give up. 'I want to meet this Gladys.'

The watchman now retracted behind the iron gate. 'That I cannot do, saab, until I have her permission.' Raghu took out a thousand-rupee note this time. The watchman almost salivated. His hand darted out but before he could take it, Raghu had grabbed his wrist.'Open the gate first,' Raghu hissed into his ears. The watchman gulped and unlocked the gate.

The watchman locked the gate behind them and whispered.

'I will take you to her, but I will say that you are from the BMC.'

Raghu nodded.

◉

In comparison to other local railway stations in Mumbai, Bandra station in the mid-afternoon is not very crowded, However, Samir, who had arrived after a bumpy ride on the autorickshaw, was still taken aback by the number of people standing in front of the ticket counter. Not sure which queue he should join, he stood in a corner of the ticketing area but was still jostled by people hurrying to join one queue or the other. Finally deciding that he would risk it, Samir stepped forward and joined what seemed the shortest queue. After a long few minutes, he got his turn at the counter. He fished out the thousand-rupee note. 'Churchgate' he said. The man behind the counter pointed to a sign above. The sign read, 'Please tender exact change.' Samir was about to request the ticket-seller to make an exception in his case when the irritated people standing behind him started making a noise, asking him to leave the queue and not waste everybody's time. He was pushed aside by a clucking, no-nonsense lady in a polyester sari. He stood by the side of the queue, not knowing what to do, till an old man took pity on him and said, 'Go to a food stall and buy something. They will give you change.'

Samir thanked the man and headed inside to the platforms. As he walked towards the food stall, a man with an open tin canister on his head rushed past him, spilling some of its contents on Samir's hand. It was some kind of cooking oil. He rubbed his hands together to get rid of the greasiness but realized that he had just transferred the slick oil onto the other hand. He looked desperately around for some water to wash it off with, but all he could spot was a crush of people. Then, in a far corner of the platform, he noticed a sign for a lavatory and walked towards it.

Just as he was about to enter, a man lounging by the door raised his leg across, barring the entrance. Samir stopped, confused. The man gave him an imbecilic smile. Samir stared back. The moronic smile turned into an impatient look as the man asked, 'What? Is it your first time here? Give me ten rupees.'

Samir still did not understand what the man was talking about. 'Ten rupees for what?' he asked.

The young imbecile sneered at Samir. 'For using the toilet, of course.'

'But it is free, isn't it?' asked Samir.

'Where have you been, Uncle?' the young man snarled. 'Nothing is free in this world. Soon we will start charging you to breathe. Don't take it personally, its just business.'

Samir decided that he had had enough of the young halfwit and his attempt at extortion, so he pushed past him and headed into the lavatory. This took the young man by surprise and he called out from behind Samir, 'Hey! Stop!' But Samir kept heading into the lavatory, taking care not to slip on the dirty wet white tiles. He bent at a washbasin and toggled the tap. In the meantime, the young man had come up behind him and grabbed his shirt. Samir spun around. While trying to steady himself, he slipped on one knee. The man's grip on his shirt broke, but he lunged at Samir again. This time, Samir instinctively raised his hands in defence. The man's hands connected with Samir's and he grabbed at them to pull Samir forward. The oil smeared on Samir's hands acted as a lubricant and the young man's grip slipped. He went careening in the other direction with the force of his own backward momentum. His foot slipped on the slick floor and he fell backwards. His head connected with the edge of a washbasin. The crack of his skull reverberated within the empty environs of the lavatory. Immediately, he was rendered unconscious. He might have survived this skull fracture, had he not fallen on the floor head-first, at such an angle that his neck snapped on the spot.

◎

Rishi was shouting, papers spilling out of his agitated hands. His aristrocratic features were contorted with anger.

The papers were some sort of account statements. He was obviously not happy with them, as he threw them in the air and walked out in a huff. Samir called out to him. Rishi turned and walked back, stopping almost an inch away from Samir's face.. 'This is not personal, its business,' he said.

Samir slapped him in response.

A shocked Rishi stood still, unsure of how to react.

Looking at his downcast face, Samir hugged Rishi, begging forgiveness. It was personal. After all Rishi was his own—more than his business partner—his cousin, his blood.

◎

Samir walked towards the young man's prone body, shaking. Bending down, he shook him. The man was still. Samir rolled him over and his lifeless eyes were open, staring at the ceiling. A scream from behind him dragged Samir's attention away from the dead young man. A boy stood at the entrance to the lavatory, his wide eyes fixed on Samir, his mouth spewing incoherent, shocked words. Samir rushed towards the boy in an attempt to pacify him and explain what had happened. But the boy, ran back to the milling crowd on the platform, shouting his first coherent word: 'Murder!'

Samir emerged on the platform to be greeted by a host of accusing eyes. Scared, he put up his hands, 'It was an accident,' he shouted to no one in particular. Two men rushed past him into the lavatory. A few others started advancing towards him. Samir made a dash for the far end of the platform.

'Stop!' one man yelled from behind him, but Samir had no intention of doing so. He ran up the stairs to the footbridge that was not very crowded at the time of the afternoon. Unfortunately, he ran headlong into a railway police constable who was coming from the other side. The constable saw the agitated men behind Samir and registered the scared expression on Samir's face. He reached out to grab Samir, but Samir ducked. The constable lost his balance and went rolling down the stairs. Samir continued his flight up the stairs. As he reached the bridge, he turned and ran towards the eastern side of the Bandra station. Luckily for him, a train had just come in and deposited a large number of commuters on the far eastern platform of the station. Samir merged into a bunch of commuters who were climbing up the stairs. Cutting through them, he ran down the stairs to the platform. When he reached the platform below, he hopped into the stationary train. Not stopping to look behind, he jumped onto the railway tracks on the other side. He searched for a gap in the metal fencing that separated the railway tracks from the Behrampada slums. Finding one a few hundred yards ahead; he quickly jumped through it and entered the slums. He ran headlong through narrow, maze-like gullies and came to an abrupt stop as he tripped over a man who was huddled near a door. A high-pitched voice cried out, '*Teri jaat ka baida maru!*'

Samir turned his face to see that the man was a bag of bones. He had a thin, bony face that was scrunched up in agony as he rubbed the spot on his chest where Samir's foot had connected. As Samir lay on the ground, gasping for breath, he looked the man up and down, incredulous.. His bones stuck out through his T-shirt and his ribs could easily be counted. Still in pain, the man now shook a thin fist at Samir's face. 'I will break two for every bone of mine that you have broken,' he shouted at Samir. 'I will break your jaw with one punch. I have watched *Dabangg* five times.'

Samir couldn't help breaking into laughter at the living skeleton's threats.

'Sorry. I am very sorry, bhai,' said Samir, placating him.

'That's right. I *am* a bhai. A gangster, Gardullah bhai.' The emaciated man proclaimed.

Samir lowered his head in obeisance. 'Please forgive me, Abdullah bhai,' he said.

'Not Abdullah, Gardullah,' said the man. 'Gardullah, the king of all the garad, all the smack in Bandra East. Not pansy stuff like marijuana or fancy-vancy cocaine, but hardcore, pure, fully-adulterated brown sugar.'

Samir raised an eyebrow. 'You are a drug smuggler?'

Gardullah sneered. 'I am bigger than a drug smuggler. I am a drug user. I have used every drug known to man and nothing has happened to me. See,' he pointed to his body.

Samir looked him up and down once more. 'Yes, I can see,' he said with a straight face. Suddenly, Samir remembered what he had been up to, before he ran headlong into Gardullah. He did some quick thinking. 'Gardullah bhai, please help me.'

'What is the matter?' asked Gardullah.

'There was an accident, it…it…wasn't my fault. People are after me.'

Noting the urgency in Samir's voice, Gardullah motioned Samir to follow him. 'Come on, I will show you a place to hide.'

A grateful Samir followed Gardullah through a maze into an open garbage dump. Samir held his breath as a rancid stench rose from the dump to his nostrils. Gardullah stopped in front of a section of a giant pipeline with pieces of metal welded onto it. He understood their purpose only when he saw Gardullah expertly use these metal pieces as handholds and footholds to clamber over the giant pipe. Gardullah hopped onto the pipeline with his lithe frame. As Samir too crawled on top of it, he saw an empty space that lay between the two adjoining sections of the pipeline. Gardullah had used the space to create a living area that could comfortably accommodate two men. As Samir eased himself into the space, Gardullah threw a ratty cushion at him, motioning him to use it to rest his back against the hot metal pipe. He smiled and said, 'Welcome to my Pipe Star Hotel.'

◉

Raghu's SUV cut through the crowd of autorickshaws buzzing around Bandra station. He had spent the last forty-five minutes pretending to be a BMC water inspector who was trying to improve the water supply in Sherly Village and seeking the advice of prominent residents of the area, one of them being Aunty Gladys. She had been very kind and, thankfully, garrulous. In between her water woes, she had also passed on details of how she had met a man whom she had believed to be dead for almost twenty years. In a somewhat sketchy manner, she told Raghu all she had told Samir. Raghu had come to the quick conclusion that he had to now follow Samir to Colaba. He left, after thanking Aunty Gladys profusely for her hospitality and her expert ideas about improving the residents' water supply. As he headed towards the Bandra–Worli Sea Link, somewhere near Mount Mary, he received a call from Inspector Pandian. The call was regarding a message received over the police wireless about a madman, attired in hospital clothes, being involved in some sort of murder incident at Bandra station. Raghu could not believe that this could be Samir, but decided anyway to investigate this. He turned his vehicle towards Bandra station.

Raghu parked the SUV right in front of the station in the 'No Parking' zone. He reached below the backseat and pulled out a police inspector's regulation cap and a wooden police baton. He placed the accessories on the dashboard, in full view of any casual observer. He had used this trick many a time, to park wherever he wanted to. The menacing presence of the police officer's cap and baton were enough to ward off any curious traffic constables. He stepped out of the SUV and entered the teeming station.

As he entered the platform area, he saw crowds gathered at the far end. The presence of so many police personnel made his pulse quicken. He hoped that nothing serious had happened to Samir. Increasing his speed, he made his way through the crowd to the centre of the commotion. A police constable tried to push him aside, but sensed from Raghu's imperious manner that this was a person of some importance, not to be messed around with. He gave way in deference. Raghu peeped over the heads of the gathered policemen and saw the crumpled body of a young man. Instinctively, he heaved a sigh of relief.

It was not Samir. He caught the eye of a young sub-inspector and signalled to him to step forward.

'What happened here?' asked Raghu.

'Who are you?' asked the sub-inspector in return.

'I am a municipal corporator.'

The sub-inspector shrugged, 'He was just a local tapori... slightly slow mentally. He used to collect hafta from the station stall owners and liked to harass people on the platform for fun. Apparently, someone didn't like his sense of humour. A madman.'

'Where is the madman? Is he in your custody?' Raghu maintained his deadpan gaze.

The sub-inspector could not hide his irritation any more. 'Saheb, if he was in my custody, do you think I would be here? He has escaped.' A constable called out to the sub-inspector. The constable had been talking to a couple of youths in the crowd. 'Saheb, these two chaps say that the dead man is the brother-in-law of Kundalik Kadam.'

Raghu stepped back into the crowd, stunned. 'Kundalik Kadam!' He knew who that was. A slumlord who commanded a lot of respect in Bandra East. He had his finger on the pulse of every illegal activity going on in the Behrampada, Indira Nagar, Bharat Nagar, Navpada and Garib Nagar slums.

A knot started forming in the pit of Raghu's stomach. He began to fear that he would not see Samir alive again.

◉

Kundalik Kadam had spent the past forty years doing real estate dhandha in the slums of Bandra East. Even though the opportunities to expand his business by becoming a genuine legal 'builder' had been tempting, Kundalik had not yielded to those urges. He was smart enough to realize that he was best dealing with the poor or illiterate, over whom he held complete sway. He didn't want to risk going out into the big bad world and dealing with white-collared customers who seemed wary of his uncouth ways. He had quietly built an empire in the slums, from the bottom of Khar East to the upper tip of Dharavi. No one knew that most of the slum shanties belonged to him, through proxy holdings. The amount of rent that he earned every month far surpassed what many bigshot builders could earn in a year. His small army of thugs ensured that the rent was collected on time and business operations were 'smooth'. He had made it a point not to recruit any family members into his dhandha, as he thought them weak links in his chain of command. He feared that sooner or later, one of these weak links would give way and the intricate infrastructure that he had built would come crashing down.

Now, as he stood listening to his weeping wife, he feared that that day had come. The one family member that he had allowed to be a part of the dhandha, only because of his disability, had now caused a tremor in his ranks. Kundalik would have to take decisive action, or he would be seen as weak himself. He wanted to tell his wife to shut up, because her snivelling, imbecile of a brother deserved to die anyway. Instead, he phoned his deputy and barked, 'Find this madman. Bring him to me alive.'

◉

The sharp ring of a mobile phone woke Gardullah up from the drug-induced slumber that he had fallen into. At the same time, Samir had been trying to clamber back onto the giant pipe while leaving Gardullah's 'Pipe Star Hotel' to continue onwards. Samir, too, was startled at the ringing and lost his footing on the curvature of the pipe. He slipped back down to where he had been sitting earlier.

Through his haze, Gardullah reached into a small cloth bag and pulled out a mobile phone. He put the phone on speaker mode and loudly croaked out 'Gardullah Home Delivery Service. What is your order?'

The person on the other side didn't find any humour in Gardullah's attempt at a joke. 'Abey chutiye, have you seen a madman wearing a hospital patient's clothes?'

Gardullah looked towards Samir, who was holding his breath. 'Behenchod, are you high as usual? Answer my question,' the man growled.

'I have seen many madmen. Everyday I see one. In fact, I may become one myself, soon.' Gardullah winked at Samir and laughed like a maniac.

The man on the other end sighed. 'Laudu, one day your nasha is going to kill you. When you get out of your haze, report to Kundalik bhai's office. And call me if you see this madman, okay? Everybody is looking out for him. He has killed Kundalik bhai's brother-in-law.'

Gardullah seemed upset. 'What! That haraami yeda is dead? He owes me money for the last three consignments I scored for him!'

'That bastard had borrowed money from me, too, but what can we do? Instead of thanking his killer, we have to find and kill him instead.'

The line got cut. Gardullah and Samir stared at each other. Finally, Gardullah reached under his mattress and took out a wooden box that was wedged in a corner under the pipe. He took out an old police service revolver from the box.

'We have to get out of this area immediately,' he told Samir. He grasped a welded piece of iron and clambered on to the pipe. Standing atop the pipe, he looked down at Samir and said, 'Are you waiting for a shubh muhurat to come up?' Samir smiled, held on to the iron and, using all his strength, joined Gardullah on top of the pipe.

Gardullah stuck the gun in the waistband of his pants and covered it with his shirt. Then he started walking along the pipe, in the opposite direction from which they had come in earlier. The pipe's curvature was suitable for walking without letting one tip over and fall. Samir hesitated when he saw that the pipe extended for about a kilometre across a black river of swirling sewage. He gulped as he imagined what a small sip of the black swirling water could do to a human being, were he to lose his footing and slip into it. A few yards ahead of him on the pipe, the nimble-footed Gardullah called out, 'Oye, madman, show me how mad you are. Follow me as fast as you can.'

Samir rose to the challenge. He took a few tentative steps, gained confidence and increased his speed as he began to follow the swiftly moving Gardullah.

◉

Raghu entered Kundalik Bhavan, a three-storey brick-and-cement building, standing right in the middle of Garib Nagar. It was from this place that Kundalik Kadam conducted his business activities. At that point of time in the late afternoon, Kundalik Bhavan was bustling with activity. Aggressive, brooding men were walking around, looking ready to spring into action if given a call. Impotent anger was writ on almost every face. A hefty dark man stopped him in his tracks.

'Where are you going?' he asked Raghu, his voice laced with tension.

'I want to meet Kundalik bhai,' replied Raghu coolly.

'Kundalik bhai is busy right now. He will not meet anyone.'

'He will meet me. Tell him I know who the madman is.'

The man immediately dropped his aggressive manner. 'You wait here. I will go and tell him about you.'

In a few minutes, the man was back. He did a thorough body search on Raghu, all over his limbs, chest and back. Satisfied at not finding anything, he asked Raghu to follow him to a large inner chamber on the second floor, which resembled the inside of a temple. Statues of gods and goddesses were placed in various niches and walls. Small diyas flickered in front of these statues. The parts of the walls that did not have niches were covered with laminated photographs of more deities. At the far end of the room was a large table, across which sat a man dressed in a red silk kurta and matching silk lungi. The man's face vaguely resembled yesteryear's Bollywood comedian Mehmood. Raghu knew that this was Kundalik Kadam but was surprised at the fact that he didn't wear the air of aggression that others in his headquarters seemed to possess.

'So, who is this madman? asked Kundalik, coming straight to the point.

Raghu walked closer to the slumlord and sat down on a chair from across him. 'He is the man who knows the details of my father's death,' he said in the cool, collected manner that he always used while dealing with authority figures.

Kundalik studied Raghu's face. 'I take it that you are looking for him too?'

'Yes, I am,' said Raghu, 'But, I want you to—'

Kundalik's phone rang. He picked up the call. 'What? Where? Accha, send men over there quickly. I am on my way.' Kundalik frowned. He snapped the phone shut.

'Your madman has just been spotted walking across the pipeline that goes over Mahim Creek to Mahim. He is really mad.' He laughed and Raghu shivered. 'Haan. You were saying something when the call came. Please finish.'

Raghu replied in a measured tone. 'I want you to call off your men. I will go after him. Don't worry, he will be taken care of. Promise.'

Kundalik looked at him, incredulous. 'Who the hell *are* you?' he asked.

'That is not important,' Raghu replied.

Kundalik reached for a bell under his table, but Raghu was quicker. He whipped out the Glock and placed its nozzle between Kundalik's eyebrows before he could ring the bell. Throughout the conversation, Raghu had anticipated this moment and was prepared for it. He had hidden the Glock securely in his underwear, tucked under his testicles, a place where no self-respecting goon would lay his hands, unless forced to. While seated opposite Kundalik, he had furtively unzipped his pants and extricated the Glock from its uncomfortable position—just in time to put it to good use.

Raghu was terse as ever, 'I am sorry for your loss, but the situation is far too complicated for you to understand.'

'Kutreya, it is you who don't understand. You and your madarchod madman are both going to die,' spat out the defiant Kundalik.

Raghu realized that any further discussion was useless. 'Get up,' he growled, with enough menace in his voice to convince

Kundalik that he meant business. Kundalik got up from his seat. 'This is my garh. Do you think you can get away from here?' he hissed.

Raghu didn't say anything, but motioned him towards a door at the back of the office. Kundalik looked at Raghu closely. He realized that Raghu knew what he was doing. The back door opened into a small private staircase that led to a shanty behind the slumlord's headquarters. This was Kundalik's private exit route that he had had specially constructed to help him make a quick getaway, should the need ever arise. Raghu continued in his businesslike manner, 'Don't try to call out to your people. I will shoot you down right here and escape through the backdoor. It is better that you come with me quietly.'

Without further protest, Kundalik opened the backdoor and walked down the staircase, with Raghu behind him. All along, Raghu held the Glock to the back of Kundalik's head. Before they emerged two shanties away from Kundalik Bhavan, Raghu covered his victim's head with a large handkerchief. Although his vision was impaired, Kundalik could make out a white SUV parked next to the shanty. Raghu bundled him into the passenger's seat, hopped into the vehicle and started the engine. Kundalik couldn't help but marvel at Raghu's level of information and planning.

'How do you know so much about me?' he asked.

Raghu replied, 'You have many enemies in the police. And I have many friends.'

◉

Samir and Gardullah were each gulping down a cold drink outside Shetty Cold Drink Shoppe, at the corner opposite

Navjivan Society, Mahim. Both of them were out of breath and needed to boost their flagging energy levels. They had walked across the pipeline over the creek without incident, except for some cheers from passengers in a local train that had rumbled past them on the adjoining train tracks. They had reached the Mahim side of the creek and hopped off the pipeline near the police quarters. Moving quickly along the path that leads under the flyover towards the Mahim railway station, they had made good time, reaching the mouth of Tulsi Pipe Road. Samir had wanted to go on towards Mahim station but Gardullah had insisted that they go towards St Michael's Church instead, as he felt this would confuse any person who might be following them. Gardullah had not disregarded the risk of being spotted on the pipeline. Samir decided to go with Gardullah's suggestion, as he was wary of trusting his own judgment.

The lemony cold drink revived Samir's senses somewhat. But the late afternoon sun was blazing and Samir could feel his skin burn. He sat down on a wooden bench under the shady awning that stretched over the shopfront while Gardullah chose to brave the heat out on the pavement. Samir watched Gardullah's eyes darting up and down the street and marvelled at his rodent-like alertness. During their journey along the pipeline, Gardullah had told him that he had been a solider in the army many years back, which was why he could brave the pipeline crossing while most others would baulk at the prospect. Samir didn't know whether to believe him or not, but as he watched Gardullah standing in the sun unfazed, he realized that it was perhaps army training that had saved Gardullah and kept him going despite the severe drug abuse he had subjected his body to.

Without warning, A jeep full of tough-looking men

turned into the lane, interrupting Samir's thoughts. He sprang to his feet, ready to flee the scene. Gardullah, instead of running, yelled out to him to grab a few of the sealed glass cold drink bottles from a crate lying outside the shop. With amazing precision, Gardullah started flinging the bottles at the advancing jeep. The velocity of the gas-filled glass bottle colliding with the jeep in motion was enough to create the effect of a small bomb, as the bottles exploded against the jeep's exterior with ferocious intensity. One bottle exploded against the windshield, smashing it into a thousand starry pieces. The driver lost control, causing the jeep to swerve and ram into an electric pole.

Without wasting time, Gardullah grabbed Samir's hand, shouted 'run' and swiftly loped towards St Michael's Church. Samir ran behind him. His energy seemed to have returned with full force, his brain seemed to be pushing his legs to run faster with every passing second. He overtook Gardullah after a couple of hundred yards. Gardullah waved him on. A loud shout from behind made Samir turn his head to see two of the goons from the jeep giving chase. One of them held a gun, aiming it at Samir and Gardullah even as he ran behind them. But luckily, the crowded road was too full of passers-by for him to be able to get a clear shot. Samir increased his pace and started dodging between the passing vehicles. By this time, they had almost reached the church. Samir looked to his right and saw an empty double-decker bus emerging out of the Mahim bus depot. He made a dash for it and grabbed the bar to heave himself inside the bus. Gardullah, was still a few paces behind. 'Jaldi!' Samir shouted, reaching out to grab Gardullah, when the man running behind him squeezed his gun's trigger. A bullet whizzed past Gardullah and Samir and embedded itself in the advertising board at the back of the bus. Gardullah whipped out his revolver. 'No! Get in the bus!' shouted Samir. He grabbed Gardullah's hand and was about to pull him into the bus when another shot rang out.

Gardullah's chest exploded in a red ball of blood. The bullet had passed through his back to the front of his ribcage. Gardullah's extended fingers started slipping out from Samir's grasp. Samir gulped large doses of air to keep from throwing up.

The bus was now gathering speed. As Gardullah fell, he chucked his revolver at Samir. 'Catch...' he said, before collapsing in a heap. The revolver bounced into Samir's outstretched hand and somehow stuck there.

Gardullah's body soon became a speck. But the men chasing them weren't done yet. Samir saw the shocked expression on the conductor's face. 'Please, don't stop the bus,' begged Samir.

The conductor raised his hands and said, 'Please, don't shoot.'

Samir was confused but then realized that he was holding a revolver. .

The conductor yelled out to the driver, 'Don't stop the bus, this man has a gun.' The driver accelerated, fearing for his colleague's life. The bus sped on, down L.J. Road towards Dadar, without stopping at any bus stops . Samir realized that he couldn't get too far on the traffic-laden main road. He shouted to the conductor, 'Take a right turn ahead.'

The conductor was hesitant. 'This is not our route,' he said, shivering. Samir now raised the gun at him. The bus conductor yelled to the driver, 'Right!'

The driver swung right into a by-lane. After that, Samir kept giving random, left–and-right instructions to the bus driver, who did as told without protest.

In a by-lane somewhere between Mahim and Dadar, Samir jumped off the bus, waving at the driver to carry on.

He then ran into another alley.

◉

Raghu Nadar was standing near the pipeline opposite the police quarters. He had arrived there with Kundalik Kadam, hoping to intercept Samir. As he arrived, he got another call from Inspector Pandian. This time, Pandian told him about another murder having taken place near Mahim Church. The police had information that a man in hospital clothes was involved in this murder, too. They were in no mood to take chances because of the impending arrival of the ruling party leader. They had labelled this man a terrorist on the loose and were on the lookout for him. Raghu suddenly realized that the back door of the SUV was open. He cursed loudly and sprang out, only to see Kundalik jumping headlong into the black waters of the creek behind. Raghu had his gun ready as he waited for Kundalik's head to pop out of the filth, but the water's surface remained placid. Sewage and assorted pieces of garbage kept swirling past, but nothing that remotely resembled a human being. Raghu lowered his gun, realizing that the toxins in the water would kill Kundalik as surely as a bullet would, except that his death would be a slightly prolonged affair.

He got back into the SUV and sat thinking. After a while, he dialled a number. 'This is Raghu Nadar. I have a request.'

A man whose voice indicated supreme authority replied, 'Sure, Raghu. I owe you a favour.'

'The man in the hospital clothes is not a terrorist.'

The man went silent for a few seconds. 'Do you know him personally?' he asked.

'Yes, sort of,' said Raghu.

'Can you vouch for the fact that there will be no more murders associated with him?'

'Well…I can't. But, do you have conclusive proof that he is the man who committed these so-called murders?' asked Raghu.

'I don't have the luxury of taking chances.'

Raghu mulled over this. 'Let's leave aside the murders. Can you ensure this man will not commit any kind of offence going forward?' said the man on the phone.

Raghu hesitated. 'Well…I…'

'You can't, right? Well, then, I can't help you.'

'At least, don't label him a terrorist…because he's not one.'

'Maybe he is, maybe he is not, but that's the only way to stop him for sure.'

'Please don't kill him, saab,' Raghu pleaded.

'We'll try not to.' The line was cut.

Raghu was left hoping that the man meant what he had said.

On a park bench in the Sant Tukaram Baludyan, a small garden tucked away in the heart of the residential expanse, close to the sprawling Shivaji Park in Dadar, Samir lay still, pretending to be asleep. Every evening, screaming kids and doting mothers crowded this garden. At present, though, in the late afternoon, there was no one around except for Samir and an old man who was catching a snooze in the shade of a tree.

Samir wanted to attract the least amount of attention towards himself while he thought out a strategy for his onward journey. Just a few minutes earlier, he had noticed some blood spattered on his hospital shirt. The realization that these were Gardullah's bloodstains sent him reeling. He entered the garden to be away from the crowded streets, the blood and the gore. Lying on the bench, he wondered if it would have been better for him to have remained in a coma. But then, he remembered what he had set out for. Today was Bahaar's birthday. There was no time to waste. He had to be decisive and quick with what he did next.

As he sat up on the bench, his eyes noticed a small single-storey house across the lane adjoining the garden. A rotund sari-clad woman emerged from the main door with two large buckets full of wet clothes. She proceeded to hang the clothes on the clothesline. Samir could clearly see that her house door had been left ajar. The house wore a deserted look except for the woman outside.

Samir rose, his mind made up. He exited the garden and crossed the road. He cast quick glances around, seeing no one, he entered the house. He found himself inside a sparsely decorated living room. He then walked into a passage beyond the living room and noticed an open door on one side. It was a storeroom. He went further down the passage and came to another door. He gently pushed it open and saw a bedroom. There was a large wardrobe near the double bed. He yanked open one of the doors; it was stuffed with women's clothing. He opened the other door and saw neatly folded men's shirts and pants on the shelves. He grabbed a shirt and a pant.

'Aai guh!' a voice screamed from behind. The rotund woman was staring at him in disbelief.

'Chor!' she cried again, her hands clamped on her mouth.

Samir pleaded: 'Please, behenji, don't shout. I...I am not a thief.' But the woman must have noticed the bloodstains on Samir's shirt, because she let out another scream. She dropped the buckets she was carrying and ran towards the passage.

But Samir was too fast for her. He jumped across the bed and slammed the door shut. The woman froze in her tracks and sputtered incoherently.

Samir spoke to her in a calm but authoritative voice. 'Look, behenji, I just want to borrow this shirt and pant. I will give you money for it.' He fished out the still unutilized thousand-rupee note and pushed it into her palm.

The woman calmed down a little and finally found her tongue. 'It's okay...take the clothes, but please don't harm me,' she said, thrusting the money back into his hands.

'I will not harm you, I promise.' Samir said to reassure her. She nodded.

Samir looked around the room and noticed that there wasn't any other exit. There was just a bathroom door in one corner. Samir steered the woman towards the bathroom.

'What are you going to do with me?' she asked.

Samir waved her inside the bathroom. 'I just want you to wait inside while I change into these clothes.'

Samir extricated Gardullah's revolver from the folds of his pajamas. He put on the trousers and unfolded the shirt. He was about the wear the shirt when his eyes fell on its embroidered label: Beekay.

◉

He had been looking for a clean shirt when he had opened Bahaar's side of the cupboard by mistake. There, he found a nicely packaged new shirt with 'Beekay' embroidered on the pocket. 'Beekay' stood for Bahaar Khanna. She used to embroider her initials on every piece of clothing. A habit she had picked up from her grandmother.

He tried on the shirt, but it didn't fit.

He called out to Bahaar and joked whether she was launching her own label, of which the shirt was a sample.

Bahaar came in and, on seeing Samir in the ill-fitting shirt, got a little upset. She had wanted to keep it a surprise, she said. Bahaar had recently spoken about wanting to do something on her own, as Sameer didn't want her to join him in his leather business. Instead, he used to always joke, she could start a family for him, with lots of children.

Bahaar now got upset and began crying. Samir pacified her, saying she could make as many shirts as she wanted. He would buy all her shirts and proudly wear her label 'Beekay' on his chest. 'But do get my measurements right, darling!' he said, twirling her around the room.

◉

'Bhaisaab, are you still there?' The lady's voice from inside the bathroom pulled him out of his reverie. He was still holding the shirt. He ran his fingers over the label: Beekay.

'Where did you get this shirt from, behenji?' Samir called out, slipping on the shirt. 'I want to buy the same kind of shirt, it fits me so well. Where can I get it?'

'Well, you'll have to go to the Beekay showroom in Colaba.' The lady replied, her voice tinged with amusement, .

'The Beekay showroom!' Samir's pulse quickened. 'Do you have the address?' he asked, while tucking the revolver safely into the waistband of his trousers, hidden under his newly acquired 'Beekay' shirt.

'I don't know the exact address, but it is in one of the lanes behind Taj Mahal Hotel. My husband shops there regularly. I could phone and ask him, if you'll let me out.' But she was speaking to an empty room. Samir had already exited the house.

◎

After reaching the main road, Samir spotted a cab parked opposite a coffee shop.

He walked up to the cab driver who was lounging in his seat, eyeing the pretty girls who walked past.

'Colaba?' he enquired.

The driver looked up at him, bored. 'No'.

'Please, I'll pay double.'

'Arrey baba, there is too much traffic and police bandobast that side today. I want to go with a lamba bhada to Borivali.'

Samir took out Gardullah's revolver and shoved its muzzle under the cab driver's chin.

The cab driver had seen enough of Mumbai's mean streets. He sprang to position and revved up the engine.

'*Saab, pehle bolne ka na, ki aap bhai hai*. Please sit. No problem, sir. I will take you there, come what may,' he said.

Samir crossed over to the passenger seat, all the while keeping the gun in full sight of the driver, but shielding it from public view with his free hand. But just as the cab was about to take off, a street eunuch appeared, clapping his hands near Samir's window. 'Mister, give some money to your sister,' he said, in a singsong manner. Samir tapped the cab driver's shoulder and told him to move on. But the eunuch leaned inside the passenger-side window. 'You give only ten rupees, sir. God will give you hundred dollars.' More clapping.

Samir pointed the revolver at the eunuch. It had the desired effect.

'No, darling, no. I am a poor girl. Please, you can go.' The eunuch scooted, swaying his hips.

Samir tapped the revolver on the cab driver's shoulder. 'Colaba,' he said.

Turning onto Cadell Road, the cab soon merged into the southbound traffic.

◉

Kundalik Kadam had just finished his latest bout of vomiting. In all, he had vomited six times in the past half an hour. His men stood around him, shuffling their feet, looking helpless. Kundalik had forbidden them from either coming to his aid or calling a doctor. It seemed that he wanted to endure as much suffering as he could.

After jumping into the Mahim Creek, he had swum underwater—if the brackish, black, liquid sewage could be called that—for almost five minutes. He was lucky that his hands had contacted with a concrete underwater pylon constructed under the train tracks that passed over the Mahim Creek. He had used the pylon for cover and raised his head above water for a quick gasp of breath. As he did so, large doses of the brackish water entered his system. Spotting Raghu at the edge of the creek, he had ducked underwater again. The foul liquid was any day preferable to Raghu's company. Using all his survival instincts, Kundalik had swum towards the Bandra side of the creek, away from Raghu's gaze. Swimming from pylon to pylon, and coming up for air occasionally, he had reached the Bandra side. He glanced back to see Raghu walking away from the creek. Kundalik had heaved himself out of the water on to marshy mangrove silt and stumbled through the tangled mangrove swamp to dry land near the pipeline. There, he had lain on the ground and vomited thrice, before he could breathe again. He had thought that he would die, but luck was on his side. A ragpicker, foraging for trash nearby, had come to his rescue. To Kundalik's surprise, the ragpicker had pulled out a high-end mobile and connected Kundalik to his deputy. He had explained that he was an expert at snatching the mobile phones of local train passengers when the train slowed down on the tracks near the pipeline.

Now, as Kundalik wiped his mouth and looked hard at the men around him, he barked, 'Madarchod, double the reward! Five lakhs for the madman, ten lakhs for the SUV man. For any sort of information.' The men quickly fished out their mobiles and got to work. Their entire network of middlemen were canvassed.

'Bhai, Rehmat Ali in Matunga has some information, but doesn't know whether to trust the source or not,' said one of them after a short conversation.

'Who is the source?' Kundalik snarled.

'A street hijra,' said the henchman. 'Rehmat says a man going to Colaba in a cab threatened this eunuch with a gun.'

'Give me the phone.' Kundalik snatched the handset.

◉

Senior Inspector Pandian was a worried man. A khabri had just called to tell him that there was a ten lakh supari out on a man in an SUV, with numbers matching Raghu Nadar's vehicle. Pandian was wondering whether he should call Raghu to inform him. Raghu knew too many of his secrets and this might be a good day for all those secrets to disappear, along with him. But Pandian realized that sooner or later, Raghu was bound to find out about the supari from one of his sources. It would be better if he was the first to inform him. In the process, he could collect a bonus for passing on the information. Pandian was not a greedy man, just needy. And he did have compassion, even if it came at a price. Last, but not the least, Raghu was from the same community as him and had been a good friend of his, mused Pandian, as he dialled Raghu's number.

Raghu, at the time, was in Dadar, near Portuguese Church, making his way towards South Mumbai, while keeping his eyes on the road in the likelihood that he might spot Samir somewhere. Pandian spoke before Raghu could even say hello.

'There is a ten lakh supari out on you.'

'Kundalik Kadam?' asked Raghu.

'Yes.'

'I'll take care of it,' said Raghu. 'Thank you. I won't forget this.' He was about to hang up when Pandian remembered something important. 'Oh, by the way, I have been monitoring the wireless since you asked me to. A lady somewhere near Shivaji Park was threatened by a man wearing a hospital patient's clothes. He was carrying a gun.'

'A lady? Why would he threaten a woman?'

'Something about a shirt from some boutique.'

'What? Hmmm...this is confusing.'

'I know. But the report said the woman was hysterical, shouting something about the Beekay showroom in Colaba.'

'Thank you,' said Raghu and cut the line.

Raghu's phone rang again. He cringed on seeing the caller ID.

'Raghu, beta,' the voice on the other side demanded, 'have I made a futile trip to Mumbai? I have just landed, but my people tell me that you refused to speak to them throughout the day. Have you changed your mind?'

It was the leader of the ruling party.

'No, sir, not at all. Your trip is going to be absolutely successful. I am sorry; today, I have been stuck with personal matters. But don't worry; I will be there to greet you at Azad Maidan, and accept your generous offer. Trust me.' Raghu rambled on with his apologies.

'Is there some illegal activity that you are involved in? Because you know...' The tension in the ruling party chief's voice did not ease.

'No, no, please trust me. There is nothing that is going to tarnish your or your party's image, sir.'

'*Acchi baat hai, Raghu beta.* I have envisioned a great future for you. For me, this is personal. I hope you will not let me down.' The party chief sounded appeased.

'Of course. You have my word, sir.'

For a few minutes after the line was cut, Raghu sat motionless in his SUV.

Then he parked the SUV and walked towards a shop selling khadi kurta-pajamas.

◉

Azad Maidan in South Mumbai is known for the numerous cricket pitches that dot it. On Sundays, many of the city's youth play cricket here. But, not many of those playing cricket know that the maidan was named 'Azad' because during the struggle for India's independence, leaders such as Mahatma Gandhi used to address huge crowds there.

Today, the maidan was bedecked in the ruling party's regalia. Party flags and banners adorned every nook and corner. A massive stage had been erected in the southern corner. The various satraps of the party were bringing in truckloads of people from their respective constituencies. The crowd was sporadically raising slogans and chants, celebrating the impending arrival of the party chief. It was the chief's first visit after the party had somehow cobbled together the margin that had brought them to power. The air was full of optimism brought about by the shift in the party's vision. The local leaders from Mumbai commandeered the microphone at this time, inciting enthusiasm in the gathered party workers, while waiting for the chief to arrive. The police presence was massive, but scattered, leaving most of the maidan under the security of the party's own 'security wing'.

Samir's cab was stuck in the early evening traffic close by, at the Dhobi Talao junction. The line of honking cars had not moved an inch for the past ten minutes. Samir cursed under his breath, wishing for the nth time that he had not taken this route. The cab had been made to wait on Marine Drive to allow passage to the motorcade of the ruling party chief. Not wanting to waste time, Samir had pushed the cab driver to take a shortcut. The cab driver, in fear for his life, had swung the cab left, over the Marine Drive flyover, past the Marine Lines station towards Kalbadevi. The going had been good till they turned towards Metro Cinema and realized that the bulk of the vehicles creating the traffic jam that evening were crammed within the square kilometre surrounding Azad Maidan. It didn't help that the early evening rush hour had coincided with the timing of the ruling party rally.

After another ten minutes, Samir couldn't take it anymore. Revolver in hand, he tapped the hapless cab driver's shoulder. 'How can I get to Colaba within the next half an hour?'

Despite his fear, the driver chose to give Samir the most honest and practical suggestion that he could. 'It would be better if you walked up to Flora Fountain and took another cab. In this jam, you will reach faster that way.'

Samir weighed the option in his mind.

'Thanks for the ride. Here, take this,' said Samir, thrusting the thousand-rupee note in the driver's hand. Samir hopped out of the cab. 'Take the short cut across the maidan and exit through the gate at the southwest corner, bhai,' called out cab driver, ecstatic at the large tip.

Samir, noting the genuineness in the cab driver's voice, waved his thanks and joined a group of party workers, raising slogans.

But, as soon as Samir entered the maidan, he realized what a mistake it was. The sea of humanity sprawling in front of him was daunting. The taxi driver, despite his best intentions, had given him wrong instructions. He turned to leave. At that very moment, the party leader whom everybody had been waiting for appeared on the stage, along with his entourage. The sea of humanity rose as one, and pressed forward towards the stage, like an unruly wave. Samir was pushed forward, even as he tried to push against the wave. Exasperated, he let himself be pushed along till the shoving stopped. Once the speeches started, Samir cut across to the left and headed to the southern end of the maidan. But he discovered to his dismay that the southwestern gate had been barricaded due to security reasons. However, there was a small entrance at the backstage area that led from the maidan to the street behind. He was left with no other option but to risk it exiting the maidan through the backstage area, even if the presence of policemen was daunting. He noticed that many people carrying garlands for the party leader were going through security and entering the backstage area. He spotted a group of old men advancing with oversized garlands in their hands. Samir walked up to a particularly frail old man and helped him hold up the heavy garland he was laden under. The old man gave Samir him a grateful smile and together, they passed through the police cordon into the backstage area.

Once inside, all Samir wanted to do was flee the maidan. But he felt guilty seeing the old man struggling with the garland. Samir called out to a young party 'security wing' worker to help the old man on to the stage. The volunteer smiled and nodded. While he took the garland from Samir, his hand accidentally brushed against Samir's waist. His expression changed as he felt something hard and metallic lodged in Samir's pajamas. He dropped the garland and ran towards the nearest policeman.

'Terrorist!' he yelled, pointing at Samir. The word was enough to make the crowd run helter-skelter. Complete pandemonium broke out, even though nobody knew who the terrorist among them was. Samir, too, tried to run, but a cop caught him by the collar and pulled him backwards. He lost his balance and fell to the ground. The revolver popped out of his waistband and landed a few feet away. 'Terrorist!' the policeman also yelled.

Hearing the shouts from the backstage, the stage now erupted in commotion as well. Senior party men ran amok and jumped into the crowd.

Raghu, who had been sitting next to the party leader, was about to follow suit when he was struck by doubt. He decided to run backstage. Sure enough, there he saw a group of policemen surrounding the fallen Samir. He ran towards them and shouted, 'What are you doing? Stop.' The policemen were taken aback at his reaction.

'*Terrorist hai, saheb*,' said the first policeman, who had

accosted Samir. He waved the revolver he had picked up from the ground. Raghu grabbed the weapon from the policeman.

'This man is not a terrorist,' shouted Raghu, so all could hear him. 'He is my personal bodyguard.'

The policemen and the crowd relaxed. Raghu helped Samir up.

A flabbergasted Samir held his silence. The policemen quickly backed off. They had bigger things to contend with at that moment. The party leaders jumping into the crowd had created a panic wave, leading to a mass stampede. Some policemen rushed towards the public address system booth and sheepishly began to announce that it was a false alarm. But not many people seemed convinced.

Samir, in the meantime, dusted off the mud from his clothes and looked at Raghu with gratitude. Raghu pointed at the open back entrance and together, they walked out of the maidan. They hopped into Raghu's SUV, which was parked one lane behind, near the Sterling Cinema.

'I have to go to...' Samir finally spoke.

'To the Beekay showroom in Colaba?'

'How do you know?' Samir looked taken aback.

Raghu smiled, 'I know a lot of things, Uncle Sam.'

◎

'Uncle Sam, are you all right? Uncle Sam?'

Through the blackness, a dark face drew near. 'Samir,' the face mouthed his name. Samir's eyes watered due to the smoke around. When his eyes cleared he saw a concerned face above him. 'Get up, Uncle Sam. Let me help you.'

Selva. Selvaraj, the manager. He bodily lifted Samir up from the ground.

Suddenly, behind him, an iron rod swung through the air and hit Selvaraj's head. Selvaraj collapsed on Samir.

Samir fell on the ground again.

His eyelids started drooping.

He noticed a face in the black haze through his half-open eyes. Rishi.

Rishi took out a handkerchief from his pocket and shoved it into Samir's mouth.

Samir fainted.

Samir opened his eyes again. Dense grey smoke. Orange flames licking at his feet.

Rishi seemed tense.

'Let me help you,' he said. He grabbed Samir by his collar and dragged him through the blackness.

Samir heard a dull cry from somewhere in the curtain of smoke.

'Uncle Sam!'

⦿

'Selva. Selvaraj,' Samir said.

It was Raghu's turn to get a start. He turned to Samir. 'You remembered something?'

'Selvaraj tried to save me. Brave man,' said Samir. A hint of emotion stirred in his eyes. Raghu was quiet, not wanting to interfere with Samir's thought process. Samir continued, 'Somebody attacked him. Hit Selva on his head with an iron rod.'

'Who?' asked Raghu, explode in a mixture of anger and excitement.

Samir shrugged. 'I don't know.'

Raghu gritted his teeth. 'You don't know, or you will not tell?'

'I don't know, I am sorry. I don't know...' Samir sighed. He was genuinely perturbed and was trying hard to jog his memory. Raghu frowned.

'I get incomplete flashes...' Samir began.

Raghu fished out the newspaper clipping from his wallet. He shoved it into Samir's hand.

Samir unfolded the clipping and read it.

Raghu pressed the pedal hard suppressing his anger. The SUV swerved dangerously close to the footpath.

'For almost twenty years—twenty years, Uncle Sam—I have lived under a shadow. The shame of being the son of a man who killed innocent people. My mother and I have always maintained that my father could never have been a killer, but no one would listen to us.'

There was determination in Samir's eyes. 'They will listen now, Raghu. I will tell them.'

Raghu relaxed his tight jaw. Samir's expression softened, too.

'You are still the same, Uncle Sam. Righteous. My father used to worship you.'

Samir looked self-conscious. 'I wish I could remember more,' he said with feeling.

'Don't you remember me? I was only eight years old when my father used to bring me to the factory. You used to give me boxes of imported After Eight chocolates and had named me "Little Rags". I still remember how I had named you Uncle Sam in return, and my father, too, started calling you that,' Raghu recalled.

Samir looked blank.

Raghu fell silent, a little disconcerted, and turned his attention to the road.

The SUV made its way through the evening rush-hour traffic at Fort and crossed Flora Fountain. At the circle near Regal Cinema, Raghu turned towards Colaba Causeway and then immediately took the first left turn.

Samir glanced at Raghu. 'You know where…where Beekay is?'

'Yes, I do. It's quite famous.'

Raghu turned the SUV into the lane directly behind the Taj hotel. He stopped after a few hundred yards. Samir glanced at a shiny neon signboard: Beekay.

Samir's eyes met Raghu's. Raghu gave him an encouraging nod. Samir took a deep breath and got down. His stomach was tied up in knots. He was going to meet Bahaar and he looked a mess. He didn't even have a birthday present for her.

As he approached the showroom entrance, two security guards started rolling down the shutters. Samir quickened his pace. 'Saab, we are closed for today,' said one.

Samir was nonplussed. 'At what time do you close?'

The other guard smiled. 'We know, sir, it's only 7 p.m. Normally, we are open till much later, but today is our madam's birthday.'

'Where is your madam? Where is she?' Samir couldn't hold back any longer.

The guards now regarded him suspiciously, looking him up and down.

'Why should we tell you? Come tomorrow morning at ten-thirty,' said one.

Samir was now desperate. 'Look, I have to meet your madam. Right now.'

'*Arre bola na*, come tomorrow.'

'Please,' cried Samir, stepping forward in desperation. The guard unceremoniously shoved Samir away.

'If you touch him again, I will shoot you both,' a cold voice called out from behind.

Raghu was standing with his Glock clutched in his hand. The guards immediately stepped away from Samir. 'Please, forgive us,' they said.

'Just tell us where your madam is right now,' demanded Raghu.

'At this time, Madam and Saheb go for an evening walk at Apollo Bunder but later on, she has a dinner party at the Taj,' said one of the guards.

'Saheb? Which saheb?' Samir's heart was racing.

'Madam's husband, of course,' said the security guard.

A light seemed to go off in Samir's eyes. He turned and stumbled back to the SUV. Raghu rushed after him. Both of them got in. Noticing his forlorn expression, Raghu squeezed Samir's shoulder in empathy.

Samir sighed. 'It had to happen, I guess. She thought that I was dead.' He let out a mirthless laugh. Raghu didn't know what salve he could offer to ease Samir's pain. He just nodded in agreement. An uncomfortable silence engulfed them.

After a few moments, Raghu softly asked, 'So, what do you want to do now?'

Samir sighed. 'I don't want to interfere in her life. She is a married woman. But I *do* want to see her once. Even if it is from a distance...'

Raghu set his jaw firmly. 'So why don't we do that? he asked. 'Let us drive down Apollo Bunder and see if we can spot her.'

Samir lapsed into silence once again. After a few seconds, he turned to Raghu and said, 'Let's do it.'

Raghu gave him a small reassuring smile and put the SUV in gear. He drove down the road and turned towards Apollo Bunder. He slowed down and drove as close as possible to the promenade.

Samir looked towards at the people milling around. on the promenade. A jumble of thoughts invaded his mind. *How does she look now, almost twenty years later? Is her hair long or short? Has she put on weight? Have wrinkles creased her flawless skin? Is the shine in her eyes still as enticing?* Samir's eyes flitted from face-to-face, trying hard to match the mental image of twenty-something Bahaar when he last saw her. The crowded promenade full of hawkers, tourists and burqa-clad ladies was not the best place for a clear view of everyone who was passing by. The failing light was not of much help, either.

Suddenly, he saw her—hair open, wearing a white T-shirt and sweatpants. She looked as stunning as ever, her chiselled cheekbones as alluring as before. Her body was still as lithe and sensual. She turned in his direction as the man she was with bent down to tie his laces. Samir urgently tapped Raghu's hand on the steering wheel. Raghu braked. As a gentle breeze blew, Samir almost feared she might fly away with the wind, vanish into the horizon. For the second time. But the wind just played with her hair, tossing it around to make her look all the more desirable. Even from this distance, he could see a hint of amusement play on her face. As if she were enjoying a secret joke. Samir wondered if the twinkle was still there in her eyes.

The man beside her finished tying his laces. He put his arm around her. She looked at him and laughed. The man turned at an angle so that Samir could see his face.

It was Rishi.

◉

The moving truck slowly sputtered to life. He tried to rise and jump out of the open back, but fell down as the truck jerked.

He saw Rishi run towards him.

'Rishi,' he shouted, 'Help!' But no sound came out of his mouth. The handkerchief.

Rishi ran a few steps towards the truck, but behind him, a figure appeared. 'Sam!' The figure called out. Selvaraj, bleeding from the wound on his head, was shouting to Samir.

Rishi turned. For the first time, Samir noticed the iron rod in Rishi's hand.

Rishi swung the rod. It hit Selvaraj on the head again. Rishi ran towards the truck. But Selvaraj held on to his left leg.

Rishi growled with rage and frustration and swung at Selvaraj once again. And again and again.

Selvaraj turned motionless.

The truck moved faster and faster away from the grotesque scene.

◉

'Rishi killed Selva,' the words burst out of Samir. Raghu looked at him intently; a fire lit his face. Samir turned towards Bahaar again. But she had vanished. Samir desperately scanned the crowd. He jumped out of the SUV and stepped onto the promenade.

'Bahaar!' He yelled. 'Bahaar!'

In the crowd, Bahaar stopped in her tracks and looked back. Her eyes locked with Samir's. The shock was palpable. She stood rooted to the spot. The crowd around them started thinning. Rishi, who had gone a couple of steps ahead, also turned now, and looked shell-shocked.

'Rishi!' shouted Samir. The three stood staring at each other, oblivious to the curious onlookers passing by on the promenade.

At that moment, from a by-lane on the right, two men emerged on a motorcycle. The man in front was Tupe, Kundalik Kadam's henchman. The pillion rider was Kundalik himself. As the motorcycle sped towards Samir, Kundalik raised a pistol and shot from behind. The bullet hit Samir on the back, passing through his left shoulder. He stumbled on to the ground, blood drenching his shirt.

The gunshot stunned the crowd. People ran in every direction, clearing the promenade within seconds. Bahaar and Rishi stood rooted to their spots, not knowing how to react. Samir rose and lurched towards them. The motorcycle sped along the road, and was now parallel to the trio. Samir reached into his waistband and drew out Gardullah's revolver. But before he could do anything, another shot rang out. Kundalik's head exploded in a mass of blood and gristle. The motorcycle skidded, and Tupe and Kundalik fell to the ground. Raghu stood next to his SUV, Glock in hand. Rishi bent down and reached out towards something. It was Kundalik's fallen gun. He picked up the gun and shot at Samir. As if in chain reaction, Raghu threw himself in front of Samir. The bullet hit Raghu's leg and he fell to his knees. Rishi grabbed Bahaar and began to run across the road, towards the Taj. From his fallen stance, Raghu shot again. The bullet went through Rishi's forehead.

Rishi collapsed in a heap at the edge of the promenade railing. Bahaar shrieked in despair.

◉

Dense black smoke. Cries. The smell of smoke.

Rishi was dragging the unconscious Samir through the factory. However, Samir was not unconscious.

A man with a murderous look in his eyes appeared in front of them.

'Take this one, too,' Rishi said to the man.

The man knelt in front of Samir. Unzipping him, he examined Samir's private parts and said, 'This man is not one of them. Take him outside and free him.'

Rishi hesitated for a minute, and then decided not to argue. He turned and dragged Samir towards the factory door.

Outside, Rishi noticed the empty truck. He lifted Samir into the truck. 'Don't worry, Sam. We'll just wait till these stupid bastards go. Then you'll have your turn.' He laughed.

A chill went down Samir's spine. He moved.

Rishi realized that Samir was still alive.

He cursed under his breath.

'I'll just be back, Sam. Don't move,' he said.

Rishi went back into the factory.

◉

By now, Samir had managed to stumble up to the fallen Rishi. He watched Bahaar crouching and crying over the body.

'Was it always him?' Samir asked.

Bahaar was silent. Her shoulders shuddered as she tried to control herself.

A single tear escaped Samir's eye. He reached out to her.

Bahaar grasped his extended hands. Her soft touch unleashed a wave of emotion that made him tremble.

Samir still had Gardullah's revolver in his hand. Bahaar gently tugged at the revolver, and Samir let go. Bahaar took the revolver out of Samir's hands, and spun its barrel towards him. Samir looked at her, confused.

'Yes', she finally replied, as she pulled the trigger.

Click. The gun was empty.

Click, Click, Click.

Bahaar kept pulling the trigger in vain.

◉

The truck was moving at full speed. Samir stirred. He rolled from one side to the other at the back of the truck, with every slight turn it took.

Grabbing on to the canvas on the side, he steadied and raised himself up to see the truck driver ahead. Samir called out to him.

But no sound emanated from his mouth. He pulled at the handkerchief stuffed in his mouth. Rishi's handkerchief.

A passing streetlight flashed a sliver of light on the handkerchief. Samir looked at it and saw an embroidered 'Beekay' emblazoned on the corner. To his shock, he saw that there was a lipstick 'kiss impression' around the embroidered 'Beekay'. Bahaar's lips.

Samir let out a scream. The revelation brought his world crashing down.

The driver spun around.

The truck collided with a tree. Darkness.

◉

The gun clattered out of Bahaar's hands.

She stood staring at Samir, dumbstruck by the turn of events. Then she reached out and wrapped her arms around him, sobbing. 'Oh Samir, please forgive me,' she whispered into his ear. He gradually softened and hugged her back. They stood entwined in each other's arms, lost to the world.

After a few minutes, Samir began to laugh. As peals of laughter rolled out of his mouth, he looked deep into Bahaar's eyes. She was confused at first, and then laughed along with him. Her laughter sounded just the same to him, and she still had that twinkle in her eye.

Samir hugged her even more tightly. Bahaar reciprocated with equal fervor.

But when he started stumbling towards the railing, Bahaar realized that something was amiss. She struggled to break away from him, but Samir's grip on her was strong. She screamed, but Samir continued to guffaw, not letting go. He had reached the edge of the railing now.

With one massive heave, he tumbled, with Bahaar wrapped around him, into the sea below. 'Happy birthday, sweetheart!' he whispered into her ear as the waves rose up to meet them.

Samir's laughter was still echoing in the air when Raghu hobbled up to the railing and looked down into the water.

There was no one there. Only choppy waves and blackness. He kept looking, hoping that Samir's head would break the water's surface. But the water had closed over Samir and Bahaar. Swallowing them up as if they had never existed.

Samir Khanna, the Coma Man had finally disappeared, forever.

Acknowledgements

⸺◆⸺

I am grateful to:

My mother, Shakuntala, whose prayers to God make my world a better place to live in.

Kapish Mehra, who won me over with his dynamism and by the professionalism displayed by his organization.

Kausalya Saptharishi, my editor, who invested her faith in my work and remains its true custodian.

Amrita Mukerji, my copy editor, whose unfailing eye has made my work a better read.

Tuhin A. Sinha, who wrote an email that started me on my journey as a novelist.

Aditi Prakash, who took time out from impending motherhood and made that all-important introduction.

Farida Haider, who was one of the first to read my work and give me the feedback that I desperately required.

Rajvardhan, additional commissioner of police, Mumbai, who inspired me in just one meeting.

Suhel Buddha, ex-Mumbai police, who triggered my thoughts so that they could find their targets.

Deepak Rao, Mumbai police historian, whose meticulous explanation of police procedure gave me numerous insights that I had not previously seen.

And last but not the least...

Goddess Mumbadevi, who protects my city, so that we may live without fear.